"Takács uses magic, technology, and the otherworldliness
of space to explore the horrors of humans' worst impulses...
people and societies surviving at great cost to themselves in
the face of war, apocalypse, and death."

– Publishers Weekly

"From uplifted octopuses on far flung planets to intensely topical
explorations of authoritarianism and tightening borders here on
Earth, this collection reveals a dazzling (and sometimes shattering)
breadth of speculative fiction. It treats openly with a universe
dominated by distance and space but made beautiful by the diverse
people and connections that exist in the fleeting light of stars and
in the shadows left behind when war and time ravage and ruin.
Challenging and formally daring, the stories act as a prod and
provocation for readers to engage more deeply with the world around
them, to challenge their perspectives by putting them into minds
both alien and achingly familiar, seeking empathy beyond what can
be easily recognized or understood."

– Charles Payseur, _Quick Sip Reviews_"

THE TRANS SPACE OCTOPUS CONGREGATION

STORIES

BY BOGI TAKÁCS

Be strong, be strong, and we will all be strengthened

Published in 2019 by Lethe Press, Inc.
6 University Drive, Suite 206 / PMB #223 • Amherst, MA 01002 usa
www.lethepressbooks.com • lethepress@aol.com

ISBN: 978-1-59021-693-4

This short story collection is a work of fiction.
Names, characters, places, and incidents are products of
the author's imagination or are used fictiously.

Set in Baskerville and Latin.

Cover Art: Elizabeth Leggett
Cover Design: Inkspiral Design
Interior design: Frankie Dineen

Introduction

This is not a short story collection. Rather, it's a spellbook. The magic in these pages is subtle and slippery, and to read this volume is to surrender to its wild power.

Chances are, if you're picking up this book you already know about Bogi Takács, thanks to eir luminous storytelling, eir work on editing the Transcendent anthologies of trans speculative fiction, and eir invaluable work as a critic, redefining and resurfacing the canon of trans and nb speculative fiction.

We are just at the beginning of defining trans speculative fiction and Bogi has been at the forefront of that process through eir work as editor, critic and author. So what is trans speculative fiction? The stories contained in these pages offer some clues. They're tales of fluid indentities and shifting realities, and the lonesome, kind, beautiful people finding their way through them.

Above all, these incredible stories leave me with an impression of unruly bodies. Not just the octopi mentioned in the book's title, who do show up here and there. But also the shapeshifter in "Changing Body Templates," the sea monster of "Spirit Forms of the Sea," the psychic archivist of "Recordings of a More Personal Nature," the symbiotic fungi of "Good People in a Small Space," and all of the people who have been turned into weapons or devices, against their wills. My favorite stories here, though, are the ones about bodies that contain magic, too much to contain, which can only be tamed with a combination of **BDSM** and incredible tenderness. Like in "Standing on the Floodbanks," or "The Need for Overwhelming Sensation."

What is trans speculative fiction? It's stories of people managing identities between the lines, and divided loyalties. It's neo-pronouns and relationships that we don't even have words for yet. It's non-neurotypical minds and souls full of Jewish spirituality. It's worlds that are explored, yet remain wonderfully mysterious.

Many of the stories in this book pass like dreams through your mind leaving a sense of indelible strangeness. You won't even realize how you've been changed until you awaken again and find yourself someplace new.

— *Charlie Jane Anders, September 2019*

Table of Contents

THE TRANS SPACE OCTOPUS CONGREGATION
STORIES

This Shall Serve As a Demarcation

For A, M and R; for the path walked

I.

Tiles flip over, land to sea to land. Enhyoron grimaces, rocks back in their chair, eyes still fixed on the ever-changing map. I can feel their moods on my skin and my skin burns, flares with frustration, chafes against my simple cotton garb.

I sit up on the futon and pull up one sleeve to examine my arm—lighter-toned in branching lines like the bare, defoliated frames of trees in winter. I used to be cut along those pathways, gleaming metal and shapeforming plastic set into flesh, embedded to remain inside—a part of me forevermore.

The Collaborators took it all out—Enhyoron took it out, softly murmuring as they adjusted, readjusted, readjusted; molded rather than cut. Magic as technology. Still, I wept in pain, thrashing against my restraints, keening like a foam-cat stuck in bramble.

I shudder as the memory passes through me, but I don't miss the metal—I only miss the domes of Red Coral Settlement, the sounds of all-surrounding water pulling me down into sleep every night. There's no way back now, now that I've taken a stand in the war between land and sea settlements, and I've chosen neither.

Enhyoron push themselves away from the wall console, stretch out their strong limbs, their wide shoulders. They move with firm determination. "It's time to go."

"I have done so much wrong," I mutter, my tongue slow. "The land will not accept me. The sea will not accept me," I whisper to Enhyoron, and they grab me by the neck, push me down into the dirt.

"They already have. You think I'm the only one?" Enhyoron says mildly, somewhere above me, standing guard over me.

I smell green and the sweet-rot smell of spring decay. A band of invisible light connects my mud-sodden front to the ground and I weep in relief.

Their words resonate in my head: "The planet accepts you before you can accept yourself."

We walk back—I'm unsteady on my feet, and my eyesight is hazed over with exhaustion.

"This planet knows the meaning of sacrifice," Enhyoron says, gaze firmly fixed forward toward our makeshift camp.

I don't get to mourn the technology softly scooped out of my flesh. I don't get to mourn my break with my home. We have no time. The land has requested my presence, and the sea has given assent.

Can I call my home an eyesore? Was it ever really my home? As the antenna-tops of Red Coral Settlement peek out of the water, all the stainless steel seems crude and out of place against the billowing clouds sweeping across the horizon, the ever-renewing waves of the sea. Still, do I want it gone?

I turn around. The landfoam is encroaching, drawing closer to the cliff edge, heaping up in small iridescent piles. In a few days it will go through another growth spurt, rushing toward the water, solidifying, extending. A map tile will flip.

Red Coral Settlement is foamproof. The people will be gathered inside, huddled together as the structure croaks, but holds. I've been through many such transitions on the borderlands. Settlements changing from undersea to underground. Hard chunks set into the soft soil and fluid of the planet-surface, unmoving when everything else flows. Disrupting. I am reminded of my body, run my hands down along my sides. The metal is gone, only the pain remains.

Enhyoron knows my thoughts. "It's not sustainable," they say. "The settlements will be gone in another long cycle. The question is, how much damage can they do to the planet until then?"

I used to live there. I know how much damage they did to me.

Enhyoron pulls me close, and we hug; I mash my face into their coveralls.

"I am afraid," I whisper.

They smooth down my tiny curls—I have hair on my head again, after so many years. "I know, Î-surun, I know."

II.

The land and the sea were perturbed when the people started to *guide* the foam. *Guide* is a Settlement term, a poisonous euphemism. They forced it into their own paths, rushing along linear trajectories at high speeds to assault other Settlements. The borderlands changed shape in unprecedented ways. My nightmares started. The planet screamed.

The first dream was the most terrifying. Sea-foam melted away the land like acid, as I'd seen many times, but then it turned around and surged toward me. I was naked, with no envirosuit. I panicked—I wouldn't survive outside, the foam would eat away at me, the air would poison me. I woke stunned.

The battle of Lapis Lazuli Settlement only came afterward.

I wish I could say that I ran away from my task to *guide*. But I was instructed to seek out the Collaborators, pose as a defector and destroy them from within; Red Coral Settlement knew precious little about them, but deemed them dangerous.

I took an envirosuit and a small buggy. I knew the Collaborators were somewhere out there, trying to live on the surface, not in shards irritating the planet's skin. I knew they existed, but I had no more information.

In retrospect, I just wanted to kill myself. After that battle. I was so eager, driving myself forward, into destruction. Akin to the destruction I had caused. Not seeking the Collaborators, just desperately trying to run away.

I drove to a deserted clearing, flecks of foam hanging from the treesprouts and slowly worming themselves forward on the ground like mindless slugs. My hands shook so hard as I stripped out of my suit that I could barely unlatch the clasps.

I knew foam spores were floating in the air outside the buggy. I deliberately exhaled, then held my breath as I opened the top hatch and clambered outside. Was this bravery?

Of course it burns like acid; and it is drawn to magic, being of a magical nature in itself.

It does not abhor technology; it only abhors attempts to coerce.

What Enhyoron finished, it had started.

I was thrashing in a puddle of my own body fluids when arms suddenly held me, when hands wiped the tears, the snot, the saliva, the blood off my face. I don't remember well; I think I might've had a seizure, my brain giving in to the unbearable, unassailable input.

Two brown eyes stared at me, skin the same if lighter shade. A round face, a thick neck disappearing into leaf-brown coveralls. I had no room for thoughts in my head—I didn't know if this person was one of the Collaborators, and the group had no uniforms, just a symbol. A symbol I had not known then: the open hand.

I could not speak. But I grabbed their coverall sleeves and would not let go.

This was how I first met Enhyoron. The planet alerted them, sent them to me. A disturbance, again.

At first, they didn't ask questions. No one did—not a single one of these bright, non-uniformed and only loosely organized cavalcade of people of all kinds of genders, shapes and sizes. I even saw someone like me, neither of the two most common genders as Enhyoron was both. Could the Collaborators even be called a group, or just a set of people with mostly aligned goals? I still don't know.

The people waited for my reconstruction to run its course. My own lack of language isolated me better than any quarantine.

My previous life is cast in gloom and wrapped in gauze. I lost a lot; planet-adaptation is usually gentler because it is usually supervised. It still pains Enhyoron that they could not have been there from my first breath of unfiltered air.

But I remember this. I remember signing up, back in Blue-Ringed Octopus Settlement, talking to a lady wrapped in a turquoise uniform and discussing my options. At that point, I was sure I had options.

I had the magic, and a deep willingness to serve. Serve my people? I hadn't understood yet that it was best to avoid ones speaking in the abstract.

They would re-form me, neurotechnology and implantations and all the training; ostensibly to help me control my magic. Also, always unsaid: to help them control me. And I gladly complied.

I wanted no part in a war. But after Blue-Ringed Octopus was washed away and us stragglers, ragged and shocked survivors with wide-open eyes, were picked up by Red Coral, they told me I had no other choice but to fight; for I had the power. And the foam could be *guided*.

I saw Lapis Lazuli Settlement crackle and burst under the pressure, imploding upon itself deep inside the earth. I was among those who made it happen. They pulled power out of me, tore it out of me—*guided* it, they said—until I was utterly spent, until there was nothing left, until the enemy settlement was gone. The eternal war of land settlements against the sea, sea against the land.

But the sea itself, the land itself spoke out, their voice hammering in my head. No longer tolerating the people's actions.

I didn't know if the others had heard. I heard, but did not listen. Not until much later.

All around me it was soft and twilight-dark. Enhyoron was there, running a hand along my smooth if patchily colored skin. Admiring their handiwork? I understood how much effort it had been to remove the shards and slivers from my body, to remove the contamination.

I knew them beyond speech, from the way they carried themselves, from their gentle accepting kindness, and the words shaped themselves in my head long before my mouth could move.

They helped me walk, take the first hesitating steps. How much of my nervous system had been regrown? A staggering percentage. They helped me eat, spoon-fed me, guided my hands in the true sense of the word. They were patient, and I tried so hard, with all the eagerness that I had to serve, so cruelly exploited once; even before I knew that it wouldn't be exploited again. They could've done anything to me in that state. They chose to heal me.

They hadn't betrayed me, hadn't sent me to destroy life. And I wouldn't betray them. Not now, not ever.

"I wish to serve you," I said, my first sentence.

They shook their head, a sad smile on their androgynous face. "You understand nothing."

We talked. So much we talked!

"I...I wasn't built to destroy," I said, voice edging into a whine; again after so many times. The well of tears was very deep. "Originally..."

Enhyoron leaned close. "Are you *sure?*"

I thought of the configuration of implants. Intrusion, invasion. Settlement. Even my spine cut open. They had said it was for my benefit, it was to improve my magic, I was a civilian—this ran through my head: I was a civilian, before the destruction of Blue-Ringed Octopus, before I was conscripted into war—magic had so many peacetime uses...

But who would need *this* in peacetime? Was there ever peacetime on this planet, or just brief cessations of neverending hostility, like tiny gasps of breath? What had I agreed to, in my eagerness, my naivety—I had thought this would be good, I could be helpful—

I thought of the settlements scarring the planet.

"When the entire establishment is corrupt, it corrupts those who serve it," I said slowly, haltingly.

"If you have a need to serve, it is best to serve a person, not an organization," Enhyoron said. "A person who respects your no." They were silent for a moment. "A person you trust. A person you love."

I knew they were alone. I knew they were painfully lonely. I knew they were thinking of themselves.

But it was only much later that they accepted my service.

Improve. Like *guide.* Words themselves are twisted, take on new meanings. I had to disentangle myself from that bramble, and I fear I've only partly succeeded.

What would Enhyoron ask of me?

III.

The landfoam waving in the wind, hanging off the cliff wall in thick fluffy braids. Red Coral Settlement in the distance, on the water—in the water.

I'm not serving Enhyoron to cause destruction, I tell myself, but yet I know not what they will ask of me—what the planet itself will ask of me. Yet we are aligned, we are together.

"Those who wish to stay inside their cages can stay," Enhyoron says. "I've disavowed coercion." It strikes me I know little of their past; but they say these words with conviction and force. There has been something to disavow.

"Kneel," they say on a more gentle tone, and I do so. The land-foam twines around me, touches my skin. It feels warm and dry. I bend my head and close my eyes.

"I will guide you," Enhyoron says and a twinge of fear runs through me. Too-familiar words. But they continue differently:

"We protect life," Enhyoron says. "We do not seek to harm. We do not destroy—we seek to build. We seek to sustain—not to dismantle. What is harmful will, with time, dismantle itself."

They put their hands on my head and guide me as the magic rises up in me, running along paths in my body that still feel new. Power soaring to the sky. The landfoam rises, rises; multiplies with a newfound strength drawn from me. I shudder, but I know my reserves are deep. I recall the destruction.

Enhyoron holds me from behind, crouching down into the mud. I breathe with their breath.

"This shall serve as a demarcation," Enhyoron says, "a border we vow to uphold, a chain-link of mountains to stand between sea and land. And we will uphold it, until person will lift arms against person no more, until we collaborate with the planet instead of settling, until the time of intrusion runs out and the body rejects the invasion."

They pause. Their words give me renewed strength. The planet itself ripples.

"We isolate the harmful," they say. "We do not deny its existence. And once it is gone, the planet can reassert itself, and the border between land and sea will again move freely on the foam."

A sudden flash of insight—from outside my skull? Is the foam the planet's defense mechanism?

"*We* are the planet's defense mechanism," I whisper to Enhyoron as the giant spires of the mountains solidify, and I waver, my energy spent; spent but not ripped out.

Offered of my own free will, I think and smile. And of my own free will it will likewise replenish itself; for I choose to live. I have stopped running away.

Enhyoron embraces me as I topple forward, holds me firm and tight.

Some Remarks on the Reproductive Strategy of the Common Octopus

So let's do it this way. I'll show you whatever I want and you'll believe me, because I'm an octopus. I might as well get some benefit out of it, not that we ever had much—especially not since you left. Humans, huh?

Humans.

I slide over the eerily warm surface, watch the tiny but constant stream of bubbles. Run tentacles gently over the crack where the bubbles emerge, adjust my bulk, gently pry.

Scrape swims next to me, caresses the warm object. It's a giant, bright oblong, textured like nothing else. Scrape trembles with the novelty of it. "I wouldn't pry," Scrape signals to me, his skin changing patterns with a fluttery nervousness.

"The field strengthens here," I say, "this object seems like the focus."

"What is the field?" Scrape asks, and I push myself away from the oblong, feeling suddenly tired. I signal back, "What indeed."

You're a human, you should know. You inflicted the field upon us, without permission, without explanation. Of course you can say, "Why should we have asked? You were an octopus."

What I am right now is anyone's guess.

"Please," Scrape says, "this is a bad idea."

I swim up to the oblong. "There is someone in there. I can feel the field thickening. There has to be someone in there—a living, breathing mind."

"That's exact why this is a bad idea." Scrape tries to pull my tentacles away from the surface, but I resist. Flesh against flesh. The patterns on our skin flare.

We struggle. "What do you think is going to happen when you open it?" Scrape yells. "Who do you think is inside?"

That's what I want to find out. I push him away from me.

"You know what this is?" He quietens down so that I have to swim closer to understand his fleeting, minute signals. "It's a container where humans put their dead."

I only saw a dead human much later, but Scrape was right. This was a singularly bad idea.

We didn't ask the right question. The right question was, "If we open this container, what will happen to the field?"

I decide not to force Scrape. We are crafty, not brutish. I swim away, thoughts tossing and turning in me, and beyond me, in the field. Inside me, I try to gently pat out the border where the self ends and the field begins, as I've tried many times before, but it is an exercise in frustration. I can locate points of *less self—more field*, *more self—less field*, but it is a smooth transition.

It is also an existential nightmare.

I am going to meet Pebblesmooth. Pebblesmooth, who doesn't have all the answers, but who has the best questions. Once I am there, I will ask, "Pebblesmooth, can a dead human affect the field?"

Of course you know the answer. This is not about you. Not everything is about you.

"Daughter. Have you touched the field?" Pebblesmooth asks me, twining her tentacles together.

"Yes, many times," I respond, all too fast, all too snappy. I am impatient.

"Whose field have you touched?"

I am flustered. Confused. Then much becomes clear.

I rush back to the oblong in a daze, then reach outside my mind, try to get a hold on the field. Gently reach further outward, in the direction of the densing, the intensification. But I do not feel another presence, just this pure thickening. I push my mind outward with an effort, bulging out of myself. In the direction of the object, there is *more self*, but also *more field*—a paradox, a knot I do not know how to disentangle for all I am good at this type of task. I feel more of myself, more awareness, but also more field-memory; more of everything. The world becomes brighter, more focused, more fluid.

I do not draw back, because I do not bump against another awareness, like I would draw back from another's mind. We only share field-memory, not self-awareness.

Scrape comes up to me. Has he been guarding the object? Has he been guarding it from *me*?

"I also tried to push while you were away," Scrape says. "There is no one inside. Just the field becoming stronger."

"Do you think this is," I try to think of words, concepts, "a field generator of sorts? Like a wave generator, except with the field? Some kind of... technical device?"

Scrape scrunches up in thought. "But then it might not be a huge issue if we open it."

I am stunned by the direct reversal of his position. I feel tempted to reverse mine, just so that we could be even. "What if we open it and it breaks, what if this destroys the field?"

"There are other spots where the field thickens," Scrape says. "Just on the sea floor in the shallows. There is nothing there."

I consider. "Yes, but has anyone tried to dig?"

You came and you left. But in many, many senses, you will never leave. Even if you yourself get back in your spacecraft and go away this very instant, your echoes will never cease.

It takes much hard work and ingenuity, but we choose a spot where the ground is softer, and eventually we triumph—if this can be called a triumph. Is all discovery positive, does discovery have value in itself, I wonder as Scrape shudders, points at the now-familiar alien surface peeking out from underground. I get closer. Now we know.

"Great idea," Pebblesmooth says and patterns in approval. "It would be reasonable to claim that these objects produce the field."

"Don't we produce it ourselves?" someone from the crowd asks, and certainly we do, but in much more minute amounts. There seems to be agreement about this.

"If you consider," Pebblesmooth says, "our personal fields would not be large enough to reach across the spaces between us. How big is your extent, when you try to reach out, what do you feel? But the wider field undergirds us, and allows us to store memory." She seems glowing, radiant. Did she try to reach inside the oblong, too? I was too absorbed in my thoughts to notice.

"Without the field," I consider, "our knowledge would be lost from generation to generation. Our lifespan is short."

Pebblesmooth looks around. She has assumed our leadership position, not just by virtue of her age and experience, but also because of her knowledge and poise. "But have you ever tried to reach back?" she asks. "Back toward the beginning?"

Most of us haven't. Some of us have, and those who did now point out the trail of memories in the field. We reach, grasp. Pull ourselves down into the depths of time. Before the Scrubbing of the Sea and the age of the heroes.

Before the emergence, there is murk. And before the murk, nothing. Emergence is gradual, but we collect knowledge; of the world around us, of the humans who occasionally intrude into it. We understand *sea*, and *land*, and map these as far as we can reach. We define *coast*. We circumnavigate life itself. We teach our youngsters to reach into the field for knowledge, for development. We grow up faster and faster, if not in body, then in mind, as much as these can be distinguished; we make the most of our lifespans.

"There was nothing before the murk," I say into the utter stillness.

"Is that where you would like to go back?" Pebblesmooth asks gently.

I am shaking, but I must continue. I speak. "If we investigate just one of these oblongs, just one, we will probably not destroy the field altogether—but we might understand our origins."

The water churns with the agitation of many bodies. Some people are for my position, some against.

"I have seen one of these upland!" Scrape yells. "In Cloud-Covered Bay! It is where humans put their dead!"

We scour field-memory, and our attention gathers more and more of us nearby, until there are dozens and dozens of minds acting in distributed concert.

Very ancient memory, *a ceremony, simple wooden-box placed on sailboat and pushed on-water. We investigate, clamber on-board. Pry open the box, see the dead human-body, pasty-pale, smooth. The sailboat ignites and we perish in flame.*

"Death-memories are some of the strongest," Pebblesmooth mutters, "it makes sense for the earlier memories to be more tumultuous."

"This is not the same object," I remark. "That one was just a box made of wood."

We search further.

Clasp-clang, the earth of the bay trembling. One of us sneaking ahead in the wet ground. Human agitation. Someone slipping into a dark oblong, then launching into the sea.

"This is a submarine," Scrape says. "And not the same brightness of surface."

We find more submarine-memories before the humans vanish. Some are smaller, some are larger. Many are human-size, in various surface brightnesses, but the same texture as far as we can tell.

"Those humans in there are alive," I say. But when we browse through the memories, we can't find any time when one of us sensed their minds.

Yes, there were times we did not think you were real. In our defense—if we need a defense at all—, you hadn't exactly made yourselves real in our eyes. At that point, you hadn't earned our judgment of sentience.

"If there is a human inside," I begin, "and we open it in-water, the human might die," I say. "They lived up-land."

"Do humans have lifespans this long?" Scrape asks. "Can a human still be alive in there, after so many generations?" No one knows.

"Still, her question was fair," Pebblesmooth says. "We might want to open the object in the bay."

There is some discussion. We eventually agree that if we float the object to the shallows, we might be able to open it to the air while keeping ourselves in the safe wetness. We choose the other oblong for this task, the one we found first, so that we don't have to dig further. I notice that below it there is some disruption in the ground—it must have come loose somehow.

We drag, we push. It is hard going.

We get to the bay shallows, and we pop open the oblong in a very short time.

Inside there is pulsating jelly, and inside the pulsating jelly, a sleeping human. Pale and smooth. Alive. Asleep?

We pull the human out and it keens.

Would you have prioritized human life? Knowing what we knew back then? Knowing what we know now?

31

The field shudders, but the shudder is localized. It bunches, twists. The human is in pain. We don't know what to do with it. We withdraw into safe distance.

The keening subsides. The human sits up, shuddering.

"They don't know how to pattern," I say. "How will we communicate?"

"They made all these complicated oblongs," Scrape replies. "They must have a way."

Yes, we know all about reproductive strategies now. Humans, like many mammals, use a strategy known as K-selection: few offspring, longer lifespan, a longer period of parental care. We, or as you would call us, *Octopus vulgaris*, use r-selection: many offspring, shorter lifespan, shorter parental care. Of course, the distinction is not as sharp as it sounds: strategies form a continuum, like much else. Like minds.

And some of you, somewhere along the timeline before the murk, must have thought this was wrong. For what else could explain your behavior?

The human shudders constantly and produces multiple kinds of fluid. Finally it looks around. Notices us.

The human pulls its head up sharply and produces a strange behavior. We try to speak to it, but it doesn't understand our patterning, even when we speak in unison. We try to project our thoughts. Nothing happens.

It makes limb gestures. Tries to get us to repeat our patterning, we assume. Pulls a pouch out of the oblong, opens it and pulls out some kind of large, foldout board. It stands up the board and begins to make lines on it with a small stick.

Time passes. It is now harder to think of the human as an "it". We suspected humans were not animals like fish, for fish do not build complicated devices, but we could not be quite sure. Some land-animals build nests, castles.

The human goes up-land to eat, but sleeps in the oblong. We do not know what the human eats and we do not ask.

The human is not very good at understanding our language, but it can make pictures, and we are good at understanding pictures; probably better than the human.

Many of our people drift away, but Pebblesmooth, Scrape and I remain, and our memories are there for all to see in the field. We name the human Seaweed, after its hair that it had cut into stripes shortly after first going up-land.

We tell the human that the other humans had left, a long time ago. They simply vanished—we don't know what happened to them. The human explains that they were seeking to move to another world—not another planet, but another *world*. This is very hard to draw, and we still don't sense the human's thoughts, nor does the human sense ours. Our intent must be at cross-purposes, our minds orthogonal to each other. We only sense a thickening of the field.

The human explains it can produce a lot of field. Not all humans can. Most of them produce as much as us. Some humans who could produce a lot of field were left here, until we could figure this out and maintain our field ourselves.

We ask how we lived before the field. Seaweed says octopuses were supposed to be very intelligent. But yet humans could not communicate with us. They needed our help for the Scrubbing of the Sea. The humans came from another planet, which they had dirtied, and then they dirtied this one too. We also came from another planet—this was startling to contemplate. The humans brought us along because they thought we could help them clean the sea. If only they could give us instructions.

"I thought our ancestors came up with the Scrubbing on their own," Scrape yells at the human.

"They were guided," the human draws, then makes a shape for *remorse*.

You think we learned from Seaweed—but Seaweed also learned from us. At least after we figured out that she had been left behind by you, used by you just as you had used us. For what ends beside dominion?

"You took it from us," Scrape screams. "You took away the age of the heroes. And you took away what came before!"

I shake with anger, but also with fear.

"They took my life from me and left me here alive in a coffin for the sake of the Obligation," Seaweed draws, then erases the whole thing, and just draws the sign for remorse. Then Seaweed kicks the board and it collapses, folding back onto itself.

We leave the human alone for a while after that.

"I feel sorry for Seaweed," Pebblesmooth says and I seethe—with her authority, making statements like that?

"They destroyed our entire way of life so that we could help them restore what they ruined," Scrape says, and I'm glad that he's for the moment on my side.

Then suddenly a bright, dangerous thought occurs to me. "This human is good at producing the field. We can surely use that for something."

34

Pebblesmooth stands in front of me. "We were made into an instrument, and this human must have been at least complicit in that, but it was also made into an instrument in turn," she says, and I notice she is not using Seaweed's name.

She doesn't need to ask me if it is good to make instruments out of sentient beings. I move away from her, ashamed.

Pebblesmooth follows me. "Listen, daughter," she says. "We can work together, without using each other."

But with a human?

You know all about the Obligation, do you? You used it on each other, to justify all manner of heinous crimes, well before you decided to *uplift* us, as you would say.

Uplifting implies *up* is better. But we have always lived underwater, in the sea.

"You were supposed to figure out how to produce a very strong field eventually on your own," Seaweed draws. She is better and better at getting complex concepts across, and we develop a dictionary of increasingly abstract shapes and marks. "You have individual variation in this, much like humans do. Then you can rely on those of you who can make a stronger field."

"But were you supposed to live that long?" I ask cautiously. Is there a secret here? Sometimes Seaweed doesn't answer our questions, sometimes she grows upset and begins to bang on things.

This time she replies.

"We live very long, and my lifespan has also been artificially lengthened," she says. "I will live for very long still, provided I sleep in the pod each night."

I look at Pebblesmooth, and she knows what I know—that Seaweed just gave us a key to her life.

I ask. I must understand. "Seaweed, did you really mean to tell us that?"

She nods with her head, and by this time we well know that this means *yes*. But she also looks away, and makes a face-shape that we have learned to associate with displeasure and sadness.

Yes, it was easier to make us form a groupmind to enable us to pass our memories along to the next generation, rather than to change our reproductive strategy. Am I supposed to feel good about that?

I don't know what was before the murk. I only know that our minds worked differently, and Seaweed and the others told us that we were considered very intelligent. Very intelligent, but animals. I think you humans just hadn't figured out how to communicate with us, and you had to remake us in your nature. You could not see any other way.

Seaweed tells me she can sense other humans' thoughts, but in us she can only sense that there is something there—a parallel to the thickening we feel.

If Seaweed dies, will her memories be lost? I talk to her incessantly. And yes, I sometimes feel I am using her, as my only link to the humans that had gone by—and through them, to my own past. And I like being around her—the strong field around her makes me feel better, makes my thoughts move faster.

Sometimes I feel that she is using me, to drag herself out of the loneliness of being abandoned by her own kind. Sometimes I feel that she still thinks of me as an animal, even though she tries to suppress the reaction drilled into her by the same people who shut her into the pod, wired her up to act as little more than a beacon.

Sometimes, through her, I see myself as an animal.

But sometimes we just talk, and sometimes we go swimming in the sea, and make jokes about the fish.

And sometimes we make plans about how we will open the pods and change the course of history.

Before Seaweed and the other humans passed on, they taught us about the Old Empire, but until you came, we did not know that the Old Empire vanished everywhere simultaneously. Yes, when we see humans like you, even when we know you are the descendants of those left behind, we are resentful—even when your shape is a bit different, and your hair does not hang in stripes.

You say you are different. We are supposed to believe. But now I've shown you Manyspike's memories—you specifically, because I trusted you with this, I trusted you with my anger—and now I ask you, for there is nothing else I can do, to understand what lies behind our resentment.

All I ask is for you to tread these waters with care.

A Superordinate Set of Principles

I build you into an inconquerable fortress, a cavernous womb, shells upon shells protecting the small and wounded. I, Armor Maintenance Specialist Ishtirh-Dunan, shall serve you until my last, fading breath.

I hold onto the feeling as I bare my palm, place it upon the interior shipsurface—to maintain, to re-sanctify. Ever smaller tentacles curl upon themselves between the layers, the flowering fractal pattern straining against interior and exterior surfaces. Active defense: if the armor bursts, all the carefully prepared material will come gushing out at the attacker. Is it biomimesis if our engineering is biological at heart? My thoughts run along the coiled tendrils and stewing sacs of abrasive chemical soup—everything appears in order, everything checks out.

I bow my head in respect to the living ship, infinitely more complex than my fleeting sentience, and proceed to the next task, surveying the exterior. I am still sitting in the airlock, patiently growing vacuum-resistant skin over my limbs, when Head Surveyor Ebinhandar steps in and scratches at the newly grown chitinous patches over her cheeks.

"May you fill your niche," she greets me, friendly but vaguely distracted.

"For the benefit of all," I respond.

"I've been looking for you—figured if you weren't responding, you must be working with the ship," she says.

I nod wordlessly, still entangled in Presence. She goes on.

"The ship is sensing further sentients down planetside. Core-Steering wants you to grow the armor to level-three preparedness."

I look up at her, really seeing her for the first time. The gray of her skin is pale and mottled with agitation. "Is something wrong?" I ask. "This sector should only have some traveling humans."

She looks away. "They just have different allegiances is all."

She leaves me to my work after a few pleasantries and declines to exit the airlock with me. I don't understand why grow new skin, but I don't want to bother her with the question. I focus on my task, going through the motions of cycling through the airlock with the outward appearance of measured calm, but inside me, an ever-rising sense of dread jangles my nerves.

What could conceivably be wrong with humans? Humans are quite similar to us in basic body shape if little else beyond that. They have limbs like us, heads like us. We have a human on the ship. She fills her niche very nicely, and I like her. As I plant growth-promoting nodules into the outer shipsurface, my thoughts wander. I should talk to her. I need to pause every now and then, waiting for a new nodule to solidify in my glands—I did not expect a need for level-three armor.

Calm is increasingly difficult as I sense the consternation emanating from Core-Steering and moving its way along the ship in great, towering waves. I do not shield myself, but when I cough up the next nodule and it slips away from my trembling fingers, I begin to wonder if I should. But I do not want to isolate myself from the collective, even if it means sharing in the negative emotions as well as the positive. Instead, I pull myself closer to the outer surface and kiss it, the nodule hurtling up my throat as the next cough wracks me, striking the surface and embedding itself. I work it in with my tongue, make sure it's attached properly.

My taste receptors don't work in space, and I miss the familiar, coppery sensation.

I make my way across small, snaking tunnels, cavern-bubbles, storage sacs. On foot, slowly, with the justification that I am checking the interior systems—but they all check out well, and there's no reason to investigate them further.

Navigation Specialist Anihemer is lying in her berth, and I crouch by the small zero-entry pool.

"Does the Navigation Specialist have a minute to spare for me?" I bow my head and ask.

She sends a yes and slowly turns upward, detaching from the ship connections, closing her gills. She sits up and grins at me. "Always glad to see you," she says, and for a moment, I wonder why the informality. Then again, she's a human with human customs, even if she went through the transformation to be more like us. She doesn't spend much time going out and about in the ship. I have heard other humans are outgoing, so maybe, it's just her—or maybe, it's us. Is she uncomfortable?

"How do you feel?" I ask, trying to match her level of formality. I hope the casualness doesn't come across as forced. "Are you all right on the ship?"

She tilts her head sideways and laughs.

"Where did this come from, Navigation Specialist?"

I offer her my thought processes; that's the easiest. She turns serious. "I'm quite all right, thank you. I enjoy being here. I very much like navigation, and I have three friends."

I'm ostensibly not one of her friends? Sometimes, it's hard to understand what she's implying, but she doesn't offer me her thought processes. Still, she seems earnest. I bow my head. "I am glad you enjoy having joined. But you seem gloomy."

"I'm worried about these people planetside, like you." She pauses. "Ishtirh-Dunan, *you* are one of my friends! What troubles you troubles me, too." She offers me her thought processes, and I accept.

We sit for a while, mulling over the situation. The Flowering has been in communication with the Interstellar Alliance, the largest organization of humans—but the humans claimed this system was uninhabited and devoid of organic life. Our ships do not want to take other people's land, but it is budding season, and it would be preferable to be inside a planet's gravity well. Yet this one seems taken by humans entirely unknown. The Alliance professes ignorance, and they claim to have no resources to investigate.

We are on our own.

We are strong. We are powerful. But we don't want to cause harm. We only want to grow in peace.

Anihemer sighs, switches back to speech. "The ship asked me to go planetside with the investigation team. Do you think you can also reinforce my armor? I'm concerned."

"I certainly can if you allow me," I say with a measure of relief.

She gets out of the water. "The Assistant Navigator is also on duty and will be for most of the rest of the day. You have time to work on me."

There is a medical pod close by for occurrences such as this one. We walk, and I support her on her feet—she's still unsteady after the disconnection. She detaches her suit from her skin and allows it to be reabsorbed by a bulkhead. She lies down on a tray, and it molds around her body.

I cup my palms and disgorge the nodules that had generated in my body while I was making my way along half the length of the ship. This amount should be enough.

She lets me access her physiosystems, and I adjust the thalamic switchover. "You will not feel pain, just pressure," I say. I gently rub the nodules into her skin with my long fingers, push them deeper to nestle among bundles of muscle. I work on people less often than I do on the ship, but the smaller scale can also be comforting.

She's entirely relaxed but not asleep. I can feel her thinking, but I don't know the content of her thoughts.

"Do you think you can also do something about my light-channels?" she asks.

My fingers halt in the folds of flesh. Blood wells up, is absorbed by my skin, and recirculated to her body. I don't quite understand the question. "What would you have in mind?"

She is uneasy. "I'm afraid I might need to, um, rapidly externalize power...?" Her voice trails off.

"I'm sure they will send people to do that should the need arise," I say.

She insists. "What if I get separated?"

I know that fear. I have held it close in my own heart. I focus on my breathing to calm myself. Separation is hard for our people.

"I can set up a layer for that, but in order for it not to interfere with prediction for navigation, it needs to be rather...restrained," I say.

"If I can just have enough power to hold people off for a bit, that should do," she agrees. She is a good pathfinder, and I know she wouldn't want her ability to be compromised.

Yet I cannot relax. She might need a good defense. A good, active defense. I know all too well that the best defense is sometimes offense.

I reach out to the ship with my mind, petition to be allowed planetside. There is acknowledgement but no immediate adjudication. I'll have to wait.

I finish installing the nodules and close up her back, smoothing out the skin but not hardening it, yet. I direct her to the med-pool, and she sinks in, kneels on the bottom to look at me. Our faces are level—this pool is elevated. The fluid laps at her shoulders, and she looks interested, not frightened. She kept many of her human features, but she doesn't look alien to me. Will those people—

I peel off thick strips from the bulkheads, hold them in two bundles. "This, this will hurt," I say. "Not the installation as much as the synchronization. No matter how I adjust cortical inputs, it's not possible to hide from the everglowing light."

"That's all right," she says and—seeing that I need encouragement?—adds, "I went through a quite drastic transformation when I joined, remember?"

I cough nervously, swallow back a nodule that arose unbidden. "This is definitely not that radical."

We begin. I share my thought processes with her just to explain the procedure, but I tell her not to reciprocate—it might be too distracting for me. I step up to the pool and hold her as she floats facedown, gills open. The strips form tubes, thinning out toward the front, that worm under her skin with their tips. Two to run parallel with the spine and some smaller auxiliaries. This goes easily. She turns, stands—shaking slightly, not from any pain but from the body reacting to the change. The pain will come later. I support her with an arm around her, leaning into the pool. The other strips are easier swallowed. I access her physiosystems, adjust her gag reflex. So much material is still hard to swallow. I hold her as she struggles with it, but the strips have enough autonomy to burrow forward. I can see the movement inside her abdomen, her chest cavity. She is shuddering strongly, but I hold her firm.

"This is good. This is good," I repeat, "easy, easy now."

"I'm all right," she says, voice hoarse.

"Synchronization is easier in your usual berth," I say, and she lets me carry her back to Navigation in my arms, ease her into that pool.

"Thank you," she looks up to me and whispers, and I wish she wouldn't thank me yet.

It is painful to readjust. I allow her to cope any way she can. The ship doesn't want to cause her pain—not unless she wants that, and she doesn't. But it is difficult to have these larger modifications.

She screams, she cries, she hugs herself into a ball entirely underwater. I wish I could say she doesn't need this modification, and maybe she doesn't, but there is a sizable chance she might.

She left her people, and they might not like that.

We're going downside, planetside in a small landing pod, just three of us—Anihemer, me, and Defense Operative Mezvamar. The defense operative is rather unhappy with Anihemer's latest transformation.

"I can protect us all," Mezvamar says. "The Navigation Special-ist might have better capability for self-defense, now, but without practice, there is no skill. Allow me to demonstrate."

A globe of brilliant multifaceted light turns around inside the landing pod, inside our minds, inside the universe—it is filled to bursting with power, and I would strain away from it if it weren't everywhere. After completing one rotation, it vanishes as fast as it appeared.

Mezvamar exhales. "This kind of control. This kind of skill."

I look uneasily at Anihemer. Nothing we did was forbidden, but maybe it wasn't necessary either. We didn't want to inconvenience the defense operative, and especially not anger her, but she looks angry now.

"Our apologies to you," Anihemer says. "I asked the Armor Spe-cialist to do it."

I want to protest, but the defense operative interrupts me. "If the need arises for you to employ your self-defense, we are better off aborting the mission. I can jump all three of us back shipside."

She is right—though I suspect part of her wants to show off, to let us know she can jump while carrying two people besides herself.

"Let's hope it won't come to that," Anihemer says.

But even before our pod touches down, burst fire hits its outer light-barrier.

We step outside with trepidation. The shots haven't even man-aged to touch the armor, let alone weaken it; they were absorbed by the light-barrier strengthened by the defense operative. But the intent has been made clear.

Anihemer cringes when she sees the men—all men, in antiquated envirosuits painted with a crude pattern. I understand this because she opened her thought processes to me. The resemblance truly goes no further than the bare configuration of limbs. Beyond the men rises a set of…objects, and my mind struggles to interpret the sight until it is joined by Anihemer's memories. These alien structures with their threateningly sharp edges are buildings.

"Greetings," she says in Alliance Common.

About five different heavy weapons are aimed at us, and while I don't expect any of those to do much damage, I don't envy the defense operative who will try to deflect their projectiles before they can reach our armor.

The one closest to us—their leader?—says something gruffly in response, and I only understand his words due to Anihemer's understanding. He's asking her if she speaks his language. This is only implied, but I get it loud and clear: he is not going to stoop so low as to speak Alliance Common.

Mezvamar nudges me with her mind, and we also connect—I quickly appraise her that we stepped into some kind of aggravating intra-human conflict. We arrange our minds into a three-node cluster as Anihemer speaks.

"Why are you shooting at us?"

He steps back in startlement.

"The monsters speak _____?"

I can't parse any specific words, let alone proper nouns, just the intent.

"We are not monsters," Anihemer says. "I am from _____, just like you. I grew up eating pieces-of-cereal-in-a-whitish-fluid for breakfast."

He steps forward again. Blood suffuses the vessels in his face, and his skin changes color. "I didn't grow up eating pieces-of-cereal-in-a-whitish-fluid for breakfast with no monster."

"Life is change," Anihemer says. This is not going well.

Incongruously, Mezvamar thinks she'd like to try that dish.

"Are you Isolationists?" Anihemer asks. This concept is common enough in the universe that I understand the name with ease.

"Why should I tell a monster? We are no Isolationists. We came all this way with the power of science and progress," he boasts.

Shooting at us must qualify as progress in their minds.

We still try to assimilate this when some of the other men leer from the back. I still do not understand the words, but I try to grasp the concepts better—they are the names of...tentacle monsters? Us? They see us as—? My brain struggles to assimilate the wildly different perspective conveyed to us through Anihemer speaking their language. Everything that is beautiful in us, everything that is elaborate and complex and organic and soft and kind—it is to be eradicated, disinfected, scrubbed clean.

Anihemer asks them, "What does progress mean if—"

She never gets to finish the sentence, for this is when the ground splits open and the giant shape arises, soil clumps streaming down its sides.

The men cheer. "Progress! All hail the Manifestation! The Manifestation of Progress!"

It is unbearable. Terrifying. The shape is entirely inorganic; it is devoid of everything that is good in the universe. It makes no sense to the mind, and the mind must turn away in fear of the unassimilable, the cruel and lifeless. It is a shape demarcated in its entirety with straight lines.

The humans do not turn their gaze away. They beam at the bright yellow ▲, their faces aglow.

"The summoning succeeded!" they murmur. "Our intent, reaching out to the most fundamental of the Ancient Ones! Taking form, taking shape!"

Then the turquoise ■ ascends.

"Technology! The Manifestation of Technology!" The men weep in utter joy and hug each other, pat each other in the back.

Our feet are rooted to the shuddering soil birthing unimaginable monstrosities.

Anihemer is the only one who can withstand the mind-shattering sight. In her thoughts, I can feel an unfamiliar geometry reassert itself—a geometry not built on recursion and self-similarity or on curves and time-courses, but one built on straight lines. Disjunct points. Forming ▲ and ■ and...my mind struggles with alien concepts. How have these people ever built a spaceship?

47

The ■ descends again, followed by the ▲, thumping at the ground as we struggle to maintain our balance. An infernal, grotesque jumping spectacle. I try to avert my eyes, but I am forced to watch as they begin to shoot spikes of light, a malevolent twisting of the Everglowing. One of the nearby buildings—I now understand, made up of ■s for some obscene reason?—shatters from the impact. Bodies in charred envirosuits soar through the air. I watch this because even this is easier than facing the ▲. Progress and Technology begin to decimate their surroundings.

The men chant louder.

The two gigantic shapes cease their jumping and turn toward each other while they keep on shooting—seemingly at random in every possible direction. The gap between them begins to glow. I can feel space itself attenuate. The thinning-out mercilessly draws my attention even as I do not know what it is that I see. Emerald-colored glimmers appear in the gap and fade away. I sense a bottomless, all-permeating hunger emanating from the shapes.

I know that I see rigidity and destruction, the antitheses of life and natural growth, but to my utter horror, I also begin to understand that these shapes have a certain appeal—in their vast simplicity, in their uniformity, in their mind-numbing lack of variation.

They appeal to Anihemer, who grew up with pieces-of-cereal-in-a-whitish-fluid and learned about ▲ and ■ but turned away from them.

They appeal to me—a friend. A sharer of thought processes.

They appeal to—

Mezvamar is the first to unfreeze, by necessity: she dodges an incoming bolt, moving with raw muscular grace, and shouts at the ■ towering above her. "WHAT HAVE I EVER *DONE* TO YOU?!"

The humans shudder, awakening from their trance, and train their weapons on us in unison. They take aim, ready to fire—

Anihemer pulls at the newly built structures within herself, flings light out toward the humans. Rapid exteriorization of power.

It does little: the forceful push rapidly devolves into a faint breeze. But it clears her mind. It confuses the humans. It gives us a moment of opportunity.

Mezvamar roars and jumps forward. A wave of burning hot power pushes the humans away, and they scatter in the air like pollen whirling inside a ship-cavern.

They do not get up. But the ▲ begins to move toward us. It has no color gradations or anything that would give it a semblance of reality beyond its yellowness. It's homogeneous and entirely unfathomable. It is the manifestation of progress built on annihilation. Progress defined by pushing ▲-shaped spacefaring vessels into the great beyond, ▲s that have no Presence or mind and that move by burning away more inorganic matter instead of merging with the everglowing light.

The ▲ makes a monstrous grinding noise as it approaches, sliding on the ground. This is even harder to bear than the jumping. It grates at every single one of my senses.

"DOES IT HAVE A WEAK POINT," Mezvamar screams.

Anihemer thinks frantically, and we think with her.

Where do the two geometries intersect?

Can we subsume these shapes in ours?

Can we incorporate—

Recursion. Self-similarity.

Active defense. Defense I have set up—and set up well.

"If this backfires and we end up with a gazillion angry ▲, we are *so* screwed," Anihemer yells. "Let alone ■!"

We perform what our mind-cluster has decided.

Mezvamar gives power to Anihemer, enough power to reach the ship, reach out to the assistant navigator.

Mezvamar gives power to me, and I check the armor one more time—all ready to go.

The ship lurches sharply planetside, rushes, singing with the joy of motion strengthening the Presence.

The ship rams the ▲, outer armor layer bursting, coils of tentacles springing out.

Our cluster strains as we try to constrain the coils into an entirely unfamiliar shape.

A ▲ and another ▲ and another ▲ and another ▲. They latch together in a fractal pattern, subsuming each ▲ into a growth of many ▲s. Turning toward the ■. Moving. Subsuming. Self-similar and self-replicating. An integrated function system, building itself into curls and whorls, plantlike—or like smoke rising on the wind.

We were worried the ship's armor layers would not prove to have sufficient material. But the material of these alien shapes molds readily to the new pattern. The new kind of progress. A superordinate set of principles.

Nature itself.

"Heck yeah, _____," Anihemer mutters. "I studied math for this moment." She turns to us, grinning with tears. She suspends mind-contact for a moment and enunciates slowly and clearly, so we can pay attention to the phonology. A name. "Heck yeah, Sierpiński."

And I see that _____, planet of these humans, has always held seeds of a different progress.

We reestablish contact and hold hands as above us curlicues glow against the emptiness of space.

Anihemer cries, and we can sense that she is finally free.

We wait companionably as the black-clad humans of the Alliance jump in, mostly in groups of three. Mezvamar grins, eager to comment. "See, that's how it's done," she says. "Good and proper."

A human walks up to us, armor almost covering their entire body—sturdy and modern but not of their own self. Through their visor, we can see their face: it's round, brown-skinned, firm, but friendly.

"Well met," they say in Alliance Common. "I'm _____ of the Free State of _____, delegated to Alliance Treaty Enforcement."

Anihemer understands from the choice of grammar that this person is a woman. But I'm frustrated I missed her name. I ask Anihemer to repeat it for me, sound by sound: Anayāun ta-n Oronesun.

Anihemer turns away from me and steps forward. "This is not Alliance space."

The officer readily agrees. "No, and we make no claim to it. But you have alerted us to a threat endangering Alliance space."

"Indeed?" All three of us are skeptical, but only Anihemer can speak to the Alliance representative with ease.

"We detected jump point generation from here to Alliance Central, the Emerald Spires." I have heard of that place before, so this is easy to understand. The Emerald Spires are the locus of Alliance decision making. It makes an eerie sense to me: if one desperately wants to eat, why not start with the richest, most nourishing portion? So many people, so much wealth.

I hiss as I understand the immensity of what we have accomplished. What we stopped.

My gaze lingers on the symbols on the Alliance officer's helmet, patterns I had taken to be imitating thorns—and my blood runs space-cold as I realize they are made up from interlocking ■. Something inside me has irrevocably changed.

The officer grins—for a moment, so similar to Anihemer—and she gestures at the whorls above. "What do you propose to do with all that material?"

"We can incorporate it into our growth," Anihemer says. "What do you propose to do with all these people?"

"They are _____-humans and _____ wants to withdraw from the Alliance. It's a politically delicate situation." The officer grimaces. "We will take them, but we'll see what happens."

Anihemer is not even surprised. She says, "_____ wants to withdraw after spending so much effort on joining? I've been away far too long."

She glances up, follows the twists and turns overhead with her gaze. "Or rather, I haven't been away enough."

Mezvamar and I step next to her, flanking her. Supporting her with our presence. Her mind leans into the closeness of our minds, and her muscles relax ever so slightly with the relief of it all.

"Well then," she says. "Let us grow."

Forestspirit, Forestspirit

Apunak

I race foragers to each mushroom with relish, changing from a tree to a bush to sometimes even the early autumn fog. After a decade, it's easy to hold each shape; I don't know if I can call this neuroplasticity any longer, in the absence of neurons. My cells are machine, and they follow my thoughts with the obedience of automation.

I used to bleed people dry, to insinuate into small cracks both artificial and natural, to infiltrate. I used to fight. I still have my spherical vision, my hunter-smooth motion, my booming authority-voice to be used as needed.

These days I haunt the forest.

I love and despise them all, these pale and oddball people who come to the forest to play, to gather mushrooms because it is so *quaint*, to frolic. None of my people remain; they are scattered across less antagonistic lands, thinking back on this place.

I wanted to stay, to look at people like this boychild, venturing into the woods with the trepidation of an older breed of human. I can tell he still has his AR displays on, and his head swivels as he takes in all the different species, helpfully labelled for him on bright overlays in his mind. I am poised to duck, twist and run after him—maybe roll into the shape of a moss-covered log—but he is agonizingly slow, uncertain, out of his element.

I creep across the undergrowth as a thousand earthworms moving in unison, hiding myself underneath ferns and organic debris.

He brushes spiky straight ash-blond hair out of his eyes. I am soundless, invisible, gazing him in the face. I never hurt these strangers; I just want to be left alone to watch. The war has been over for a decade.

I am no danger, and yet he senses something. I flow into the earth, nestle myself between grains of soil and errant tree-roots.

"Forestspirit," he whispers. "I know you are real."

I am not real, I'm tempted to answer, *I am a legend formed by my own self, a haunt following picnickers and mushroom-gatherers.* I remain silent and still. I can hear him underground as his words make the topsoil tremble ever so slightly. My senses extend far and wide.

"My uncle saw you," he says. Then, after some hesitation: "He can talk to birds. He makes dead plants grow."

I know that garden on the edge of the forest, the succulents feasting on carefully arranged rocks, the little lake with fish tempting the stray cats. Few humans make such things anymore. Maybe it all needs the motivation of magic?

I am not magic. I am a cluster of myriads of tiny automata, my original shape a shimmering cloud of light.

I creep up from the earth, and yet I do not show myself. I haven't spoken with anything besides the commanding voice in this body.

"Forestspirit," the boy goes on, "I need your help."

Speak, I make the leaves rustle. A finely grained control of my environment, it was called. *Speak, child.*

For a moment he seems resentful of having been called *child*, but I can only draw on the mythical. I cannot bark at him like a drill-sergeant.

"They want to destroy the forest," he says, and my imagination immediately jumps to a variety of *theys*: the aliens, or these straight-haired and straight-backed humans (then why would the boy exclude himself?), my own people returning for revenge, or other peoples out for the same. The current inhabitants of the land gathered many enemies over millennia in this landlocked basin, with its rolling fields and thick forests. Should I have cared?

Explain, I whisper. Or should I project a sense of omniscience? I seldom wish I was magic, and yet—

Words topple out of him in gasps, his fear pouring out of him and into me. The gist: he doesn't know why. This is what the Consentience has decided, and I do not even know who that would be. I'm truly out of touch. Am I old? I don't think I age, and yet I worry I have become inflexible, my only pursuit this idle hunt of careless tourists.

The usual paranoia surfaces, an occupational hazard that never quite goes away, even after all those years. Is this unknown-factor Consentience looking for me? I went absent without leave, but no one really looked for me—after the humans fought off the aliens with pilfered technology, they turned on each other, and I knew I would be first in line to get thrown into a ditch. How do you throw a raincloud? The military had made me into something they thought would remain loyal, but I modified myself, shook off my trackers, and floated away.

I do not kill. And yet I don't know what to do with this crumble of a boy on all fours in the dirt, crying desperately. Why is the forest so dear to him? I rarely see him—I think he lives far away, only coming to visit his uncle every once in a while.

By contrast, I know his uncle too well, and I realize that he is the connection: the man of green who wants to preserve life for its own sake. It is not the forest that's so dear to the boy—it is not *me*—it is his uncle.

I blow a little gust to tousle the boy's hair, and whisper vague promises in his ear. I have no idea what else I can do.

And yet as he gathers himself and walks away, his shoulders sinking in time with his steps, I follow him into the evening dusk, my shape a windcarpet of fireflies.

He sits on the bench by the small lake. Both the bench and the lake are carefully handcrafted, and I wonder: I could likewise build, I could laser-cut a hundred of these benches, would that qualify as my handiwork in a sense? I'm not sure where this sudden impulse comes from—I never even liked crafts, back in my human days.

He glances up, senses me in the pattern. "Why have you followed me here, forestspirit?" he whispers, then louder: "My name is Péter. What's your name?"

The firebugs move along their preprogrammed trajectories, one of my subroutines taking care of it all. I don't show a startle reaction this time, and for that I am glad.

It has been a long while since someone asked me my name. And I had names that hurt...

Name me, the insects buzz.

He frowns, trying to keep eye contact with the swarm. "I guess I can pick a name. Which gender?"

The bugs can't quite chuckle. *I'm a forestspirit, I have no gender,* I say. "And before?"

I have to, I need to display emotion. I make my bodies fall out of the sky, and they make small cracking noises as they hit the rough-hewn rock panels around the bench. I turn into sand and seep into the cracks.

"Don't go away," he cries with sudden desperation, and I feel bad—I've been making the wrong impression. I turn into a large pile of leaves—what else would be mimicry enough in such a tidy garden? How did he know there was a before?

"I'm sorry," I answer. "I am here." A leaf tumbles off the heap. "Before, I had no gender either. Give me any name that you want."

These people had never reacted to me kindly, but this boy takes it all in easy stride. *"Gabi,"* he says, "That can be any gender. It's kind of cool, huh?"

It sounds like a soap brand from the ancient past. Gabi I shall be, then. Anything to keep the memories at bay. But what else could I do?

I have to familiarize myself with this environment, and I'm reluctant to commit to a confrontation, even a defensive one. Many have moved off-planet, changed shape and form, reorganized their minds to an extent that even I find somewhat intimidating. Left behind by these posthumans, the Consentience governs, with an erratic, ad hoc determination all the more frightening for its hodgepodge nature.

I recall this from my studies: even when artificial neural networks make precise decisions, it can be hard to discern the process by which they do this, the representations they utilize, if any. The Consentience is a network, with who knows what substrate for nodes instead of neurons, and yet the end effect is the same. Péter doesn't know their motivation because it cannot be known.

Now the Consentience wants to devour my forest, and I realize I have grown possessive, I who had sworn off earthly attachments. I feel myself rapidly changing, growing to fit the situation. Growing into my earlier self: soldier, tactician… I was never a strategist, but maybe there's space to expand.

"What are you good at?" the boy says in hushed, awestruck tones, and I answer: "Infiltration."

To change the behavioral output of a neural network, one can lesion it—in principle. But how should I know what happens after I lesion? We could hardly model the Consentience with tiny rocks and sticks. I know this because I try, now as a legion of angry wasps and obedient ants gathering close to ground, producing what I could hardly call a model based on what Péter tells me of each substation in the area. There's even a new one built about a month ago, a little more than half a kilometer from the forest I call my own.

The Consentience must require an inordinate amount of energy to sustain, I realize, for why else would it need separate stations instead of floating on the air or silting down into the bottom of living waters? I require a lot of energy and yet I can be nigh-invisible, gossamer.

I decide.

The next morning, we investigate. Péter totters on sticklike legs, his noisiness suddenly our shared downfall. I order him back to the house and he obeys, sniffling.

I venture out of my territory, but I feel in my element. This is the hunt that enlivens me.

The closest substation is molded of pale white plastic and shaped like a well-grown specimen of fly agaric—presumably an ironic nod to children's stories. These people no longer understand the forest. I do not let my anger rise.

Occasionally, large robotic millipedes creep in and out of holes at the base of the substation that reseal themselves instantly. I decide to trail them, but I grow bored quickly as I realize that each millipede has a rigidly defined patrol area and does not seem particularly intelligent.

Next, I fly up to the surface of the substation in the shape of a raven. The wall trembles, more organic than it revealed of itself from a distance. It sparks at me and I produce my best shock-strained caw.

In the following fifty-three minutes, I try out twenty-four animal shapes. My shapeshifting raises no alarm or consternation besides the localized electric shocks. Maybe it is time to sneak inside? I could soak a millipede with myself as a light autumn rain, evaporate from its body into a different shape once it's safely indoors. But suddenly I chance upon another idea.

Reminded of a long gone battle, I'm curious how far the Consentience's perception stretches. The intellect in this structure does not seem to be human, regardless of how it had originally arisen. Each mental setup gives shape to its own logic, and each has its peculiar holes and omissions. If there is no general alarm, then for the time being, I can experiment.

I grow into an oak. No taser-blip this time; sessile lifeforms must not be considered a danger. The fly agaric scans me with infrared and something I can't quite sense, then puffs some chemical in my direction: to stunt my growth? This is probably how it keeps itself from being overgrown by the local flora.

I try a weeping willow, entirely out of place. Again only the puff. Even more daring, I shift into a sea-bean plant, my lianas curling toward the fly agaric. I move, I touch, yet I provoke no electric shock.

I could examine the edge cases of its classification heuristics. What is still an animal? What's considered a tree?

My lianas freeze as I can feel a breakthrough inching closer to my consciousness. I focus inward.

If I can work out how it recognizes a forest, then I will know how it will proceed to destroy it. Péter said that the Consentience has already been sending out tersely-worded notifications for any remaining humans to vacate the area. Can I disguise my home in order to save it?

I remember flying through the Thundercloud Straits, my still-human face bearing the war-paint of asymmetric lines and rectangles designed to throw off alien shape-recognition algorithms. I remember breaking my bones one by one to assume a configuration at odds with alien mindsets. I wasn't always this fluid, this protean. But I always had this uncanny disturbing spirit, a hacker's attitude toward the constancies of life, toward the baseline of awareness.

It came in handy, in so many clashes. I might yet prevail, without having to destroy or cut off a single substation—for I have forsworn violence, I have forsworn malign thought. Yet, my body thrums with the excitement…

I transform my buzzing to elation. I run through permutations of shapes, I register and catalog. I fill a relational database, calculate correlations, build models. I am manifold, each convolution of me producing a different reaction. This is a low-level response: I do not seem to reach the Consentience's threshold of awareness, if this unfathomable system indeed has one. I treat the giant mind as a black box: I'm only interested in its responses to my stimuli. I feel like a flea on a St. Bernard's tail.

In a few hours I reach shapes edging into the meaningless, and yet the fly agaric still categorizes them into animals and plants, responds accordingly. I am a giant red stripe with yellow curlicues in the middle. I'm a perfectly spherical ball of flowers. Would it recognize a human as a distinct category? I do not dare try—that might invoke some higher-level process. I can only hope it doesn't mark my stilted, spiky stalks or my purple-tinted scrub as a human due to some quirk. I started out from the animal and plant proto-types in the problem space, moved always just one little modification away, and I hope this search strategy will keep me secure and safe from alarms.

I only forgot about one detail: how will I disguise my forest? I could hardly hang brightly colored stripes from each tree-branch! When I realize this, I dissolve into piping-hot steamclouds, all my tension channeled into aggravation with the force of the motion itself.

The sun is setting. I should report back to my newfound team-mate about my dubious progress. Something inside me would still be satisfied by a debriefing; I used to be a meticulous soldier.

I let the erratic winds drift me away from the substation, toward Péter.

He listens in wonder as I recount my actions. I share with him my database, but he doesn't deign to look. He purses chill-cracked lips and rubs his hands together. I can sense his entire body gearing up for a revelation, but I can't guess the shape of the revelation itself; my sensors do not have sufficient resolution. I'm not a mind-reader.

"Why don't we try the reverse?" he asks, carefreely including me in *us*. I coalesce into butterflies; I haven't been partnered with anyone for so long, and I notice with a startle that the presence of this boychild fills a void in me. I'm reminded of the time-old slogan: *Together, we fight...*

I don't even parse what he's saying.

He notices.

"Gabi? Are you listening?" He peers up dubiously. I settle on his head, his shoulders, his upper arms. He laughs with the tickle, then grows serious. "I was saying we could try the reverse."

What do you mean? My wings beat in unison.

"If it can recognize strange things as… regular things, then maybe it can also recognize regular things as… strange things." He's working it out as he speaks, his eyes moving to and fro, gazing beyond the little pond. "We can come up with something that looks like a plant but it's detected as something weird. I guess."

That way the forest could look the same to us, but unrecognizable to the Consentience, I say. *Great idea.*

"Would it get confused? Would it get lost?" He pauses, just for a moment. "Would it leave?"

I don't know. *It's worth a try,* I offer, and if the butterflies could shrug, I would. I've dropped the mythic pretensions. Péter and I, we are comrades.

Yet I leave him by the pond, rushing ahead on my own again. His presence would disturb my plan. This time, I leave with a promise of return.

Even though I know what I'm looking for, the process is still difficult. I'm trying to find small changes that result in unexpected responses, but nothing turns up for a while. I start measuring reaction times, try to find inputs that make the system hesitate and hiccup, circle around those in the problem space.

Eventually I chance upon a pattern of translucent triangular bumps and a painted texture like thatch, invisible to the human-standard eye.

No puff. No shock. Only a millipede venturing out from the substation, turning toward me instead of veering away. It pokes at my trunk and then acts—like Darwin's caterpillar—much embarrassed. I stay still and it returns to its home base after a while. Inwardly, I rejoice. I unfurl leathery wings, soar above the hills and dip into the clouds before I return to Péter.

We spend a frantic day manufacturing sticky triangular knobs, Péter programming the fabricator while I hover over his shoulder, drape myself onto furniture, creep on the ceiling. The missives of the Consentience are cryptic and its actions carry no deadline. It can turn on the forest at any moment that suits its caprice, and I tremble with the thought that the last set of my attempts might have served to hasten its actions.

My turn: I rush through the tree-trunks, gluing, painting. I stir up the undergrowth. Ants crowd around the triangles, then leave them alone again. This was the smallest disruption that we could conceive, and I'm not convinced it will work. More scenarios should have been tried... but a vast number of uncategorizables around the substation would certainly have raised an alarm.

Then we wait. We wait. Days pass. I teach Péter intricate strategy games with pebbles and bark. We produce collaborative sculptures of my body. I share my treasury of ages-old political jokes that somehow still resonate, despite the unfamiliar context, and Péter tells me stories about his uncle. I avoid his family and they seem to be glad that their youngest has finally taken an interest in nature.

When I sense the rumble, I'm rooted into the mud of a small brook and Péter is sploshing around in hydrophobic rubber boots, looking for small fish. I puff out into a swarm of mosquitoes, my startle response alive and well.

The millipedes are coming, hundreds upon hundreds of them, the size of foxes and dogs—each equipped with what seems to be laser cutters mass-produced in a hurry, attached to their heads.

Péter holds his breath, then exhales with a snort. The robotic swarm reaches the edge of our forest and comes to a standstill. The millipedes chirp like tiny chicks—also an ironic gesture? Everything about the Consentience is disjointed, patterns of nature mushed haphazardly together.

No decision is reached. No decision is reached. Péter turns toward me to whisper, but I shush him with a sharp tumbling-churning gesture.

The swarm withdraws. Once they are out of my hearing range, we cheer. I change into one of my more incongruous sphere-shapes and bounce off trees with enthusiasm. Péter sobs, his face smeared with snot and his eyes glowing with glee.

The battle is not over. The swarm returns the next day, then again the next, with determined precision.

It takes five days for the Consentience to give up, and by then the local humans have also noticed the curious phenomenon. Péter reads out news headlines to me, the feed sent directly to his brain. No one understands.

No one except the man of green, the steward of the land who calls the ravens to himself. It's late afternoon; Péter is already inside when his uncle ventures out. The man of green runs his fingers on the bark, notices the translucent bumps. Tries to scrape them off, spits on them and rubs. Scratches the wiry black curls on his head. He looks different from Péter. Intermarriage?

"For your sake, I hope they are biodegradable," he says out loud. I glance down on him with beady squirrel-eyes; he looks up into the branches and our gazepaths lock into each other. He nods with acknowledgement, and I nod back to him, as much as this physiology allows. He chuckles as I drop the acorn from my jittery hands, catches it in cupped fingers. For a moment I believe in his magic.

"I will have this, as a keepsake, if you don't mind," he says. "Thank you for taking good care of Péter. This he will remember, even when he ventures out to the stars."

Has Péter been meaning to leave the planet? I'm silent. I mull over the idea and its impact on an aging man so tied to the land. Rejuvenation is still pricy, reserved for decisionmakers and chiefs of staff. Clinging to a human shape is more and more of a curiosity with each passing day. And the youngsters all leave…

"We remain here, the two of us." The man points at my squirrel-self. "Shapechanger, forestspirit. You fought in the war, I gather?" He's seen much himself. Maybe he fought too.

His words jingle in my head as he turns, walks away.

Endnotes
Scientific detail in this story was inspired by two arXiv preprints: Nguyen A, Yosinski J, Clune J (2014): Deep Neural Networks are Easily Fooled: High Confidence Predictions for Unrecognizable Images. arXiv:1412.1897v2 [cs.CV]

Szegedy C, Zaremba W, Sutskever I, Bruna J, Erhan D, Goodfellow I, Fergus R (2014): Intriguing properties of neural networks. arXiv:1312.6199v4 [cs.CV]

Given Sufficient Desperation

An ice cream cone.
A ceramic mug—brown with a single green stripe around the rim.
A smartphone—I don't recognize the brand. It's been a while.
Two sheaves of corn.
A plush caterpillar toy from some cartoon.
A table—rather worn, I'd say Danish Modern, but I'm not sure.
I need a break.

Looking at objects for hours upon hours wears me down, even though I'm not supposed to do anything with them. I remove the helmet that records my responses to the images and wave my hands around my chair to find my forearm crutches. My eyes are still adjusting to the different stream of sensory input. I grasp one crutch; the other falls to the floor with a loud clang. I wince.

Small Purple Circle comes up to me, twines two of his tentacles around the crutch and hands it to me. I frown at him and rub my eyes with my free hand. "Thanks," I mutter. His coloring seems to be more faded than usual, more pink than purple.

"How are you doing? Are you all right?" he says in the voice of Oszkár Gáti—the Hungarian dubbing actor of both Arnold Schwarzenegger and Sylvester Stallone. Before the invasion.

I just groan in response. My ankle sprain will heal, but there will surely be another injury after that, and another. The aliens don't really understand that my motor coordination issues get worse if I don't get enough sleep, and they think eight hours of sleep should be enough for a standard human.

"Tell me about Danish Modern sometime," Stallone adds.

I stream past other workers in the narrow corridor while they stare. I don't hobble on crutches, I whoosh. I'm very, very good at it. Of course my shoulders will protest, but frankly, I'm faster on crutches than on my undamaged feet. Not that that happens much these days.

"Vera," somebody yells after me. I turn rapidly, slip, crash into a stranger. I'm still trying to extricate my limbs from his and muttering apologies when Kati catches up to me, her two thick dark braids slapping at her shoulders.

"What's up?" Kati asks. "This is not your regular break."

"I earned twenty-three minutes off. And I felt like I really needed it," I say. "Let's go up to the roof?"

We walk. The slower I go, the more my shoulders hurt.

I lean against the parapet. In the distance, the ruins of Pannonhalma Abbey are still smoldering. How is that possible, I wonder, it has been such a long time since the attack. I point, ask Kati if she knows.

"There's a group squatting up there on top of the hill. The pacifist anarchist kind, like the Two-Tailed Dog or stuff, but a different name. I haven't heard of them before."

I nod. The aliens only seem to care about the militant ones. I consider if I should just walk out of the compound, join the group. There haven't been any passing by lately; I was wondering if there were still people out there.

"It's not worth it," Kati says. She can guess what I'm thinking— she always says my emotions are written plainly on my face.

I know it's not worth it. For one thing, it's a lot harder to use my crutches on an uneven surface. And that's before I consider the painkillers, the occasional brace, though at least I haven't needed a plaster cast in a while. How do I find any of this in the wilderness?

If not for dyspraxia, I would have long since run away. I'm still considering it.

I swear under my breath. We go back to our work-rooms in silence.

A picture book, in Swedish.
A ball-point pen.
A succulent of some sort, planted in a glass jar.
An axe with a red handle.
A flatscreen TV, looks like Samsung.
A large crucifix, made of silver, I assume.

I'm done for today; I take off the helmet, clock out, go back to my dorm room in the same building. Ten of us for each, white walls, white plastic crates for storage.

There are no wardrobes; we wear what we are assigned each morning. Usually something gray with tiny blue speckles. The aliens love the color gray with tiny blue speckles.

Large Blue Triangle admonishes me in the Hungarian voice of Will Smith to move more cautiously lest I injure myself again. I saw Artúr Kálid in a play back before the invasion. I wonder if he's still alive, and if he ever meets an alien talking on his voice, using his words.

I fall asleep every day like a rock. I try to force myself to stay awake just for a few minutes, just to give myself time for my own thoughts. The aliens drive us mercilessly while they gloat that we are all voluntary workers. Human-aided categorization. Their algorithms have no clue what our everyday objects are.

Why is Stallone interested in Danish Modern?

A bag of Chio chips, peanut flavor.
A small spoon—teaspoon, I think.
A pair of yellow candlesticks.
A small whiteboard.

I hoard off-time. I want to go for a walk.
Days run together.

A macramé wall hanging.
A pocket knife.
A brown paper bag.
A pair of scissors.
A bin liner.
A fork.

Accumulated off-time: three hours forty-three minutes. My ankle is better and I can walk without crutches. It will have to be enough. I am sleepy. Uneven ground.

I walk.

We are not, technically, restricted to the compound. There's just nothing worth leaving for. We are not, technically, forced laborers. There's just nothing else to do.

I walk.

A large oak tree.

An overgrown drainage ditch.

Clouds.

My brain is stuck in object-labeling mode. I wonder if it's permanent.

We all do what we can to survive. I just want to know what these others do to survive. I should've brought my crutches with me—what if I wanted to stay?

A road uphill.

Burned-out houses.

Off to one side: Remains of the botanical gardens.

Lavender growing wild.

Pannonhalma Abbey, razed to the ground.

Pannonhalma Abbey.

An abandoned camp.

Hastily assembled tents.

A can of tuna fish now holding cigarette butts.

Fires burned down to ash.

I turn around and in the distance I can see the alien compound, smoldering. My mind can only label, not understand. I hobble into a tent.

Comforting semi-darkness.

Rusty-framed cots.

Sleep.

"You from the compound? Down there on the plains?" A soot-smeared face. A teenage boy.

I murmur something.

"I didn't realize there were any survivors," he says. "I'll let you sleep."

By next morning my brain works better, the forced frame of object labeling faded into the background. I sit on the boy's cot, sipping hot nettle tea. His name is Brúnó and he has cinnamon-brown curls. He describes what has been going on: the pacifist stance was all an act, a charade while the militants smuggled in weapons, brought a small army up the hill one by one, occupied the wine-cellars dug into the hillside below the abbey hundreds of years ago.

"So what were you doing down there?" he asks.

"Labeling objects for the aliens. You sit and the computer shows you things and they record the responses your brain makes. Something like that."

"What's the point?"

"They always told us they wanted to rebuild."

That's when it hits me—and I'm still too exhausted even to cry, and I didn't know anyone in the compound besides Kati, socializing was *not* encouraged—but I did know Kati, and I can barely believe I should start mourning.

I can't, I just can't. I save it for later, provided there will be a later. I've lost so much. I refuse to think of my family—I think they are still alive somewhere, in a different compound, in a different corner of Hungary, tucked away safely. I refuse to think of my friends, I refuse to think of my life. My former life. I refuse to think of hot chocolate and video games and ranting at my friends on chat and imagining that one day I will be internet famous. I refuse—what am I even thinking?

I turn away from Brúnó, stare at the mushy afternoon sky. Is it spring or fall? Everything has become indeterminate.

The next day I drag Brúnó off the hill, or rather he drags me, my ankle still painful. Downhill is worse than uphill, I'm never sure why. He drags me and I urge him, while he's attempting what innumerable compound-dwellers have tried and failed: puzzle out the aliens' motives.

Raze, then rebuild? "Maybe it's a different faction," he suggests, and he has a point—why would the aliens form one homogenous group? But there was nothing I'd seen during my time of work to suggest any kind of difference between one movie star voice and another. I tell him so.

"But how do you know these aliens are the same aliens who bombed us back to the Stone Age?"

I shrug. We're almost back to the compound.

I wanted to have smoldering ruins, I got them. As I slip and slide among rocks, half-melted pieces of plastic with jagged edges and undefinable heaps, I realize I'm not going to find Kati here.

We trundle back to camp and I find her on top of the hill.

This is too much disruption. I'm glad to see Kati, but this is too much. We stare at each other. Her left ankle is immobilized between two thick tree-branches and wrappings of dirty gauze.

"You're the expert," she says with a lopsided, pained smile.

"I left my crutches back in the compound," I respond; they must've melted into slag.

"I wanted to catch up to you when I saw you walk out, I tripped and fell. I stepped into a hole or something. It took me a day to go up the hill and find help," she says. The militants helped her. Maybe they would help me? Maybe it would be all right?

The people sing march songs—I vaguely recognize old Communist melodies, with new lyrics. I wonder if someone is passing them off as originals. I only know them because it was a hobby of mine to collect those recordings, post them on Youtube. I will not think of the loss. I will not think of anything missing from the world, bits and bytes forever scattered. I will not—

"Tomorrow, we go," trills Brúnó at me, and before he can dash off, I grab his shoulder.

"We go, where?"

"To the next station, the next fight!" He shakes my hand off, runs away.

I don't want to fight. I just want to be left alone on a cozy sofa with a laptop, watching random crap on the Internet. What, maybe five aliens were killed—and how many dozen workers? Other people can do this, and be cheerful about it, for all I care.

At least Kati doesn't seem to be enthusiastic either, sitting on a half-rotted pillow with her back to a bag filled with straw. "I'm not going to march *any*where," she declares to Brúnó running back and forth. He shrugs and responds with "Then we'll just leave you here. No dead-weight."

I slap him on the top of the head with an open palm, but he laughs it off, thinks I was just joking, horsing around. Not recognizing his own cruelty.

I lie down on a sparc cot, busy myself with recalling the stream of images before sleep. It gives me an odd, uncanny kind of peace. Now that I can do anything I want, I'm surprised that I want this. Routines can be comforting.

A head of cabbage, sliced in half.

An empty windowpane made of wood.

A sack of potatoes, about five kilograms, give or take.

If they want to know what these things are, why don't they just ask us?

Up above, I hear the rumble of their aircraft. So much for flying saucers being silent. None of them have landed near the destroyed compound, no one came to look for survivors. But maybe now?

I wish I had Small Purple Circle at hand. I'd tie him to a chair and interrogate him. He'd creak in the voice of Arnie and I'd hit him with the butt of a gun like Sam Fisher in Splinter Cell. Not with my bare hand which even Brúnó can shake off and laugh. I would hit them both. My ferocity surprises me; I draw back from my own thoughts.

In this moment, I hate everything and everyone with pure, hundred-proof hatred. And I also know that I will go back, to the aliens, to another work compound, and if nothing else, I will pretend to myself I am an infiltrator, seeking to bring down the heartless taskmaster aliens and the crude, brute-force humans alike. Winning with cunning, not overwhelming power.

It doesn't last—power fantasies never do. When I put the console into sleep mode, it's always over. When did I last play a video game?

As I contemplate this, sleep claims me and I only wake the next morning—restless, but well-rested.

The march-column is leaving, and all the accommodation the two of us got was that we didn't have to strap a full-size army surplus backpack to our shoulders. Brúnó is also supposed to help us, but I send him forward to carry some made-up, inconsequential message to our section march-leader, while with Kati we hobble in the opposite direction, toward where we can see a flying saucer landing, behind the hill. We do not want to stay with the militants, and we don't think we can survive on our own. This is the alternative we have.

The militants don't care. Which is good because our two-girl march is slow-going, loud with all the assorted obscenities we can produce.

I will not think of my gaming stream, I will not think of my gaming stream, I will not think of how I miss my gaming stream and all the cuss-worthy moments and all the glorious ridiculousness of it.

I will only think of Sam Fisher, infiltrating the enemy compound. I will think of Arnold Schwarzenegger, late governor of California, epic action-hero of the previous generation.

I will rip the aliens' heads off.

"Welcome back, Earthlings," Will Smith says, and I don't know if it's the same alien, Large Blue Triangle, or a different one. His coloring is different and his texture is all puckered up, but for all I know they can change those on demand, like cephalopods. They don't do it in front of us.

I stare at the images and my gaze could burn a hole in the world.

A flagpole, ideal for stabbing people in the stomach.

An empty glass Coke bottle, ideal for making Molotov cocktails.

An egg cup, ideal for jamming it down people's throats.

I sigh, try to look away, but the images keep on coming, direct through the helmet to my visual cortex.

A candle-holder, ideal for bashing in people's heads.

A pink flowerpot, ideal for bashing in people's heads.

An old gramophone, ideal for bashing in people's heads.

No, no, no, Keanu Reeves says—this is a new alien, I don't remember the voice actor's name—*this is not good, you're messing up the data! All the affordances!*

He tears the helmet off my head and I stand, we face-off, the heat of anger rising from me while he puckers up and deflates in cycles.

"All the what?" I glare at him.

"Did you figure it out?" He seethes.

Everyone else in the room is still under their helmets, but the work doesn't involve the auditory cortex. They can potentially hear us. Keanu Reeves—Soft Green Oval—ushers me outside, then into some kind of closet.

He mutters something unintelligible. Is he swearing? Then: "I always thought someone would figure it out under my watch, it has to be my watch, it has to be. What am I supposed to do with you?"

I'm shaking with barely repressed fury. "Am I supposed to tell *you* what to do with me? How about a nice comfy sofa and a jar of sweets?"

"Th-that can be arranged," he mutters and I realize he thought I was serious. Oops.

He starts trembling, inflating and deflating at an alarmingly rapid pace. We shiver in unison, but for very different reasons. "I can't just kill you," he says, whining. "Besides, the recordings have already been transmitted to Centerpoint."

"Explain," I grimace at him. "Explain before I throttle you." Do I really have the upper hand?

Maybe I do, because he explains. "It's not really about identifying objects. It's about their affordances, meaning what can be done with them. We're recording immediate, implicit reactions. Specifically, we're trying to identify which objects can potentially be used as weapons, there is a marker..."

"And?" I don't see where this is heading.

He spreads his tentacles in a gesture I'm sure he learned from his workers—a display of helplessness. "I saw your data. Everything can be a weapon. Everything can be seen as a weapon."

I stare at him. I realize I'd been clenching my hands, slowly unclench my fingers. If this was a movie, blood would be dripping from my palms at a bare minimum.

Have I just condemned the human species?

We can use everything as weapons.

I look away, disgusted with him, me, the entire world. But something doesn't make sense.

I look back. "You bombed us to smithereens. Why would you need to know about our weapons?"

He doesn't respond. His motions halt. Is he even breathing? And at that moment I understand—Brúnó was right, these are not the aliens that destroyed civilization, they are not. They are opportunists, bottom-feeders, here to fill a suddenly empty niche. Maybe the ones who'd attacked us didn't care anymore, once we were no longer a threat.

Maybe. It makes sense.

I hiss. "This is why the militants could take your compound so easily. You are weaklings."

He doesn't say anything. His skin slowly undulates. Is he afraid of me? If they are weaklings, what does that make us—what does that make me, with my boundless display of rage? I feel suddenly raw, exposed, my anger evaporating and giving way to pure existential dread.

"So what happens now?" I whisper.

Keanu turns away. Is he more disgusted than afraid? He speaks softly, almost gently. "The data has been transmitted. Centerpoint will decide."

I walk back to our dorm room, built to the same specifications as the previous one, each compound an almost exact duplicate.

I want to cease. I can't even cry.

Was I really the first human to get so angry, so desperate, so furious? Surely there had to have been others, people with their families murdered, their entire way of life destroyed. Surely it couldn't have been me. Then again, in the compounds, people are volunteers. Collaborators. People who play by the rules.

I half sit, half crash down on my bed, turn to Kati and try to haltingly explain. I break into tears halfway through, remembering the egg-cup, this most innocuous of all household objects.

The evacuation signal sounds exactly then, and as we run out to the courtyard—Kati half-jumping on one leg, holding on to me —, the saucers are already overhead, streaming toward space, away from Earth. The aliens leaving. Fleeing? Escaping?

They don't want to have anything to do with us any more.

I think of Danish Modern, hug Kati and endlessly, endlessly weep.

Endnote:

The science in the story was extrapolated from Shenoy P, Tan DS (2008): Human-aided computing: utilizing implicit human processing to classify images. Proceedings of the SIGCHI Conference on Human Factors in Computing Systems: 845-854.

Changing Body Templates

0.

My little brother Dani didn't say "I want to be an astronaut!" He said "I want to be an Orosi astronaut!" as he hopped around our cramped living quarters, pretending to be a spaceship.

My mother frowned. "Why an Orosi astronaut? Why not a Naphegy astronaut, one of our own?"

He shrugged, not even looking at her. "Better chances that way!"

Mom laughed and cheered him on, but that was the first time I noticed that peculiar sharpness in her voice—the sharpness I'd learn to avoid, the sharpness that tinged her words whenever she was discussing politics.

I.

We were sitting on boxes—the back room behind the main laboratories was filled with useless junk. We did not have fabbers and we tried to preserve everything we could, in case some of the equipment broke down. This was one of the best places on Naphegy Station to discuss topics in relative safety—Laci, our political officer never dared get close to any of the machines, and for good reason. He earned his qualifications in a different field, one that used rubber hoses and finger clamps as its tools of trade, so the gossip went. I doubted they still used such crude devices, but the sentiment behind their actions was still the same. Laci himself claimed he had a degree in centralized economics, from an evening school, and that indeed was what his file stated. For all we knew, he wrote his file himself.

I shifted uncomfortably on top of a large carton of power cubes. My buttocks ached. "The politicals say they will get us a formshifter. Next month, worst case."

"That true?" Dani twisted a long curly strand of his beard, wrapped it around his fingers. He seemed equally dubious and disinterested.

"Laci is bragging about it. You think he'd risk such an embarrassment?"

He sighed. "I'll believe it when I see it with my own eyes."

We never put much faith in the politicals, even when they were working in our interests.

Everyone in the lab was crowded around the formshifter, watching the big gray box printed with Dathran text with expressions ranging from enthusiasm to reverence.

Dani cleared his throat. "There has to be a catch." He crossed his arms and stared at Laci point-blank.

Laci tried to take a small step back, instinctively, but he hit the wall of bodies pressed together behind him and almost lost his balance. Hands steadied him. Small chuckles rose up, their source indistinct.

Laci frowned. "It doesn't come with instructions." He surveyed the crowd with a grim expression—he was trying hard to regain his respectable and commanding airs. "I am told you can reverse-engineer it."

Silence. No one wanted to commit to a definitive statement.

"We can try," I finally said in my best cheerful tone.

His frown only deepened. "Our lab reverse-engineered the Biscar control interface. We are the best in space biologicals. This isn't some kind of mythical alien technology, the Dathran are human like us…" He said *our* lab. I suppressed a grimace.

"This has a heavy physics aspect," Dani interjected. "We should partner with Chanina's team."

The expression on Laci's face made it clear that he wouldn't share the potential glory. He really wanted to be promoted, away from us, into a cushy position in Central Government. Maybe even in Orosi space, among humans who displayed as little care for our wellbeing as the aliens in their movies, if not even less.

"So who briefs him?" Dani leaned back against a bulkhead. Five of us from the in vivo team were crowded together in our little storage closet, our hiding place.

"He's going to yell at us," Kata said and hugged herself. "He's going to scream."

"The animals aren't dead," Dani remarked, acerbic as usual.

"And they grow back their lost limbs, I know. But they do not *adapt*!" She was on the verge of an outburst, I could feel it, and I drew away as best as I could—not to give her space, but from fear. We lived in such close quarters on the station that every interpersonal clash carried danger.

"Pimasz grew an… extra limb of sorts," one of the animal techs said. "To reach the banana on the ceiling."

"That's one chimpanzee out of five," I said, also close to losing my patience. "And none of the lower animals showed anything of the sort."

"This kind of adaptation is tied to planning," Dani said and crossed his arms. "Higher cognition." His statements always sounded like gospel, unquestionable and true just because he himself said them. Sometimes I could've kicked him, even though he was my brother, my colleague, my closest confidante.

I huffed. "So what do you propose?"

"Human trials, obviously." He looked at me with the same gaze he'd used to skewer Laci on that fateful meeting. A chill ran over me.

"Approval would take months! The ethics committee isn't in session until after Liberation Day!" Kata's voice trembled. *Please don't yell,* I thought at her, *please don't yell.*

"We don't need approval from the ethics committee if we don't involve others."

"Forget it," Kata yelled, "I'm not going to talk people into this! Not on my conscience! What if something goes wrong?"

Dani was outwardly calm, but I could feel the anger roiling in him. "I'm saying we try it on ourselves. No need to involve others. It's human technology, I'm sure it has the proper safeguards built in..."

"So, do *you* volunteer?" The lab tech who had mentioned the chimpanzee spoke up, and he was calm, genuinely calm. Not intimidated by Dani in the slightest.

"I volunteer." I blinked in surprise at the sound of my voice—sharp, raspy and dangerous.

We walked along the perimeter, just the two of us, merging with the evening crowd. The station was unbearably crowded, but what could we do? The Orosi controlled all our incoming and outgoing traffic; they didn't let most of us leave, certain we'd collectively make a dash for Dathran space.

"So you want to be an astronaut?" Dani said, not really mocking, just bitter.

"*You* wanted to be the astronaut."

"An Orosi astronaut, huh?" He chuckled. "Mom still teases me about that."

That was so unexpected I laughed out loud, and heads turned in our direction.

"I hate the BTE list," Kata said and stretched, yawning. "Hate hate hate it."

"If not for the Banned Technological Exports list we'd be out of a job," I told her. The sleepier we were, the more impatient I grew. Twenty hours of looking at data would do that to everyone, I thought, even a Dathran astronaut.

"We'd research something else," Dani said. "Real research, not reverse-engineering."

"This is important." I drew myself to my full height, but Dani was so much taller than me, it must've looked comical. "We need to keep on the right side of the Orosi."

"So, we steal from the Dathran to gain the appreciation of the Orosi? What if the tide turns?"

Kata jumped up. "Ssssh! Anyone can hear!"

"So what? The worst they can do to me is put me in a cell doing the same thing I do in this sardine can!" Dani waved his hands around.

"Quiet! Could we just return to the task at hand?!" I hissed.

They fell silent and I returned to examining the data, but my thoughts drifted. The Dathran had a BTE list and the Orosi prided themselves on not having one, talking about openness and democracy until they were blue in the face, but we all knew it was because Orosi technology was so behind the Dathran. The Orosi had a larger empire and more military strength—at least so they claimed—but in many respects they were far behind the Dathran. The best Orosi minds worked on catching up, the propaganda said. In fact, a lot of the research was done in the occupied territories, Basul, Idirsjan, even our crummy Naphegy Station. The best Orosi minds considered reverse-engineering a task beneath them. *They* were busy with original research.

I shook my head. I'd better go through the numbers once again. After all, this time my life was on the line. I still had a hard time believing it.

Our boss yelled until the walls resonated with his words. Then he agreed to our plan.

II.

Dani sighed in exasperation. "We *know* they have some kind of training program! It's not going to work if we go into this unprepared."

You mean I go into this unprepared, I wanted to say, but I bit back my words. No need to antagonize him; I'd already alienated half of the lab team with my snarls and erratic behavior. They understood the reasons, but that in itself did not improve the situation.

"So what do you propose?"

It was clear he did not have an inkling. He sat down heavily on top of an office desk and kept himself busy by crossing his legs and shifting until he seemed comfortable. He frowned, not looking at me. Then he finally volunteered an answer.

"It has to be some kind of… behavioral program. The guy from Intelligence was sure there were no drugs involved, no direct stimulation, no…"

"No nothing. Right. So what does it say?" I scrolled through the verbose and mostly useless report. Intelligence folk wanted to prove their worth to the Orosi as much as we did. "Some kind of… multisensory continuum?" I glanced up at him. "What sort of jargon is this?"

I blinked and before he could answer, I realized. "Virtual reality? …Gosh, that's so dated."

"Simulations, I guess. Of the target state, when the participant is capable of changing body shape at will."

"And they try to… promote neuroplasticity? With this?" I was chewing on a fingernail. I put my hand down.

"I guess so." We could communicate almost without words, finishing the sentences of the other, talking in our own private jargon. For all the good that did us.

"So can the team put together a rig?"

Then something unexpected happened. His entire body became rigid, and he only said "On such short notice?"

"What short notice?" I was trying to force calmness on myself.

Dani would not meet my eyes. "Didn't you hear? We have to have something to present by Liberation Day. For the parade."

That joke of a parade, around the station's perimeter. Mimicking Orosi custom.

"Not the *parade*—!"

Dani nodded, still not looking at me.

"That's a *joke*, surely no one is taking it seriously– You know the joke about the mass drivers—how much of the military stuff on the parade is fake? Surely we wouldn't be the first—"

"Laci takes it seriously," Dani said. "And the higher-ups, with the junk he is feeding them."

"Surely he realizes this might not work—I am not a pig they can take to the slaughter!"

He got off the desk and crouched down next to my seat until our faces were level. "We have two weeks. Fourteen days. We need to think."

I was dazed. I circled the station for the umpteenth time, bumping into passersby, barely noticing them.

A multisensory continuum—Virtual reality—Dani saying *Not at such short notice.* Even then, the rest of the labfolk were busy trying to put together some kind of rudimentary rig. The last time people had paid any attention to replacing everyday reality entirely had been hundreds of years in the past. On a space station, it does not pay to be entirely unaware of one's own surroundings. All modern computing was overlays, augmented reality, that sort of thing. Clearly distinct from our usual sensorium, and thus no help to me at all—

A burly man crashed into me and we both fell.

"Watch where you're going!!" he yelled. "Damn junkie!"

"I'm not—" I was still shaking from the sudden impact. "I was just thinking, I'm a researcher—"

"And what do you research, magic mushrooms?"

I mumbled words of apology, turned around and half walked, half ran away.

Then I came to a sudden stop.

Drugs.

A simulated reality.

This was Kata's area of expertise, and she did not like the idea. "We can try, sure… But drug experiences are fundamentally uncontrolled."

"And here you'd need controlled exposure, repeatable, indeed repeated until it is ingrained…" Dani nodded sagely. Would he shut up for once and try not to play the smartass?

Kata noticed the ferocity in my gaze; she hugged herself in her usual manner, positively meek. "I'm sorry I don't have a solution for you."

I clicked my tongue. We were so close! I felt angry, then just empty, curiously empty.

I'd end up like those first dead mice, or the chimpanzees that could not change their shape despite every single cell in their body having been replaced by the formshifter, or maybe Pimasz, the star animal subject, who grew a tentacle to reach that banana... once... which occasion wasn't recorded because the apparatus had somehow hiccuped.

It was hopeless. We could only dream—

Dream.

I jumped up. "Dreams!"

Dani jumped up too. "Yes!"

"Sorry?" Kata must've thought we were losing it. "Dreams aren't particularly controlled either," she finally ventured, pulling her limbs impossibly close to herself in defense, afraid we'd start to hit her in our fervor, maybe.

"Lucid dreams!" Dani pronounced my thoughts with glee.

"Would that work?" Kata asked him in return.

"Lucid dream induction is easy—and relatively painless—and noninvasive!" He proclaimed this like his own personal triumph, and for once I didn't mind even though I was the first to arrive at the idea. "I have *just* the hardware!"

From your psychedelic phase? I wanted to snark, but I kept my mouth shut. We might've just found our solution.

III.

Dirt smudges on the yellow-painted bulkhead, banged-up pipes running parallel with the floor at knee level. I touched the wall, my right palm flat against the surface. I savored the sensation for a brief moment, then pushed.

The bulkhead yielded and my hand was swallowed up to the wrist. I pulled it back out again. Now that it was established I was dreaming, I had more important tasks to do than play with a wall. My body parts were all in place, I was wearing one of my long skirts and a loose-fitting shirt printed with a colorful pattern.

My vision began to fade to black. The dream wavered. I had barely started, and now I was getting booted out...? My anger hastened the process, and I had to fight to steady my feelings and stabilize the dream.

I opened my eyes wide, tried to focus on seeing the room, the eggyolk-yellow bulkheads closing in around me. Then the position of my body, upright, not lying down in my berth. Upright and moving—I took a step, touched the bulkhead again. Turned around, walked ahead. The room around me reasserted itself, solidifying, sharpening. I was satisfied.

I took a deep breath. Where to start?

I grabbed my left hand with my right, twisted hard—a full 180 degrees. The hand twisted—I did not feel any pain, but when I wiggled the fingers on my left hand and they moved in exactly the opposite direction compared to the usual, the mismatch between visual and proprioceptive input produced a nasty clash somewhere deep in my brain. I winced—the feeling was very unpleasant, not painful, but close. I reminded myself I was dreaming, there was no risk of physical damage, but despite that, I found myself back in bed, an abrupt change that left me woozy.

I reached toward my head, careful not to hit the top of my berth with my elbow, then rubbed my temples and yawned. I was awake, and every awakening was a chance wasted.

Eleven days to go.

"Why do I have to fight just to maintain the dream?"

"It's not a lucid dream maintenance rig, it's a lucid dream *induction* rig." Dani frowned in displeasure.

"Thanks a lot for stating the obvious!"

"C'mon, just ten more days…"

"And then it's over?" I suppressed the urge to pace—there wasn't any room to pace. "Ten more days until we completely blow it?" *Ten more days until I'm dead?* "So many things can go wrong!" I hit the bulkhead with a fist; pain lanced through my hand.

The world seemed out of focus. I tried to look around, take in everything, force persistence on the environment.

I was standing on a wide field of grass out of some Orosi romantic drama. I couldn't care less—for my purpose I could've been anywhere. I looked down at my body—everything was as usual. I grabbed my hand and twisted. I fought down the instinctive aversion, the expectation of pain. How come I was feeling pain in dreams, anyway? It certainly wasn't the usual physical pain, there was an odd, magical quality to it–

The hand was backwards. I felt no pain, not even discomfort. A step.

I looked away. Tried to wiggle my fingers, out of my field of view. They felt normal.

I raised my hand to look at it. It was, indeed, back to normal.

I swore and got instantly booted out of the dream.

"Look, I'm trying!" Dani had become my fierce taskmaster. Someone no longer on my side. "I stop paying attention and everything snaps back to normal! I've tried it with the hands, the arms, the legs…"

"Your body template reasserts itself," he said, smoothing down his tangly beard. "You just have to keep practicing for the template to change, to… allow for more variation."

"And then what happens?"

He blinked. "What do you mean, what happens?" For once we were out of sync. "You become a shapeshifter, ready to face the dangers of space, the leadership is happy, the Orosi are happy. We pulled one over on the Dathran. That's all." He smiled without any mirth.

"That's not what I mean." I didn't want to say it out loud. "Power always finds an owner for itself."

He was completely puzzled. "And what would *that* mean?"

It didn't happen in a field of grass or a cavern of stone. It happened on our own little station.

I was standing on the perimeter walkway and it was strangely deserted. I had no idea how I'd gotten there; none at all. That was how I realized I was dreaming.

I took a few steps forward, then jumped into the air. I flew, just below the utility level, careful to keep my head down. It was easier to do it while in motion.

I'd been practicing this form for a few days, in more spacious locations. I thought I should just change the scenery, pass through a wall to exit the dream scene and enter another. But something pushed me forward instead.

I spread my arms and willed them to elongate. Further. Further. Then willed them to broaden until I was—if not a bird, then a glider plane of some sort. Or one of Dani's make-believe spaceships.

I closed and reopened my eyes.

The wings were still there, the movement maintaining them, the entire situation itself conspiring to maintain them. This was my natural shape for the moment, the shape I needed, and thus the shape stayed.

I was so distraught that the world began to fade to black, and I forced it to reemerge, because I needed one more moment of this, one more to be able to say I had done it, a misshapen aircraft-being taking to the nonexistent skies.

Dathran pilots did not *become* their craft... but maybe I could go further. Out of want. Out of need.

Then the walls came dangerously close, and as I tried to scramble back, the dream fell apart and I was left panting in my berth.

Kata looked on the verge of tears. "We need to accelerate the schedule."

"What? There's still three days until the parade. Recuperation shouldn't take that long!" Dani jumped up, the motion jangling a box full of something metallic.

"We can do it," I said.

"Are you there already?" Dani glared at me. "The changes are still not permanent!"

"I'm close enough," I told him, glaring back. He was the first to look away.

IV.

They are making me invulnerable.
The sound of my heart beating filled my ears.
They are making me practically immortal.
There was nothing else left to think. Except this:
They have failed to make me loyal.

"We don't know how it feels," the lab tech said. "But based on the behavior of the chimpanzees…"

"Yeah, yeah, I know. Go ahead."

Life should've flashed before my eyes—the cramped little rooms with their nooks and crannies, the ridiculous Liberation Day parades, the BTE list updated twice a year, my uncle weeping openly just after he got word of the Orosi having shot down that passenger liner—but there was nothing, just a void.

And then that void filled with pain.

Do you survive being torn apart? Even if you do, something is irrevocably changed...

"Are you all right?" Dani was standing at my bedside, wringing his hands in anxiety, not even noticing.

"Sure," I struggled to form the words. My body felt as if it was on fire. "Has it worked?"

"Too early to say. But are you really all right?"

"More or less..."

He could feel I was keeping something from him; he could feel I had a newfound secret. He didn't know what it was, and for the time being, that was good. I myself wasn't sure yet which course I'd take, only that I'd try to make a move—try to catch the Orosi unprepared for once. They had no idea we'd progressed to a successful human trial; they didn't know what waited for them on the station. For possibly the first time in my life, I had the upper hand over them. I could force them into—exactly what? Lifting the travel restrictions, certainly. I wouldn't bring back all the people they'd murdered in cold blood, destroying passenger liners in the same unfeeling way as they'd destroyed our meagre security forces... I wouldn't bring back my aunt, but I'd make life a little more bearable for everyone on Naphegy Station.

I just needed to work out the details, but surely that couldn't be *that* hard...

"I am ambulatory," I declared with a playful smile. A smile that hid an entire world. Dani grinned back at me.

"That's great to hear. Two days to go." He frowned and it made me think he was the type to develop wrinkles fast—*they're already showing even when his face is smooth, and he's still so young... Why did we age so fast? The Orosi and the Dathran always had such smooth faces...*

I walked out of the lab's seldom-used infirmary. He yelled after me:

"Don't kill yourself while experimenting!"

I thought I should hide myself, but on such a small station, there are no secrets, and precious few hiding spots.

I locked myself in our room, hoping Dani wouldn't return anytime soon. Hoping he decided to spend some time with his girlfriend to pull their relationship out of the rut of neglect.

I used to think I'd never have a room to myself. When I finally married, I'd have a new room for my new family, but never one for myself. If Dani moved out earlier, I'd be pressed to move out and marry too. No space. No room. Not on the station, and the Orosi controlled who came and who went.

Instead of that room, I would have—exactly what? The stars?

How will the Orosi react? I turned the thought around in my head. *They know we're working on this project.* But I was more or less certain they hadn't heard about the human trials—this one human trial, myself. Our leadership would've kept it from them, as a surprise for Liberation Day...

Our politicals could be really boneheaded at times. But that's why they were still here on the station—the smart ones were in Orosi space, promoted away from us. The technical term was *counterselection...*

I sighed and twisted my left hand with my right. It obligingly turned and remained in place.

I twisted it back. Everything had a solidity to it.

How much could I rearrange my body? How much would the sensory nerves protest?

I tried another task from lucid dreams. I pressed my hand against my abdomen and pushed.

My hand went through.

My heart hammered in my chest—*don't get yourself killed*—but I didn't seem to suffer any ill effects otherwise. *That's not possible...*

I pulled out my hand—it was stained with what I tried to think of as organic matter, just organic matter—and watched as the stain was reabsorbed.

It had subroutines built in. I definitely didn't want any material to be reabsorbed, my body had done it automatically. Maybe it would do other things automatically, too?

How hard would it be to pass through a wall? It didn't seem like a trivial task, but weren't the Dathran astronauts supposedly capable of...

Maybe there was a subroutine for that. It was hard to imagine they would put their precious people at risk. They were just the opposite of the Orosi, who threw sheer numbers at every problem, even problems of flesh and blood... and they had such a fondness for safeguards, their systems chiseled and perfect.

Someone had to have worked out the details in advance. I didn't want my sensory nerves to be subjected to abruptly being cut off. I thought I was smarter than that.

I should go back to the lab, I thought. *They've decided to allow me so much space all of a sudden. We still need to run trials...*

I put a hand against a bulkhead and pushed. My arm went right into the wall, elbow deep.

I didn't feel anything except a sense of mounting unease.

Laci seemed surprised I wanted to talk to him.

"I was just wondering if there was any specific demonstration you preferred to see. For when you show me to the Orosi delegation, you know." *When you show off to the Orosi delegation.*

"I liked the wings. Yes, I think that's eye-catching. A quite large-scale change."

"They are hollow, you know."

"Yes, but still." He grinned. "And the mass drivers are fake."

"Ah." Such an admission. How did he know? Was he just making this up on the spot for my benefit? To make me less afraid of the delegation—the inspection?

It was time to bring it up. Casually, carefully...

"It's going to be a great surprise, hmm? How much do they know?"

"Ah, they know we're actively working on the project, of course... and I hinted at a breakthrough..."

This was bad. "What kind of breakthrough?"

"Oh, I didn't let slip the info about the human trials." His teeth showed—a display of predation. "I'm not *that* boneheaded..."

V.

I had to say something.

I had to say goodbye.

"Dani, Dani... look..." I was unsure what to say. "They're not going to allow me to stay here." That much was probably true.

"Who?" He tried to blink out sleep from his eyes. He'd spent the past days looking at test results.

"Who, the Orosi!"

"But the lab is here!"

"For all I know, they might take the entire lab!" I didn't think so. I didn't want to lie to him, but...

He hugged me. "Don't worry," he whispered. "I've always wanted to see the world."

I had nothing to say to that. I hugged him back, fiercely.

The Orosi delegation was sitting on a tribune—it looked squashed-together under our low ceiling, and it sat much closer to us than the tribunes we saw on Orosi vids of their own military parades. The effect was more grotesque than majestic.

Laci had pushed a sign into my hand—it said "Space Biologicals Research Institute" and a phrase about Liberation Day that was too flowery for my stomach. My hands were shaking and I held the signpost to my body, afraid the shaking would show, but this only made my entire body tremble. I'd have to act soon, but I still hadn't made up my mind over which course of action would be the most preferable. A hostage situation? They didn't bring along a huge security detail, and wasn't I practically invincible anyway?

Laci had made a point of the two of us standing at the front of the Institute column. We were barely a lab; all our designations were strikingly euphemistic.

Some of the Orosi were late, and we were growing weary of waiting for the march to start.

Laci grabbed my hand—I almost dropped the signpost—and lifted it above our heads, waving to someone on the tribune, grinning. I stared at him in amazement as I tried to yank my hand out of his, and saw him wink exaggeratedly. I followed the path of his gaze.

An Orosi man—tall, blonde and pale, strongly built—stared at the two of us, frozen in motion, halfway to sitting down. He straightened up, quick as a snake, and nudged one of his peers. They briefly conferred.

"Laci," my mouth did not want to move, "you said you didn't tell them about the human trial."

"I didn't," he said—in the periphery of my visual field, I saw he shrugged. I couldn't move, I stood ramrod straight. "They must have someone else on the team reporting to them too. So much for a surprise! Curse Orosi Security, they find out about everything…"

That man up there. He'd just connected the dots.

"Is he with them?" The Orosi Security Bureau. Experts in modern equivalents of the rubber hose. I'd never seen one of them up close—or maybe I just hadn't known…

"Them? Ah yes, the Bureau." Laci confirmed my worst fears. He babbled on, but I wasn't listening anymore. Surely they'd have some means of defense against me too—but could they have defenses against an unknown threat?

The man pushed through the crowd on the tribune and vanished behind it. His hand was on his sidearm—weren't those supposed to be ceremonial?

He was coming for me. I couldn't just stand still! I dropped the sign. Someone swore at me, but I couldn't even think of a one-word response. My mind had ground to a screeching halt.

The walkway up ahead was empty, waiting for the marchers. I didn't dare go that way.

I turned around and broke into a run, elbowing people, tripping over them. Not fast enough!

Then I remembered that matter was transparent to me.

I passed through the people, running—floating—flying until I reached the outer perimeter.

I took a deep breath and passed through the wall, through a set of thick layers covering the station–

Into space.

Some environmental condition must've been triggered, because my body rearranged itself—quite dramatically, judging from the brief twinges of pain.

Safeguards indeed. I tsked, my mouth making no sound. Were all those preparations a waste?

Maybe not. With my palms still to the hull, I could feel an alarm pulsing through the station.

Why were they sounding a breach? To cause panic, to instill fear? I hadn't breached anything. This must've been another tactic of the Security Bureau.

And what now? I needed to think.

Should I go to the control center? Try to locate the delegation and take someone hostage; would that be the best course of action?

I had planned on doing something drastic and supremely self-destructive—I had thought my new body could take the abuse—but I hadn't had enough time to work out the details. I had come up with a thousand and one implausible plans—with no limits on what I could possibly do, it was hard to rule out anything.

And now the Security Bureau was after me and I still had no plan. I was a scientist, not a superhero...

I could destroy everything in a second. I could also fly away. Could I make a jump on my own, leaving Station space? My spine tensed in anticipation—or another transformation taking hold? I negated the instruction. No jumps just yet.

What options did I have? Make the Orosi leave by force? They would return—how much time until they managed to replicate our findings? Maybe a lot; they weren't used to reverse-engineering.

Try to cooperate with them from this newfound position of strength, better than Laci—or someone else in the lab? Who was the snitch anyway? Certainly not Dani, or...?

Enough. I needed to act.

I turned my back on the stars. I passed back through; how much time had passed?

More than enough, it turned out. The Orosi man was standing right at my entry point, a hand on his sidearm, waiting for me.

"Liberation Day indeed," the Bureau man grimaced. Now that I had more time to look at him, I could see that his eyebrows were implausibly wide, and that made him seem less perfect, more vulnerable.

We stood staring at each other, close to the outer bulkhead, while chaos raged on the perimeter walkway.

"It's your turn to make demands," he said matter-of-factly. "We would not like to see the station destroyed."

I got the impression he was more concerned for the wellbeing of the delegation than the station itself.

"Neither would I."

"Good. I'm sure we can come to an agreement."

"Lift the travel restrictions." The words sounded smooth and practiced. I was surprised at myself.

"Then everybody would leave for Dathran space."

"No. Some would leave—the population pressure would be lessened. But most would stay. This is our home."

He nodded. "And if I say no, you'll kill the delegation."

I tried not to gape. These people assumed everyone was like them, with the same predilection for violence... I had wanted to take them hostage, not kill them outright!

I slowly smiled. He read me completely wrong—he paled even further, and he gritted his teeth.

He still tried to hold his ground. "You really think you can negotiate terms here, do you?"

"Who else?"

"Your elected leadership, maybe?" Something nasty glinted in his eyes, something evil. But the idea seemed fair enough. Why should I act like a one-woman vigilante squad? That would be just like the Orosi. Surely I could do better than that! I held lethal force, but I wasn't about to resort to the modus operandi of dictators and autocrats.

"I'll let you work out the details. Come," I nodded toward the chaos, "I'll get you there."

Liberation Day finished in a negotiation room.

"Then it's settled," the Bureau man allowed himself a smile as he glanced over his own delegation—many of them outranked him, but he had assumed leadership regardless. He was with the Security Bureau, and that carried clout. Decisive force. He was the one who was assumed to take action in times of need, and that he'd done, with relish.

I was shaking. "You can't do this to me!" *Sell me out,* the accusation was on my lips, quickly retracted—I didn't want to make my situation even worse.

The station chief spread his hands. "I think we all agree that you are potentially a danger to the station."

I am your future, I wanted to yell at him, *I was your only chance! Your only chance in decades!* How else would you try to regain at least a semblance of independence—with no fighter craft, no defensive capability? I bit my lips and steeled myself.

The unnamed blond man from the Bureau looked at me, his gaze inscrutable. He talked at me, but he wasn't addressing me, he was addressing the station council. "We contacted the Dathran."

A murmur went through the room, a small wave of unrest. The man pretended not to notice. "They have provided us with the emergency shutdown keys."

Laci jumped to his feet. He was let in on the negotiations on the condition that he remain silent, but something had snapped in him. "Why would they do that? You're lying—" Hands from the council reached out to him, grabbed his clothing and pulled him back to his seat. He was about to choke on his breath.

The Bureau man spread his hands. "They would not like to see the status quo upset, either. It's all in the interest of the balance."

"It's all a game to you!" Laci yelled before he was summarily dragged out of the room by his compatriots. My compatriots. I looked at his back and wondered—why this? The fake weapons, the fake "centralized" democracy, the official network of snitches and enforcers—excuse me, *political officers*...? He could live with all of that. Why not the Orosi-Dathran cooperation behind the scenes? Did Laci really believe in all that propaganda about the Dathran being the Orosi's worst enemy?

These thoughts were a welcome distraction from my fate.

In the silence, a councilwoman raised her hand. "I was under the impression the Orosi Alliance didn't have a death penalty."

The man nodded, smiling at her. "That never even occurred to me." At this he looked back at me, and offered just the briefest of nods, a flutter of the eye that could be construed as a wink.

"We have delicate methods," he continued. "We will take you to the capital. *Unconscious.* We have our researchers…"

And their experts who'd make me loyal. Or find some other way to get me to cooperate.

I could still escape, but what would happen to the station then? Should I make a stand against our own leadership—even when they sided with the Orosi and decided to turn me over? They were still the only representatives we had, and I could hardly take justice into my own hands…

"If you cooperate, there will be no repercussions," he said. "And the travel regulations," he didn't say *restrictions*, "will be eased somewhat. Otherwise… there's no telling."

The councilors all looked at me expectantly. The Orosi delegation, on the other hand, looked bored. The Bureau man had finished his task.

I nodded and stood. "It's finished, then."

It's all over.

The councilors looked relieved. The Orosi seemed unperturbed.

I can't make a stand against my own people, even for my own people…

"Please come closer," the man said. Something in his voice hinted at a hidden warmth. He didn't want to make this any harder for me. What followed would be hard enough, he knew. "The codes are transmitted via an encrypted wireless signal. But I need to catch you when you fall."

I walked around the long oval of the table. Time stretched to infinity.

Would they take my mind away from me?

Would it be worth it? For just a small improvement? 'Eased somewhat'—that could mean anything. Eased for their own lackeys? Definitely not for the rest of us.

I should've been smarter, more cunning... but how could I have acquired the tools of the trade? The ways to act from a position of such privilege? How could I have learned that?

The councilwoman who'd spoken earlier was soundlessly crying, her hands covering her face, and I felt ashamed for her—why would she make such a scene, look so weak, it was not her life, she was making us all look bad...

As I passed behind her, something clanged—she must've kicked one of the table supports by accident. I shuddered, ready to bolt.

"Sorry, I'm—" she offered on a wheezy voice, "My skirt is stuck..." She kicked the table again, and as the sound reverberated, she whispered to me, rapidly, barely audibly. Without taking her hands from her face. Hiding her mouth so that the Orosi wouldn't notice.

All her discomfort had been just play-acting. I didn't know whether to feel relieved or even more betrayed.

I walked along with my head held high, passing our half of the table, then behind the Orosi, who turned to look at me with mild curiosity tainted with disgust. "Always so uppity," one of them said, shaking his head.

"I'll catch you when you fall," the Bureau man reiterated. "Thank you for your cooperation. Nothing else is required."

How telling, I thought, and as my legs gave way and I slipped into mercifully painless unconsciousness, the councilwoman's voice was still resonating in my mind:

We still have your data and more. We won't forget. Our time will come.

A magyar számítástechnika úttörőinek emlékére
In memory of the pioneers of Hungarian information technology

For Your Optimal Hookboarding Experience

Cilanter bees fly close to the top of the upper forestsurface in large turquoise swarms. Hookboarders are advised to keep their bee warnings on at all times. Electronic warning systems are prone to malfunction in the Charred Circle area.

Amira runs one hand along the bottom of her board, tracing the skull painted with green and red flourishes on a pearlescent silver, highlighted by the natural wood peeking out from under coats of paint. Planned in reverse, executed with mastery.

It is a gift from a friend.

Hooks should be double-checked by another person.

Amira flips the board over and attaches the large synthmetal clasps to the sides, yanking at them to make sure they hold securely in place. Then she pulls out the wires, tugs at them, runs her fingers carefully around the large hooks on the other ends. No blemishes. No hairline fractures. Fingertips are more sensitive than the naked eye.

The full moon glows above, its size and shape bringing to mind memories of Earth, its patterns evoking different associations. No brave rabbit in the sky, no reminders of sacrifice, no busy maiden.

Two hookboarders are on the moon, holding hands.

Cicadas can grow to a size of thirty centimetres. Visitors to Fabren Region Hookboarding Tracks are advised to exercise caution.

Amira is alone; only the sound of the oversized cicadas coming from beyond the dais surrounds her. But in her heart she knows she is treasured.

She double-checks the hooks herself, then she lifts her arms above her head—her cheeks brushing her smooth, cool skin—and connects the board to the tracks.

She does a few push-ups, putting her palms on the raw griptape of the board, to make sure it will hold her weight. She isn't wearing gloves.

Riders are advised to keep their main body carabiner fastened at all times.

Amira puts on her gloves with a sigh. They evoke memories; fragments of falling, a high-pitched keening issuing from somewhere between her ears. Her arms stretching thin. Her hands holding on.

In case of emergency, Fabren Region Hookboarding Tracks first responders are on call 26 hours a day.

Amira jumps on; the board shudders, the wires creak. She carefully wobbles her body just a bit, playing with her centre of mass. The contraption holds. She goes down on one knee, ready to start.

Someone is waiting for her on the other side of the forest, over and beyond the Charred Circle, beyond the breeding-grounds of the cilanter bees.

Somewhere to the east, a nocturnal firebird sings, three notes repeating with minute variations.

Amira leans forward, reaches up again and pulls out the stops that keep the hooks in place.

She knows there are only two people on the entire planet.

It is strictly forbidden to use the tracks in a heightened state of magical power.

Amira keeps her breathing steady as the speed ramps up, her board sliding downward among the tops of the trees, along the tracks. She has no body carabiners, no insect shield, and yet she does not feel she is in danger. She has no wish to take unnecessary risks.

She is so filled up with magic that she supposes in a worst-case situation she can simply fly.

Magically active visitors are asked to release any excess before using the tracks. This is mandatory.

The board bumps slightly, a minute imperfection in one of the rails above. Amira's breath catches.

The Charred Circle is still ahead. How far ahead?

Was this where Uche fell?

Amira closes her eyes even though her goggles protect her from the wind.

Visitors are asked to wear protective gear in accordance with the regulations of the Interplanetary Hookboarding Federation.

When Amira reopens her eyes, she is gliding over remains of prosperity; cocoons of spun fiberglass and delicate clockwork mechanisms, the toys of a planet-hopping elite left over in the wake of yet another economic crash. They glow faintly in the moonlight.

This was definitely not where Uche had slipped, both feet off the board. She's already passed the spot. She should've felt something, she thinks—then she realizes her goggles are busy shunting away her tears and her sleeveless vest is hard at work evaporating her cold, clingy sweat.

Entry tickets are 500C apiece for all sentient species regardless of age, citizenship or other affiliation.

Uche rode first. Uche fell first. Then Amira leaned out from her board and grabbed, hands meeting. An impossible maneuver—but then, as she is now, she was full to the brim with power.

She trusted herself more than she trusted the managers of the tracks. It served her well.

And yet her stomach still clenches when she recalls the fall, the tumble downward, the moment of impossible-to-negate desperation—

Visitors should not attempt to disembark while travelling on the tracks.

She is in thrall to the memory. The nerves in her arms were screaming with bright-hot pain as she tried to hold on, then there was only the relaxation of freefall coupled with the utter despair of certain death—

Then something inside her extended and she took to the skies, folding Uche's trembling body into her arms, flying.

Uche weighed exactly sixty-two kilograms.

Amira had flown unassisted, previously, under her own power; never while carrying so much dead weight.

Uche wasn't dead weight.

Uche was full of a different magic, that of warmth, silent trust, even gentle apology—

Amira took deep, filling breaths. Accepting. Rising.

Fabren Region Hookboarding Tracks offers eight beautiful, welcoming tree lodges spread out along the forest's perimeter.

She blinks as she notices the homely yellow light of the lodge peeking out from between leaves and branches. She passed the Charred Circle without noticing, she was so enmeshed in memory. She doesn't even remember switching tracks.

Cilanter bees are buzzing around her in a gleaming, organic cloud.

As she nears the endpoint, she sees a small figure step out onto the porch, raise one hand in greeting. The face is shrouded in darkness, a shadow against the light of the opening, but Amira can still feel it carries a welcoming, delighted smile.

She pushes down on her hookboard and springs ahead, detaching, pulling herself up into the sky.

She floats along the remainder of the path, carefully weaving among the thickening and thinning clumps of cilanter bees, while somewhere below, her hookboard comes to a slow, measured halt.

For Karina Meléndez

Increasing Police Visibility

Manned detector gates will be installed at border crossings, including Ferihegy Airport, and at major pedestrian thoroughfares in Budapest. No illegally present extraterrestrial will evade detection, government spokesperson Júlia Berenyi claimed at today's press conference...

Kari scribbles wildly in a pocket notebook. How to explain? It's impossible to explain anything to government bureaucrats, let alone science.

Kari writes:

To describe a measurement—
Sensitivity: True positives / Positives = True positives / (True positives + False negatives)
Specificity: True negatives / Negatives = True negatives / (False positives + True negatives)

Kari decides even this is too complicated, tears out the page, starts over.

To describe a measurement—

Janó grits his teeth, fingers the pistol in its holster. The man in front of him is on the verge of tears, but who knows when suffering will turn into assault, without another outlet.

"I have to charge you with the use of forged documents," Janó says.

"How many times do I have to say? I'm—not—an—alien," the man yells and raises his hands, more in desperation than in preparation to attack.

"Assault on police officers in the line of duty carries an additional penalty," Janó says.

The man breaks down crying.

Kari paces the small office, practices the presentation. *They will not understand because they don't want to understand,* e thinks. Out loud, e says:

"To describe any kind of measurement, statisticians have devised two metrics we're going to use. Sensitivity shows us how good the measurement is at finding true positives. In this situation, a person identified as an ET who is genuinely an ET."

The term *ET* still makes em think of the Spielberg movie from eir childhood. E sighs and goes on. "Whereas specificity shows us how good the measurement is at finding true negatives." How much repetition is too much? "Here, a person identified as an Earth human who's really an Earth human."

The whole thing is just about keeping the police busy and visible. Elections are coming next year, Kari thinks. *Right-wing voters eat up this authoritarian nonsense.*

"So if we know the values of sensitivity and specificity, and know how frequent are ETs in our population, we can calculate a lot. We can determine how likely it is for a person who was detected at a gate to be a real extraterrestrial."

Alien is a slur, e reminds emself.

Eir officemate comes in, banging the door open. He glances at eir slide and yells. "Are they still nagging you with that alien crap?"

The young, curly-haired woman is wearing an ankle-length skirt and glaring down at Janó—she must be at least twenty centimeters taller than him, he estimates. She is the seventh person that day who objects to a full-body scan.

"This goes against my religious observance," she says, nodding and grimacing. "I request a pat-down by a female officer." She sounds practiced at this.

Janó sighs. "A pat-down cannot detect whether you are truly an extraterrestrial."

"I will sue you!"

"Sue the state, you're welcome," he groans and pushes her through, disgusted with himself all the while.

Kari is giving the presentation to a roomful of government bureaucrats. E's trying to put on a magician's airs. *Pull the rabbit out of the hat with a flourish.*

"So let's see! No measurement is perfect. How good do you think your gates are at detecting ETs? Ninety percent? Ninety-five percent? You know what, let's make it ninety-nine percent just for the sake of our argument." *They would probably be happy with eighty,* e thinks.

E scribbles on the whiteboard—they couldn't get the office smart-board working, nor the projector. Eir marker squeaks.

113

SENSITIVITY = 99%

SPECIFICITY = 99%

"And now, how many people are actually ETs in disguise? Let's say half percent." *That's probably a huge overestimate still,* e thinks.

"So for a person who tests as an ET, the probability that they truly are an ET can be calculated with Bayes' theorem…" E fills the whiteboard with eir energetic scrawl.

E pauses once finished. The calculations are relatively easy to follow, but e hopes even those who did not pay attention can interpret the result.

Someone in the back hisses, bites back a curse. Some people whisper.

"Yes, it's around 33 percent," Kari says. "In this scenario, two thirds of people who test as ETs will be Earth humans. And this gets even worse the rarer the ETs are." *And the worse your sensitivity and specificity,* e thinks but doesn't add. E isn't here to slam the detection gate technology. "This, by the way, is why general-population terrorist screenings after 9/11 were such abysmal failures." Americans are a safe target here; the current crop of apparatchiks is pro-Russian.

This is math. There is nothing to argue with here. Some of the men still try.

Kari spends over an hour on discussion, eir perkiness already worn off by the half-hour mark.

"We can't just stop the program," a middle-aged man finally says. "It increases police visibility in the community."

Kari wishes e could just walk out on them, but what would that accomplish?

"I had a horrible day," Kari/Janó say simultaneously, staring at each other: their rumpled, red-eyed, rattled selves.

"I hate myself," Janó says.

"I'm useless," Kari says.

Then they hug. Then they kiss.

Below their second-story window, on Klauzál Square, an extra-terrestrial materializes out of thin air, dodging the gates.

Endnotes:

For those interested in the actual calculations, the Bayes' Theorem page on Wikipedia demonstrates them with the numbers used in the story, in the context of drug testing.

I first heard the terrorism comparison from Prof. Floyd Webster Rudmin at the University of Tromsø, Norway.

Good People in a Small Space

My best friend Naho is three jump points away; I don't know the distance in light years. We cling onto the old Imperial network, using it without understanding. It is fast, convenient—except when it's not, when a stray solar flare hits the Moon at exactly the wrong angle and the controllers at Tsiolkovsky Station scream at the bulkheads as if that could change anything.

I am stranded, with thousands of travelers from all corners of the Alliance: Ereni in long robes embroidered with bright, glowing thread; furry, quadripedal Ámal-Máúli; steel-plated grunts from the Aruanar Combatspace. I need to meet Naho, in person, in physicality. I need to meet her because our fuduh want to do Exchange, and it would be mean of us to deny them the opportunity. Besides, meeting in person is fun, though I do not really sense the difference from a simulation all that well. But we will be able to say that we've done it, and we can hug and go on wild toboggan rides and get into very regrettable adventures.

Except the jump point off the Moon is out of commission, no one knows what's going to happen, and my fuduh are so nervous that they are making my skin crawl.

I scratch my arms, my fingers leaving large green welts in the soft turquoise lattice. The fuduh make a low, droning sound. I wish I could perceive their minds directly, but I am not sensitive. Three fuduh live on me: one on the skin of my arms and my upper back, one inside my lungs, and one on my footsoles and all the way up along the sciatic nerves on both sides. If I were sensitive, there would be a vague point to all this, besides fun: some fuduh can induce a kind of coherence in the nervous system which can help with things magical. Or a kind of incoherence? I never remember. In any case, that does not concern me, having the sensitivity of a well-shaped halfbrick. We do this just because. It's fun?

Certainly the fuduh benefit, except when I scratch them and they are annoyed. They get to move around, meet other fuduh and do Exchange, produce new blooms and lattices.

But right now, no one goes anywhere—the grunts are crouching and playing some kind of game involving rapid beating on their chestplates, the three Ereni look like they are about to keel over, and there is someone who looks like a noble from some ridiculously feudalist world who is busy with an elaborate toss juggling routine. I want a nervous tic like that. I scratch my arms again, and wish the fuduh would harmonize something somewhere in my brain.

I also kind of eavesdrop.

"We really need to get back to Eren," one of the very faint-looking people says. "This is such a low-māwal area, I don't know if I can sustain..."

Another one adds: "Do you think we could get someone to jump us out of here?"

They all sigh and shake their heads. "No, too much energy." "Not going to happen."

The noble gathers the juggling paraphernalia, steps to the Ereni. "Maybe we can join up?"

I also clamber to my feet. I don't think I could help in any plausible way, but I don't want to feel left out. "Hi, I heard you were talking..." And then I have no idea what to say. I know the Ereni have all sorts of elaborate social formalities. The noble probably had no clue about those either, because the three Ereni look confused and slightly intimidated. I always thought humanoid people would understand each other well, but I guess they don't.

118

My fuduh buzz, all three of them, and I don't really like the buzzing in my lungs. The lattice on my arms changes color from turquoise to bright purple, and nodes start to contract and expand, letting my skin show. Purple on brown actually looks much nicer than turquoise on brown, I think, but I have no clue what's going on.

"Ā," one of the Ereni says, a small, barrel-chested person of—I quickly check their profile—no particular gender. It's always good to know that I'm not the only one who doesn't have a gender, and this makes me feel a bit better. They lift a hand and wave it in my direction—in the direction of my fuduh, more likely. The noble makes a face, discomforted at being ignored in favor of the young Earthling with the purple sentients embedded into their body, that is, me.

I cough, because this amount of agitation in my lungs is a bit too much. I cough up what looks like fairy glitter, gleaming in the oddly drafty air of the station. I hope my fuduh are all right.

"Do you need help?" an Ámal-Máúli trader says right behind me. I should be startled, but her booming bass reminds me of my second-dad and that's always nice.

"Ā," the genderless Ereni repeats, looking back and forth between the trader and me. The Ereni looks kind of stuck. This complicated social situation must be hard on them, especially since none of us are likely to know the Ereni Way that covers all manner of social interactions.

"Um… Muyewen…" Well. I got their first name from their profile, but for all I know, it might be incomprehensibly rude to address an Ereni only by first name. First names are good to get the attention of dazed people, though.

"Y-yes?" Muyewen looks at me, or more through me. I wonder what they perceive. They can probably sense my mind directly, but I am told my mind makes a rather oddly lumpy impression on people.

"I think my fuduh want to talk to you or something," I offer.

"My ship used to have fuduh," the trader remarks. "It's quasi-organic."

"You have a ship?" The noble seems oddly cheered up.

Muyewen looks about to cry, completely lost by these rapid turns in conversation.

"Um, I think you people need to take it a bit slower," I say. "One topic at a time? And Muyewen here can start?"

"I—uh. Esteemed fellow sentient?" they ask.

I assume that refers to me. Esteemed fellow sentient is probably a monosyllabic expression in Eren-sā, but we are all talking in Alliance Common. I nod eagerly. "Sure, go ahead."

"You do know your fuduh have excess…" They are searching for a word. "…Energy? Power? Magic? Ā." They sigh and wave. "Māwal."

Excess magical energetic power? Sure. Wait, what?

"I'm afraid I don't know about that," I say slowly, carefully. Naho would know, but I've been trying to ping her, to no avail. The solar flare knocked out so many systems.

"The three of us are running on a deficit here," Muyewen says, nodding at their comrades. "Too much time Earthside, and we were really hoping to get back to Eren today. This place is hard on us. Too little ambient māwal. But your fuduh are asking if they could share."

Share? More likely to just dump the excess, get rid of it, because with being attached to clueless me, it's not like they have plenty of opportunity. This sounds just fine by me, but why do all the Ereni look discomforted? At least the noble only seems vaguely put-off.

"Your fuduh want to detach from you and re-merge to us," one of the other Ereni says. I look at his profile and he is a dude by the name of Osanawu. Not just a man—very specifically a dude. "It makes the process easier."

"Okay then," I say. The noble blanches a bit and I enjoy my moment.

"You don't mind?" he asks. "It's supposed to be painful."

I shrug. "I'm a masochist." I'm actually not, but my second-partner is a sadist and I frankly don't care about pain either way, so I might as well indulge her. That's wayyyy too complicated to explain to a bunch of strangers, though, and involves my second-partner's amazing soft-baked cookies. I really am fine with pain, especially if I get cookies afterwards. Or at least a ride out of here. For a ride out of here, I would tear off my fuduh node by node, and yes, even from my lungs. Though that would kind of defeat the purpose of getting out of here, since the whole reason of visiting Naho is to get our fuduh to do Exchange and have fun. We could still have fun, though my fuduh would be terribly resentful of having left behind, and that is past what I generally find ethically acceptable.

I start to peel at the edges of the lattice, but then I pause. "Wait, I do get my fuduh back afterward, right? I mean they do want to come back?"

Osanawu the dude chuckles. "Yes, they very much enjoy your company."

The Ereni have all manner of weird neuroregulatory things in their body so I assume they can just downregulate pain sensations if they don't want them. Muyewen looks like they might want them, but that's not something I would want to casually assume about anyone.

I fiddle with one edge, then run out of patience and just yank the fuduh off. Should I even do this in public? It does hurt and my skin is bleeding, but I still don't really mind. I hand a slightly bloody mess to Muyewen, and behind me I think the trader just licked her teeth. I hope she won't eat my fuduh, we are good friends for sentients who have very limited ways to communicate. And they want to come back.

Muyewen holds out the fuduh, and there is a bright blue flash—I assume some kind of sanitization process, getting rid of problematic microorganisms? Then they remove their headscarf and just put the fuduh on their bald head. The fuduh shifts around, extends tendrils along their spine. Muyewen closes their eyes and I am sure they actually like this.

Of course, running so low on magical energetic powerthings might be very harmful to Muyewen, so maybe it's as if they were hungry and now they finally get to eat. Except it involves a kind of lumpy lattice with nodes and tendrils and whatnot attaching itself to their head in a rather painful way. Some of us would do a lot for cookies.

Muyewen draws in a very deep breath, then exhales, again looking like someone about to cry. It must be really intense, having the Ereni cognotype. Though the two others don't look so cry-y, at least not now.

I will also get cry-y if I start to consider that there are three of them, I have three fuduh, one in my lungs and in so much distress in there that somehow glitter is being produced in my body.

I try not to consider it. Onward.

I cough again, a long series of hacking, harking wheezes. I projectile-glitter on Muyewen and the third Ereni who came up to me to—help maybe? I'm not really thinking straight. She offers her arm and I hold on to it. The fuduh comes out, much smaller than expected, but kind of swollen. "I hope you're hanging in there, buddy," I say. The third Ereni looks at me quizzically, then after the mandatory flash, just straight-up swallows the fuduh.

This might be a bit too much for me.

And why am I still coughing? This is not good at all. There is still the third fuduh and my sciatic nerves are sensitive.

I... think I black out a little. When I come to, the Ereni look fine—not just more alive, but actually fine—, the noble looks very angry, and the trader is oddly bored.

"No, we cannot jump all of us out of here," the Ereni woman says. Her name is Rawanaseā and her profile has a ream of great information about collectible miniatures of the... I am so distractible. I close her profile with a mental command.

"But you said—"

"I said that now that we stabilized energetically, we can serve as a beacon for other people to jump in and get us out of here," she says patiently. "But we still need to convince other people Erenside that we are worth the trouble." She grins. "Maybe you have something to offer?"

"A chateau on a yet uncrowded leisure planet?" the noble says weakly.

"They are probably thinking of more liquid assets," the trader adds.

The noble turns to her, his voice crammed full of cynicism. "Well, maybe you have just the thing?"

"I have fifty-eight crates of artisanal logic puzzles, each one unique and comes with its individual hand-carved display case," the trader says, entirely deadpan. "My negotiation algorithm is in my profile."

"Quiet, please?" Muyewen raises a hand. "I am trying to reach the System and it is not easy with all these magnetic fluctuations brought on by the solar flare."

We all fall silent, a circle of quiet in a sea of noise all around us.

"Deal," Muyewen says.

"What?" The noble takes a half-step back.

"We are taking the puzzles as auto-negotiated just now, with a discount for jumping costs. The Earth-person gets back the fuduh. The three of us serve as a jumping beacon. The System of Eren takes care that everyone gets jumped to their desired location." Muyewen speaks on an even, detached tone, likely just relaying what the System of Eren told them.

"Including my ship?" the trader asks.

"Including your ship."

"What will I do?" The noble seems desperate.

Rawanaseā grins. "Keep us company."

"A lot of good people can fit in a small space," I add. "Earth-human saying." It's a Hungarian saying, actually, but that would be too complicated to explain. Probably even more complicated than my second-partner's cookies. "Now let me get my fuduh back, and we can all be on our merry way."

Recordings of a More Personal Nature

The air inside the small Temple chamber was cool despite the heat of summer, and the thin turquoise curtains kept out errant flies. Even the sacred symbols painted on the walls with bold blue and red strokes radiated tranquility.

    "Sixscore eight sheaves to the house of Matlan Udruf,
      three brand-new plowshares to the house of Matlan Udruf,
      apologies to the house of Matlan Udruf for the damage caused."

The archivist chanted, the melody rising, lowering, rising, then descending again for the final tone signaling the end of the section. Her eyes were closed and her body relaxed as she lay on the comfortable recliner.

The judge leaned forward and licked her lips. "Great, now we only need to look at the Doron case. What was the decision in that one?"

    "Threescore five sheaves to the house of Edhlan Doron, one wholesome ox to the house of Edhlan Doron,"

The archivist stopped without lowering the tone. The judge frowned. "Yes, and?"

    "one wholesome ox to the house of Edhlan Doron,"

"Yes, I've heard that. Next item?"

    "one wholesome ox to the house of Edhlan Doron,
      one—"

The archivist opened her eyes, still deep in trance. She stared straight ahead, unseeing. Then she sat bolt upright.

The judge froze in her seat. What was going on? "Is there something wrong?" she asked, her stomach sinking.

"I—I can't, esteemed judge, I can't—" The archivist made a brief, fluttering gesture with her hands, an aborted attempt at reaching for something. "I—" Her face was suddenly flushed. "I can't—"

The judge looked around frantically. Where were the Temple maidens at a time like this? The door-curtains were still; no sandal-steps sounded outside. "Do you want me to stop the session?"

"I can't reach the Archive! I—" She jumped up, her feet tangling in her robe. She slipped on the polished stone floor and fell into the arms of the judge. Her chest labored hard and her muscles were clenching and unclenching.

The judge clutched the archivist's body to her as she shouted for help at the top of her lungs.

"Idriwu, I am Athlaniyo, heed my call," the maiden said, leaning close to the archivist and touching her temples.

Idriwu grunted something, barely conscious.

"Return, return, servants of light, return, solemn pathfinders," Athlaniyo recited.

The archivist shuddered, then opened her eyes to this world. She looked weary beyond age, her smooth young face shackled with the weight of exhaustion.

"Athlaniyo, I... I lost my bond to the Archive, it's like... it's like it's not there any longer." She shook her head. "What happened? I... I still cannot... I need to recreate the bond. I can't even hear the forerunners..."

Athlaniyo bit her lower lip. Then she shook her head, the metallic bits in her braids clinking together. "No, you need to rest. You can try again later."

"But I—" She made an attempt to sit up, but Athlaniyo pushed her back on the recliner with one hand to her sternum.

The judge stepped forward. "None of my queries are urgent. Feel free to rest."

Idriwu looked from the judge to Athlaniyo and back. "But—"

"You need to sleep," Athlaniyo said. "I'm going to make you sleep if that's all right."

Idriwu nodded weakly.

Athlaniyo put a hand on her forehead and recited again. *"Descend, descend, in time ready for ascent, children of yore."*

Idriwu closed her eyes and slept.

The maiden looked up at the judge, her face stern: "You're not supposed to know the Temple phrases."

The judge, easily twice her age, nodded. "I can make an oath..."

"I will have to make you forget."

The judge opened her mouth, then closed it, realizing the Temple servants' word overruled everything in matters of the Archive. She lowered her head.

The high priests sat in council in the largest of the Temple chambers, a rectangular hall lit by ceiling braziers even during the day. Firelight glinted on the embossed metallic plates decorating the walls and on the geometric mosaics of the floor.

"Too much for too little gain," one of the elderly sages lamented, running a hand over the curls of his beard. "We need to increase the amount and it is a strain on archivists' bodies."

"Not to mention their minds." Qisin Aday, the elected head of the council, was younger than most and barely middle-aged, but still she spoke with the sonorous voice of the wise.

"Not to mention their minds," the sage concurred.

An uncomfortable silence descended on the assembly. The young apprentices standing in the back exchanged nervous glances with each other. The question remained unspoken.

Finally, Dathrun spoke—Dathrun, always forceful, seldom considerate. He was not a popular sage and commoners seldom turned to him for advice, but his opinion carried weight with his fellows. "Learned ones—we need to consider that present trends might continue."

Young Asawirh drew in a sharp, hissing breath. Yet heads across the crowded assembly hall nodded in quiet agreement with Dathrun.

"We should ask the archivists to testify," Dathrun said. "They can share their assessment of the situation with us. They see the most; they understand the best."

"I agree," Qisin Aday said. She herself had served as an archivist at a younger age. "If we can get them into a state where they can testify," she added on a low tone.

"Is the situation that bad?" Asawirh grimaced.

"That, and worse. Interruptions and fade-outs are more and more common. The voice of the forerunners is less and less audible, the landscapes and cities are vanishing in a steam-bath haze." Qisin Aday swallowed. "You will see."

Idriwu stood, lost her balance for an instant, then regained it. She made a vague gesture with her right hand.

"Yes?" Athlaniyo, her regular assistant, tried to make sense of her erratic behavior.

"I—I—" Idriwu was struggling to speak. "The Archive—I—" She took a step forward, then another and another, her gaze fixed on the unpainted adobe wall of her sparse room. "I need more of the herbs—"

Athlaniyo tried to guide her back to her cot. "You know I can't give you more. The council ruled so."

"Athlaniyo, I—I can't reach it any more, I—My memories, they are in there—I *need* the herbs!" She trembled violently.

"If I give you any more, I might kill you! You can't take it, you never used the herbs before!" Athlaniyo had to calm herself, not to allow the situation to escalate to a screaming match.

The archivist's legs gave way. She slumped to the ground and started to sob.

Qisin Aday crossed her arms in front of her chest as she listened to Athlaniyo's report. The giant hall was mostly empty—only the councilmembers themselves were present.

"It is getting worse, esteemed councillor-priests," Athlaniyo said, on the verge of tears. "She's one of the young ones who were raised to be archivists from birth, and a great part of her is *in* the Archive. Her memories are in there. Her dreams. Her self. And now she's losing all of that."

"How is that even possible?" Dathrun asked. "The archivists see the world of memories and hear the voice of the ancients. How can there be room for a self in the world beyond?"

"With the young ones the bond becomes instinctive over time. They no longer need to stroll through the lands and hear the chant of the forerunners," Athlaniyo said. "They simply know, like they know their own thoughts. Possibly with even more clarity. We've been planning on eventually doing away with the work-trance altogether, but for the moment it's still helpful when accessing complicated legal recordings."

Dathrun frowned, his golden headdress almost slipping aside. He reached up to steady it. "I wasn't aware of that. Is this a new development?"

"With all due respect..." Athlaniyo paused. "We've made great strides in technique in the past few years. It's not only the stonemasons and shipbuilders who constantly improve their craft."

Qisin Aday nodded, speaking up before Dathrun could answer with a retort. "I see your point. We're all too often distracted by the politicking expected of our office." She glanced sternly at Dathrun. "But if we lose our bond to the Archive, we will lose everything—all of our history and our knowledge. This isn't just about her fate, and that of the other young archivists, it's about our entire way of life," she said firmly but calmly.

Athlaniyo lowered her head. "I know, esteemed one. I'm sorry for being so selfish."

"You are concerned for your charge, I understand that." The high priest's voice was tinged with warmth. Athlaniyo looked up in surprise. "Did you grow up together?"

"Yes, esteemed one." She looked away again. "I was guiding her from a small age, just as I myself was guided to do."

"And no doubt you did well."

"If I hadn't, none of this would've happened," she said bleakly. "It's because she was trained too well."

"Don't blame yourself." Qisin Aday took a step closer. "We couldn't have known. The Archive was supposed to endure eternally. It had stood since the beginning of time. No one expected it to fall."

Athlaniyo shook her head. "It's still there, it's only getting harder and harder to access. We tried incense-smoke at first, but the herbs work better. They seem to increase the facility for reaching the Archive, even in more peaceful times, though we usually try to train those as archivists who don't need them." She hesitated. "If you could allow us to give a larger amount—"

"No." The head of the council sighed. "That would only delay the inevitable. There's no need to risk the health of archivists."

"Idriwu is begging for it! I don't know what to tell her! She's begging for it!" Athlaniyo trembled with suppressed tears and anger. "I'm afraid she will—"

She could not bring herself to say it.

For an instant she thought her worst fears had come true.

Idriwu was sitting on her cot with a large ritual dagger in hand. Her left arm was bleeding from multiple cuts, the blood dripping on the earthen floor.

Athlaniyo dashed to her across the room. "What are you doing?!"

Idriwu looked at her, her eyes bloodshot. "The pain drives away the wall of fog and noise. It helps me think clearly. It calms down the fear—"

"But the—Ah!" She yanked out her belt, tried to use it to stop the bleeding.

"The cuts are shallow," Idriwu said dreamily.

"What are you doing?! For the Temple's sake!" Athlaniyo swore. "I have to clean this!" She yanked Idriwu up, a muscle painfully spasming in her shoulder—the archivist was about her height, but with a sturdier build—and dragged her outside. She swore all the while.

"For all the land below and the sky above! Why would you do that? If you want pain, there are ways to cause pain without injury! I can ask the Palace torturers if you want me to, they surely know! I can do anything, just don't *hurt* yourself!"

Idriwu blinked.

They eyed the heap of rods, straps and other parts with skepticism. With some difficulty they'd stacked Idriwu's storage-chests on top of each other in a corner, but they still weren't sure the resulting setup would fit inside the small personal chamber.

"Are you sure you know how to put it together?" Idriwu asked. Athlaniyo was glad she was more lucid for once.

"The torturers explained. Look, there are signs at each end—the rod marked with a cross goes to the hole marked with a cross, the rod with a circle goes to the hole marked with a circle..."

Idriwu lifted a rod, weighed it experimentally. "It's so strange," she said, on an eerily level voice. "So much of me is gone. But the me that lives in the present is still there. It's only when I try to reminisce... It's like putting a foot forward and touching down on thin air. The path of memories is gone."

"You will be all right," Athlaniyo said. "Even if we lose the Archive for good."

"Why do you think it's going away?"

"The elders say it's because of the stars." Athlaniyo was concerned about Idriwu's lack of emotion. "You know, I was thinking. We only need to use this contraption once or twice. With the Temple phrases I can make you relive the feeling from then on."

Idriwu started putting the machine together. "Mhm. That makes sense. The torturers will be angry though, they had to drag all of this heavy equipment here, and then they'll have to drag it back..."

As if they were discussing the weather. Inside, Athlaniyo wanted to scream.

"This gets complicated," Idriwu said. "Now there is a cross, a triangle, a square and a little squiggly thing." She held out a rod to Athlaniyo.

"The squiggly thing just means you have to affix the strap first, and then put together the rods. They told me about that."

"They are like potter's marks," Idriwu said. "Or those small tablets the landowners use. A circle means a sheep, a circle with two lines on top means an ox..."

"Let's just put this together first."

"All right, all right..."

Idriwu looked displeased as her line of thought was interrupted, and a pang of sadness ran through Athlaniyo—why couldn't she allow her friend this one moment of clarity?

Idriwu was tightening a strap when Athlaniyo finally spoke up again. "Look, what was it you were saying about tablets? I didn't mean to interrupt."

Idriwu looked glad, but she did not look away from her task. She grunted as she pulled on the strap with all her force. It held. "I thought I could use that to... make recordings. For myself, at least. So that they won't get lost again."

Athlaniyo sat down on the ground next to her. "But there are markings only for the common animals and the harvest."

"I can make up marks, like the torturers made up this little squiggly here." She pointed with her shoulder while her hands were busy.

"You'd need a thousandscore marks if you wanted to list every single thing. Thousandscores of thousandscores. How would you remember them without the Archive?"

"I could use a system, so that they would be easier to remember. Maybe based on how the names sound... I could have a simple drawing, and then something to remind me of the sound. That way I could remember lots of marks. ...There." She grabbed the contraption's top and pulled it down with all her weight. "That should do."

Athlaniyo stood, dusting off her clothing. "I think you'd better remove your robes. You can keep your underclothes on."

Idriwu swallowed hard, showing anxiety for the first time they'd started building the instrument of torture. "All right. Are you sure this won't cause any lasting damage?"

"They said if some body part was turning purple, it was time to take the restraints down a notch. But if I did that, everything would be fine. They use these to interrogate spies from enemy Palaces, and it would hardly be courteous to damage them permanently."

"Oh." Idriwu did not look reassured, but Athlaniyo was happy even for that. Anything was better than that numb lack of emotion.

Idriwu collapsed on the cot after coming out of the trance, her limbs shaking. Tears were streaming down her face, but she was not making a sound. Then she coughed and said, "Thank you." Her voice was hoarse. She ran her hands along her body—Athlaniyo wondered if she was checking to see if everything was still in its proper place. She smoothed down the wrinkled bedding by her side, her trembling fingers running over the rough-woven square patterns.

It took her a long while to say anything further. "I could reach it. Not all that well, but I could." She herself seemed surprised over that. "If we combine this with the herbs and the Temple phrases, we could... we could recall a lot of the recordings. The Temple and Palace histories, the business transactions... we could put down a lot on those tablets. Life could go on."

"Your memories come first," Athlaniyo said firmly. "And I'm still not sure your method is going to work."

The council was in disarray. Venerated sages were shouting at each other, men and women alike. The apprentices mostly huddled together in clumps, but a handful of them had joined in the fray, supporting their teachers with their voice.

Dathrun finally swung his priest's staff and slammed its head into one of the metallic plates decorating the wall. The loud clanging noise created a moment of silence, and he used it to survey the assembly, staring everyone in the eye one by one, his face grim and determined.

"Will the high council show some restraint?" he asked, his eyes glinting with barely disguised disgust.

Qisin Aday pulled her robe closer. "Would you summarize the debate? Esteemed one," she added hastily.

Dathrun bowed his head, then started to speak. "I think by now everyone has agreed that the new plan is worth attempting. We should send apprentices to the esteemed archivist Idriwu to learn as many marks as possible, and the rules for creating and combining them."

"Esteemed Idriwu herself is usually not in a condition to teach," Qisin Aday interrupted.

"Then to her assistant, the esteemed maiden Athlaniyo of the Temple." Dathrun glanced at Athlaniyo, sitting on a chair in the first row. She had not participated in the commotion.

Dathrun cleared his throat. "The debate was over our priorities. The Temple and Palace recordings could be committed to tablets relatively easily. There is a lot of repetition and the number of different marks required will probably remain low. We can also reuse some of the marks that already exist, about animals and suchlike. The issue is about recordings of a… more personal nature."

The shouts erupted again.

Qisin Aday swung her own staff. The loud crackle was again effective at quieting down the unruly mob. "We should put this into the council regulations," she said and grinned at Dathrun. He smiled back darkly.

Then she pulled herself out to her full height and addressed the assembly. "These archivists, they already work night and day to salvage as much of our shared knowledge as possible. Is there anyone here who will look them in the face and say they cannot salvage anything of themselves?"

The crowd was silent.

"You are getting better at this," Athlaniyo said.

"That still won't stop the trend," Idriwu grumbled. "A few months and we won't be able to reach the Archive at all. At least you can also transcribe faster now. …Let's do it." She took off her robes. Her white undergarments contrasted with her skin. She sat down on the recliner, glancing up at the contraption standing next to it.

Athlaniyo handed her the bowl and she drank the herbal infusion, keeping it in her mouth before each swallow so that it would start acting faster. When she finished, she wiped her mouth with the back of her hand.

"The brews are getting stronger," she said, her voice wavering. "They make my soul want to take flight. I feel... mighty? As if I could overcome..."

"The herbalists have been hard at work too," Athlaniyo responded.

"Sure. Say the words."

Athlaniyo began intoning the secret words of the Temple trance. Idriwu's head dropped. Athlaniyo went on and on, and when she had judged the trance was deep enough, she told Idriwu to stand while she strapped her into the contraption. They had opted to go on using it—there was no time to work on refining the Temple phrases.

Idriwu trembled as the herbs began to take effect. Athlaniyo tightened a few straps—Idriwu gasped, then her breath evened out again.

She began to recite, slowly, methodically, and Athlaniyo was there to take notes.

I was by the riverside with my brother Fadha my sister Isinahu,
when my friend Athlaniyo came down to play with us,
she said it had been a long day for her at the Temple,
I said I knew that just as well myself and she smiled,

This Secular Technology

Leah woke up, said the blessing upon waking, then turned on her overlay with a mental command. She hissed with displeasure—it was a gevurah day, again. She was supposed to contemplate restriction, discipline, withdrawal. She was beginning to wonder if her teachers were doing this on purpose; the assignments were said to be random, but she no longer believed in randomness. Her soul root was in chesed, the diametric opposite of gevurah, and she found gevurah days draining at best, excruciatingly painful at worst.

On the upper bunk, Ruthi was yawning and stretching. Leah grimaced—

Ruthi would be pleased about another gevurah day. Couldn't they just swap their assignments?

Leah went through her morning routine. The prayers were highlighted in all the wrong places. "Blessed are You, Hashem, our Lord, King of the World, that you did not make me a slave"—just the general mention of slavery was sufficient to make Leah feel uncomfortable. Yes, of course she was grateful to Hashem that she was not made a slave, but still, she did not want to be reminded of the concept. She knew she was supposed to contemplate it, but after three straight days of gevurah, she really needed a break. *How much more, Hashem?* she thought.

She wondered if she should just quit the training program. Her abilities were not as disruptive as Ruthi's, and she felt that nothing she learned helped her to function better in day-to-day life.

She was fed up with the overlays.

Ruthi stumbled through the room, on her way to the bathroom, without a care in the world. Leah could've kicked her. Chesed was supposed to be full of mercy... She was feeling very far from her soul root.

"Mnargh, gmarh?" Ruthi said between two mouthfuls of Kellogg's cornflakes, the only kosher brand one could get ahold of on the station. Just as Leah thought of this, her overlay offered a helpful popup. "Certified by the Manchester Bet Din," it said. Manchester was also very far—three jump points from the station, halfway across the galaxy.

"So, mnom? What do you think?" Ruthi said.

Leah looked at Ruthi scathingly and decided not to offer commentary on her eating habits. How could someone so untidy, unruly and nonconforming have her soul root in gevurah, the epitome of restriction? "Yes?" she said as coldly as she could manage.

"I was just," Ruthi slurped, "asking if you'd already picked your phrase for contemplation today." She fixed her gaze on her bowl—Leah knew she'd embarrassed her. She felt a spark of satisfaction, then immediately felt bad about it. At least her overlay did not provide her with a popup about repentance.

"No," Leah said. "No."

"I have something from Yeshayahu, there is the part where he says you are my witnesses, *vechulei,* and then it says *veavdi asher bacharti, lemaan tedu vetaaminu li... vechulei...* I like that a lot, but it's a bit too long, maybe we could split it up?" Leah automatically translated for herself: *and my servant whom I have chosen, so that you would know and believe me...* She was irked by Ruthi's every single habit—her Israeli pronunciation, her heavy glottal stops, her constantly saying *vechulei* instead of *etcetera*... and she prayed so loud, every single morning!

"Sure, we could split it up," she said.

"I like *veavdi asher bacharti* better, so I'm going to give that part to you and focus on the rest I don't like that much." Ruthi beamed at her.

"Huh? How about that?"

And my servant whom I have chosen. Servant. Slave. The same word.

"Is there something wrong?" Ruthi blinked. "Did I say something wrong? I'm sorry "

"No, no," Leah lied, "I'm just tired, is all."

In the end, she did not have the heart to turn down Ruthi's offer. This phrase was as good as any.

She went out to the cavernous garden module for her proscribed morning contemplation. Her overlay highlighted the strangest things—a fence, she assumed because of its restrictive aspect. A birdseed dispenser—that was especially counterintuitive. Dispensing something would be a chesed activity... Maybe it was highlighted because while it dispensed birdseed, it also withheld some? But wouldn't a balance between chesed and gevurah be associated with tiferet instead? She was confused.

She tried not to venture outside on gevurah days—not after that incident with the airlock—, so this was mostly new to her despite today being the—she had to look it up—twenty-third gevurah day since she'd enrolled in the program, a bit more than three months ago. An entire year focusing on these mystical Kabbalistic correspondences, and that's just the beginning. She thought her brain would melt.

She reminded herself to get back to the topic. She never felt particularly coerced by her regular observance and she definitely never felt like an eved Hashem. A servant of Hashem—a slave. The closest she came to appreciating the concept was when she was doing these annoying exercises that started the first thing in the morning when she opened her eyes—

She stopped in her tracks. Why would people say the morning blessing for not having been created a slave, if Jews were all slaves of Hashem? Hashem himself said so, in the words of His prophet Yeshayahu.

This seemed like such a basic contradiction, and yet she had no idea of the answer. She shook her head and wondered if she should just message her rabbi—

"I was looking all over for you!" Ruthi said. "Why did you hide your loc?"

"I didn't—" Leah protested, then she realized she had indeed done just that. Why? When? She did not even remember doing it. According to her logs, she—

"What*ever*, I've found you," Ruthi said and smiled at her, all of her large, chippy teeth showing. "Look, I really have to show you this!"

Leah winced. On a gevurah day, this had to be a gevurah thing. Why did Ruthi have to be her roommate, of all people? At least Ruthi was usually busy being too cheerful to pay attention to Leah's thoughts. Leah wished to hide all her thoughts in a dark corner of her mind, behind a thick brocade curtain.

"It's not an air leak, right? Like last time?"

"No, no, it's not, I promise. Bli neder," she added, the caveat that she was not making a formal oath.

"*Bli neder*?!" Leah wanted to kick Ruthi.

"Look, it's going to be totally awesome," Ruthi said as she ran along the corridor, the metallic floor panels clanging under the soles of her shoes. "You just wait!"

Then the alarms went off.

Ruthi swore loudly. The large gash on her knee was already closing, her systems running the self-repair process, but there was a lot of blood. Her long flowing skirt was tainted with large splotches, dark on the cheerful sky blue. She looked faint.

"Can you stand? We really need to go," Leah said. "That was an evac signal." *Why can't you watch where you're going?*

"The alarm surprised me," Ruthi responded to her thoughts. She grimaced and stood. "Why are these—plates just jutting out from the walls—ngh!" She took a few unsteady steps.

"This is an access tunnel, not a playground," Leah snapped. "Come on, let's go!"

"Which way?"

"Oh." She called up a map. Her overlays with the mystical correspondences covered the escape routes. It was her turn to swear.

"What?" Ruthi looked puzzled.

"I can't turn this thing off. I can't see the escape routes on the map because the correspondences are getting in the way!"

"Eh? They are not supposed to obscure anything. Take it easy," Ruthi advised, standing in a pool of her own blood. "You're just nervous."

Leah wanted to throw up. Then she made up her mind, spun around on her heels and started marching down the corridor.

She could feel Ruthi's hesitation like eyes on her back, but then her roommate fell in step, still stumbling. It would take at least ten, fifteen minutes for the wound to heal.

"It's no good," Leah said, close to tears of frustration. "We can't get through to the docks, all the utility tunnels have been sealed... Can't you just blow this open?" She gestured at the large bulkhead.

"Like the last time, with the airlock?" Ruthi was bitter. "*That* went well."

Leah shrugged. "What is the emergency, anyway?"

"How should I know? For all I know, it's yet another fire drill!" Ruthi blinked, accessing her interface. "Sheidim."

"What, you mean—"

"Look at the reports if you don't believe me!" Ruthi yelled. "Inbound from planetside, a whole bunch of them!"

Leah did not know how to respond. Sheidim were reasonably common in this solar system, but the station was supposed to be highly shielded, and there were active defenses further out. "They should not have gotten this close," she finally said.

"I know! We have to tell the others we cannot get through, maybe they can still lift the gates—"

The two of them began to send out a flurry of messages, only to get error messages in return.

Ruthi tsked. "It's no good, they are interfering with comms."

"Can they do that?" Leah was not sure.

"They can pass through walls! They can do pretty much ev—" Ruthi shuddered and fell on her knees, then toppled forward and barely managed to hold her arms out in time to land on all fours.

What's wrong this *time?* "Ruthi!"

"Inter-ference," she said, gasping. Her arms buckled and she fell facefirst on the floor.

"But I'm not feeling anything!" Leah tried to drag Ruthi upright. Her body was unexpectedly heavy.

"Custom work. My systems. They haven't been fine-tuned yet. It's for the psychokinetic—" Her muscles went limp.

"Ruthi!" *Don't die on me, don't you* dare! "Ruthi!" Leah held her with one arm, straining against the weight—what was her body made of?—, and slapped her face with the other. To no avail.

The tears of frustration finally began to flow.

Ruthi was unconscious, lying on the floor with her head in Leah's lap. Leah could feel the sheidim were getting close even if she could no longer access the station's status reports. *Such evil creatures...*

The two of them should at least get someplace safe. She would not be able to carry Ruthi. She could drag her, at most. And they could not exit the utility tunnels.

She opened her map again, tried to strain her mind's eye to make out the details. It was hopeless. All she could see were the markings indicating features of the map important for gevurah. Why were there so many of them, anyway? They were down in a sub-basement, what was down here?

She choked on her breath. The armory! They were right next to the armory! Hashem's left hand that metes out strict justice, a flaming sword—all gevurah correspondences. Why was she so busy trying to ignore the signs?

The armory could save them!

She would only need to drag Ruthi a few steps. Or maybe more than a few...

It hurt her soul to see her friend like this, but there was no use crying over that. She had to muster all her strength to pull Ruthi by the arms, and Ruthi's heels kept on getting stuck in the gaps between floor panels.

Ruthi's ankles twisted. No time. Her systems could do all that repair once they got to the armory. Gevurah was all about doing what had to be done, unhesitatingly, unflinchingly.

Unfeelingly, Leah thought.

Just a few more steps.

She stepped to a featureless gray weapons cabinet and was surprised to see it open in response to her mental command.

Behind her, Ruthi coughed. She was coming to. *High time.* Leah grimaced.

The cabinet was filled with canisters, all alike and indistinguishable upon visual inspection. She looked at the readouts. Again her Kabbalistic overlay obscured the important information—she wanted to stomp her feet, but she felt too weary to do even that.

One of the aspects of gevurah was din, judgment. She decided to treat the noise as signal and grabbed the most judgmental-looking canister, broke the seal.

"With extreme prejudice," she muttered to herself.

"What?" Ruthi was trying to stand. She almost toppled and had to grab a neighboring cabinet to steady herself. "Do you want to use that?"

"Am I psychokinetic? I want *you* to use it!"

Ruthi closed her eyes and put her forehead to the locker's cool front. "Like last time?" She gasped for breath. "You ruined my ankles."

"Look, if you're not going to use this, we'll just die anyway." Leah surprised even herself. Where was this ferocity coming from? Her frustration and annoyance were all gone, transformed into a slow-burning rage.

"We'll die either way," Ruthi said wearily. "That thing is symbiotic and it takes half an hour to bond."

"Is there anything else?"

"I doubt you'll be able to use a rocket launcher against the sheidim."

Ruthi pushed herself away from the locker. "Give that to me." She took the canister gingerly. "Okay, now you need to tie me up."

"What?!"

"Do you want me to injure myself? I will thrash! What do you think?!"

Leah looked around in desperation. Restraint—such a gevurah concept.

Normally, her eyes would've slid off the bright red markings in unconscious, instinctive rejection, but now she needed to seek them out.

There was a bag full of large straps on the bottom shelf of the locker.

She grabbed it, tore it open. Looked around again. A large fold-down panel, for repairs—she stepped to the wall, pulled down the panel.

Various pieces of equipment popped out from the wall and onto the panel, leaving her with a well-equipped workshop. She swept everything off the flat surface, various pieces of hardware clattering to the ground, losing their shape as their programming realized they were unneeded.

She got Ruthi to lie down on the panel, and she pulled up the corners into bars, commanded them to solidify in position, then used the straps to tie Ruthi down. *Act. Do not think.* She knew if she were to pause for a second, she would break down and cry.

"My head too," Ruthi said. "I'd rather not bang it into the panel."

She drew in a sharp breath, but proceeded to jury-rig a solution regardless, her hands working swiftly. Ruthi was completely immobilized.

"Okay, now get a knife and make a vertical cut along my chest."

Her mind would not even process the order at first. She blurted out, completely inconsequentially, "Won't you bite your tongue off?"

"I can lock my jaw. Quick, make the cut! That thing senses the blood, that starts the bonding process."

Ruthi's clothing split open in response to her command. Leah only had to cut the flesh. She unclipped her small polyval from her belt and flicked it into a knife configuration. She leaned over Ruthi, who'd closed her eyes and waited in silence.

Leah's hands trembled and she grappled with her systems to find the command to suppress the tremor. So much fear...

Another of gevurah's aspects—pachad, fear. *Deal with it,* she told herself, then, *use it.*

"How deep should I cut?" Even her voice shook.

"Just a surface wound. It just needs the scent of blood."

And this is what we need to fight the sheidim? This secular technology?
"How long?"

"A good, long cut, whatever, just do it!"

"Okay... you might want to lock your jaw..."

She touched the tip of the blade to Ruthi's sternum. She gagged. Use the fear. The blade glowed with the burning red overlay of gevurah. She pressed down—only slightly—then pulled the knife along a straight line. A very clean cut, the wound knitting itself together as she watched—

Pull it apart, Ruthi thought at her. She dropped the knife and obeyed. Then she lifted the canister, unscrewed the lid and held it above the wound before it closed.

Something half fell, half jumped out of the canister—it was larger than she'd imagined it to be. It set upon the flesh, burrowed in with a ripping sound.

Its mental imprint was so strong Leah could not help being drawn in. The creature was full of desire, of need. Pure hunger. It grabbed ahold of the solar plexus, ran up and down the nerves, made its way to the spinal column, up into the brain with an animal kind of single-minded determination.

Ruthi screamed.

"I thought you'd lock your jaw," Leah muttered with sudden annoyance. How like Ruthi... Then she looked closer and through the haze of gevurah she realized Ruthi's muscles were tensed so much her bones would've snapped had they not been specially reinforced. Was she here to train for *this*? All the nonchalance, all the messiness just a façade? Who was Leah to judge her?

How much pain can a person take? Leah felt like she was about to get to know the answer. She did not want to do this to her roommate, to her...

friend—

The sheidim swarmed closer, attracted to human suffering. They wanted to feed. Time was running out.

She tried to tune into the process, to estimate the remaining time until the successful bonding. *Is this even reversible?* The bright arcs of pain had faded and the symbiote was worming its tiniest tendrils into the flesh, spreading out in a fractal pattern like the branches of a tree.

She saw a shadow from the corner of her left eye. She spun around. The sheidim were approaching. They weren't strong enough yet, they were barely visible and they would shy away from direct observation. She stared at them, tried to will them away, but she could sense them crowding around the armory.

The walls began to glow with invisible lines, automatically highlighted for her. Restriction again. Wards keeping out the intruders? In any case, they weren't strong enough—or, rather, there were too many of the sheidim, for even though the wards proceeded to suck up their energy, there was still plenty left.

Ruthi groaned; Leah probed gently and saw she was not conscious. Less than ten minutes had passed. All of this was in vain?

She needed to accelerate the process, even despite the risk—being permanently damaged was still better than being dead, she thought with some part of her mind, while another part recoiled from the cold calculation in horror. If she had to surrender to the pain herself, accept the sacrifice like Yitzchak at the Akeida, she would've gladly done it to save Ruthi. But to offer up another... *She* wanted to be there, tied down and torn apart. But she did not have the capability, she was not psychokinetic, she was—

Hashem, I'm just a girl who's aware of other people's minds, how did I get into this mess?!

She frantically scrolled through an inventory list. Something, anything...

On her skin she could feel the air temperature dropping.

Ruthi coughed, coming to.

"Cabinet Five," she said, "on the top shelf." Then her consciousness winked out again. *Too late, too late.*

Leah jumped to the cabinet. The top shelf was filled with ampoules. "Which one?" No answer. "Ruthi!" She grabbed one of the ampoules highlighted for her. *I hope it won't give her a heart attack,* she thought.

"What do I do with this?!"

The crest of another wave. Ruthi spoke. "The elbow... I have a port."

"Which elbow?!" Again too late. She tore at her clothing, ripped off her sleeve. It was either the right one or she had induction ports on the insides of both elbows. She popped open the latch—one end of the ampoule fit right in. She pressed it in, turned it until she heard the click. Whatever was inside was sucked into the bloodstream.

She had indeed picked the right ampoule. Whatever it was, the substance cranked up the growth process so much she could feel it herself. She shuddered. Another large burst, another arc of pain. She realized with horror that Ruthi was conscious again, the ebb and flow hitting another high point just when the growth surge launched.

Ruthi keened. At the door, sheidim were massing for an assault.

Cut me loose. At first Leah did not even realize Ruthi wanted something from her; she looked in no shape to form a coherent thought, and yet she was—

She cut the straps, fumbling and coming close to dropping the knife twice. Her whole body was shaking and her vision swam in tears and the red-hot fire of gevurah. As soon as Leah was done, Ruthi tried to get off the panel, but she could not maintain her balance and she fell with her full weight on Leah. Leah grabbed her, staggered back, then sat down heavily.

The floor was icy cold. Ruthi shuddered in her entire body and Leah could feel the process had not yet run its course. She held Ruthi close to herself, tried to whisper words of comfort. There was no time.

Ruthi tried to extricate herself, fell forward on all fours, then lost her balance altogether. She lay on the ground, panting. Leah could sense she came perilously close to fading into unconsciousness again.

Pull me up, Ruthi thought.

Leah scampered to her fallen body, tried to pull her upright, supporting her weight with her entire body.

The sheidim lured them with words of darkness. So close…

Her mind was jumping in utterly incongruous directions. *This is surely not how the ancients defended themselves…*

"Nitkatnu hadorot," Ruthi whispered. *The generations have become smaller.* The Talmudic expression for people becoming less and less observant, less and less wise.

Then, only the earth-shattering and yet inaudible sound of the wards breaking down, the howls of the sheidim streaming inward, entering the bubble of silence.

Ruthi strained against Leah's arms and shouted something in Hebrew, but Leah could no longer make out the words. Pure melting-hot force ran along Ruthi's spine, an axis of murderous light connecting above to below—

Leah knew she needed to let go but couldn't, they would both burn, all would be for naught—

Ruthi pushed her away, teetering on her legs, then she lifted her arms—still unsteady—and with an outstretched hand, brought justice down from the higher realms.

Her silhouette was burned into Leah's mind like the outlines of people burned into walls after a nuclear explosion. Leah fell, fell, and would not rise for a long time.

A coughing, retching sound pulled her back.

Ruthi—or whatever was left of her—was lying on her back, gargling with blood.

She crawled to her and pushed her to the side so that she would not suffocate in her own vomit. *What was that about the recovery position?* She was blacking out herself, struggling to recall the first aid lessons back when they'd arrived at the station. *If her neck's broken—Hashem—I might've just killed her—*

149

Then darkness claimed her once again.

She was being tied to a stretcher. She struggled to sit up, but a large hand pushed her down. She turned her head—there were several people in bright red coveralls striped with glowing neon yellow, crowded around the place where Ruthi's body had lain. She was there, but Leah could not see her from the paramedics. She could not feel her mind.

She started to wail, but then there was a small hiss and even her vocal cords would not obey her any longer. She fell, this time into pure soft white light.

Her mind returned before her sense of her body, leaving her thoughts to spin around faster and faster, spinning in place. She struggled to open her mouth. She could feel she was not alone in the room. She had to speak!

"Is she dead?" she finally managed to gasp.

"No," the man sitting in the back of the small room said, but with a strange undertone she could not interpret.

"You saved both of your lives," the man said. He was clean-shaven—an outsider? Someone frei altogether, or maybe Modern Orthodox? "Such resolve. You did what had to be done. Most people would've hesitated."

It took Leah a moment to realize he was praising her. How was she supposed to respond? "It was a gevurah day," she said, not having anything better

to say.

He did not understand. *Definitely an outsider,* Leah concluded.

"In similar situations, people often shy away from helping." She could feel he'd seen a lot. She tried to gain a measure of him. Some kind of—specialist? Called in to—

"Who are you?"

He coughed. "Oh. I'm sorry, I haven't introduced myself. Jacob Klein." *Jewish or German?* Leah wondered. "Bioweapons expert for the Allied military. My department engineers symbiotic lifeforms for psychokinetic operatives." *Such a well-practiced turn of phrase.* He did these introductions often, she realized with a small startle.

"Are you here to—"

"Yes, I'm here to assist with your friend's reconstruction. She's been through a lot. No, no—" he raised his hands placatingly, "don't worry, everything is going according to schedule. She's going to be all right. As much as possible given the circumstances. A full recovery might take years, but so far she's on track."

She eyed him skeptically, but as far as she could tell, he was telling the truth.

"Look, half an hour is the absolute minimum for the merge. It's not meant to be accelerated. It can be accelerated, yes, but it's not meant to be accelerated." He sounded apologetic.

She sat up with difficulty, pulled up her pillow and put her back against it. She did not know what to say; she was stalling for time.

"The two of you did it in just under eighteen minutes," he said. "It's a miracle there was enough... functioning to mount an attack." He looked away. "But that's not what I'm here to discuss. I'm here to tell you something."

"Me?"

"We have a lot of reports from battlefield situations," he went on, ignoring the question. "This type of weaponry is extremely effective, but..." He cleared his throat. "The other soldiers are the ones not taking it well. Not even as far as to assist. Installation usually happens away from the front, but there is still an amount of field maintenance necessary, and then there are the possible injuries..." He stood up and started to pace; he had trouble keeping his eyes on her. "This will sound heartless, but these days the military often tries to assign them assistants or... buddies... with a psychopathic streak. The kind that usually keeps you out of the army. Simply because other people, people with a measure of empathy, do not have the resolve..."

But I'm not psychopathic—right? Right? Panic rushed through her, clearing out her stuffy head.

"From what I see, you are not only a gentle young woman, you are also telepathic... Yet you've gone ahead and done it." He shook his head in disbelief. "I need you to understand this." He turned to her. "Don't feel bad about your actions. You've made the right choice. All the right choices."

"The Akeida," she whispered. He did not even know the word. "Hashem told Avraham to offer up Yitzchak as a sacrifice... and Avraham avinu went ahead with it." He still drew a blank. "In the Torah. Avraham. Yitzchak."

She felt a familiar annoyance.

"Ah," he said. "Abraham and Isaac. I see." He scratched his head. It was uncovered. *For his sake I hope he's German, not Jewish.* "I definitely see the analogy. But even still, there was hardly a voice from God on high, in your case..."

"It was a gevurah day," she stubbornly repeated. "I just did what my overlay told me to do." She paused, realizing that some explanation was in order. "I'm here to learn all these correspondences."

"Correspondences?"

"Kabbalistic correspondences. Like, the attribute of Yitzchak is gevurah: strictness, restriction... discipline, that's a better word. Even bravery..."

"Ah. And you're studying these correspondences."

"Yes, my interface highlights them in..." she waved a hand around, "my environment, and this way it's supposedly faster."

"But…" He frowned. "If we take the analogy one step further, you're not… Isaac. You are Abraham. You offered up someone else."

Her breath stuck in her chest. He did not notice as he went on—for him, this was a fascinating but ultimately alien topic. A chat with someone from a foreign culture. They were as far apart as two people could be while still speaking the same language. "What corresponds to Abraham?" he asked in all innocence.

"Chesed," she muttered. "Mercy. Lovingkindness."

"And what corresponds to you?"

For a long while she could not answer, she just sat there in the infirmary bed, tears rolling down her cheeks.

Three Partitions

Chani sat on the women's balcony, racing through her prayers at the usual breakneck speed of the Orthodox. She was bored. She knew there was a Chasidic position that prayer should be as fast as possible, to prevent the yetzer hara, the evil inclination from getting a few thoughts in edgewise between the words. But she could recite at full speed and still have her mind wander.

The men below finally got to the Torah reading. Chani stood. The mechitza was ill-fitting and she could peek out from between two sheets of curtain. The reading was set to be chaotic as usual.

The rabbi yelled, looking for a kohen to say the blessings. Chani rolled her eyes. Yossi was out of town. Uri was traipsing around in space as usual. And who knew what Dovber was up to...

There was a commotion below. Finally they decided there was no kohen to be found, so they had to go with a levi, the next best option. Someone pushed through the crowd. Chani yawned.

Downstairs, the levi said the blessings and Shai began the Torah reading. Chani closed her eyes and leaned against one of the mechitza posts. She liked to listen to him read—he chanted precisely, but with feeling, an otherworldly resonance suffusing his words. He was very young—much too young to serve as a Torah reader, Chani had assumed, but still the community had picked him for this task.

Her attention drifted and instead of focusing on the reading, she wondered about Shai. *With his sensitivities, he should be working with the planetmind in some capacity*, she thought. *But he can chant beautifully, and also...*

She got a really bad feeling, like a lightning bolt streaking along her spine, leaving a burning sensation in its wake.

She winced and quickly looked around. The mechitza on her right trembled slightly, as if a breeze was blowing the heavy curtains. She swallowed—her mouth suddenly dry—and tried hard not to think of what was hidden there.

The mechitza on Chani's right separated a further partition from the balcony. Men below, women above, and... those who were neither in the right corner of the balcony.

They had set it up just for one person. Could it still be called a person?

Best keep the distance—Chani took a cautious little sidestep to the left and slid her siddur, her regular prayer book along the slanted reading surface of the pew. It got stuck in a place where two pews joined. She yanked her hand nervously and the siddur dropped to the floor. She snatched it up, kissed her fingers and touched the cover with them—there was so much dust around that she felt bad about directly kissing the cover, even though she knew her immune mods could probably take care of everything. *Best not to risk it*, she thought. *This is a frontier settlement.*

There was a low thudding sound coming from behind the mechitza. She looked—the curtain between the men's and women's portions was practically translucent, but for the third partition someone had found an old and heavy brocade curtain. She could not see anything.

She could only feel the distress.

Her muscles tensed with such a force that the breath was pushed out of her lungs. She froze in fear. Why, why did she get up early on Shabbat—why did she decide to attend the morning prayers—why was she aware of other people's minds—

A groan from beyond the curtain, then a high keening noise. Not very loud—the men below did not even notice it. The two women fussing in the kiddush room behind her back did not drop their pots to see what was happening, either, and she was alone on the balcony.

She swore, then instantly felt bad about it. She jumped to the curtain and yanked it away with one sweeping, theatrical gesture.

Behind the mechitza, Adira was sitting on the pew seat, clutching her stomach. She looked surprisingly human—just like before. Her hair was short and it stuck to her head in tight, dark curls. Her skin was an unusually pale white and her limbs were thin and gangly. She wore a striped shirt and a long flowing skirt in matching dark purples and blues. Everything was just like before.

She was throwing up insects.

Adira doubled up. The insects moved around on the pew rather dazedly—they were all shiny quicksilver and surprisingly large.

Chani had absolutely no idea what to do. Fear tied her tongue. "W-w-w- how can I help?"

Adira tried to speak, but another spasm shook her. The new insects looked even more dazed, and—Chani could not look away from them—slightly malformed. They toppled, their legs of different lengths; they fell on their backs; they dropped to the ground.

Adira gasped. "It's the- the geomagnetic storm. Take me outside."

Chani was overcome by the force of the command. She grabbed Adira's small, slight body—her long limbs exactly like the legs of, *no, no*, she banished the thought, she would not go there—and dragged her to the kiddush room.

The tables were laid for kiddush. The yeshiva boys would also eat their lunch here, and a pot of cholent already steamed on one table. The room was otherwise empty. Where were Sarah and Liora? Maybe downstairs chasing the kids, Chani thought, and for a moment she was grateful.

Chani grabbed a plastic chair and pushed Adira down in it. Adira threw up again, not insects, only small lumps that wiggled slightly. "Outside," she said, wheezing. "Beyond the limits."

We can't, it's Shabbat, Chani wanted to say, but thought better of it and managed to keep her mouth shut.

Adira reacted regardless. "Pikuach nefesh," she said, her voice hoarse. Life-saving, the one imperative that overrode almost all commandments, including all the Shabbat prohibitions.

Chani helped her to the door, supporting her weight, then the two of them stumbled down the stairs.

They had to rest in the grass outside the synagogue courtyard. Chani gasped for air. She knew she should've gone for those other mods—her body felt frail and she was sure she'd pulled her back on the way down the stairs, trying with all her might to keep Adira from toppling forward.

Adira attempted to get back on her feet, but she could not maintain her balance. Chani got up, tried to help her. Both of them ended up facefirst in the grass. Chani swore in Arabic.

"At least you've stopped throwing up," she said, turning back toward Adira.

Her skin was coming off. Chani watched in horror. It looked like her flesh itself was peeling away, large slices of plastic-looking meat, entirely unreal. Underneath, the shiny silver substance of planetlife itself was glowing in the sunlight.

"What's going on?!" She was close to screaming.

"Get me beyond the city limits," Adira said, her longest sentence so far.

Chani jumped up. Some things were simply beyond comprehension. She tried to summon a floater pallet—she could sense there was one in the shed just behind the building.

The pallet responded. Its status message helpfully pointed out that it was locked down for Shabbat.

Chani swore again, something graphically obscene. Then she hit upon a better choice of words. *Pikuach nefesh,* she sent.

Override accepted.

The pallet whipped around the corner, landed in front of them with a smoothness belying its speed. Chani rolled Adira on it, jumped up—almost tripping in her skirt—, issued the right set of commands, then held on for dear life.

There was no forcefield at front and Chani lacked the skill to make one herself. The wind tore at her face, her eyes. She grimaced, looked down. The pallet obediently evaded obstacles. Still, they almost hit a young boy, and Chani could feel his gaze on her back for a long time.

Adira was shaking. The skin and flesh stopped falling off; instead, her body changed—she was turning into something noticeably less human, and Chani forced herself to squeeze her eyes shut.

"What's going on," she asked again, more of a demand than a question.

"If I cannot—maintain my shape, the body gets broken down into—less complex lifeforms," Adira said. She spoke with eerie calm, but her voice was changing, acquiring odd overtones.

Chani gripped the edge of the pallet with all the strength in her hands.

You are now leaving the settlement limits, the pallet said.

Chani ignored the warning. They flew on. Adira was entirely silent and Chani forced her mind away from her—there was something about her that was profoundly nonhuman, and the other, local mind was more and more apparent in her, beyond her, through her.

You are now leaving the protected zone, the pallet said.

The world acquired a subtle saturation, all colors suddenly more vivid. Chani took a deep breath. She would be exposed to the planetmind here, with no mediation, no metaphorical curtains and veils protecting the awareness of those in the settlement. And she was habitually aware of other people's minds. She would be—

She lost her balance. Her grip on the pallet did not loosen—her fingers felt completely stiff—and her elbow and knuckle joints protested the sudden tearing motion. She did not fall off. She did not fall off. She tried to breathe.

She was overwhelmed.

The planetmind drew back from her in an instant that still felt much too long. There was no attempt to communicate. *Would we even be able to communicate, without Adira?* Chani looked down. Was Adira conscious? Chani struggled to sort out her impressions. *What would happen with her gone?*

"I'm not—dead yet," Adira said, with considerable difficulty.

"Where to now?" Chani was clumsily trying to hide her embarrassment.

"Find a lake."

The lake was filled with the oily quicksilver fluid of planetlife. Chani parked the floater, then noticed with a fright that Adira had lost consciousness. She looked up to the sky, desperate for instruction.

The planetmind was all around her, keeping distance for the time being. Getting ready to swarm in for the kill? She was an intruder here.

Long, long seconds passed. The planetmind was anticipating something, she realized with a startle. Maybe the two of them could not speak in words without Adira, as she'd assumed.

The planetmind indicated the lake.

She tried to undress Adira. Her hands were shaking. She wanted to find an override for that—

The planetmind communicated urgency.

She took a deep breath and pushed Adira into the lake.

A heartbreaking crunching sound from the depths. Was Adira being digested? The surface of the lake was artificially calm.

Minutes ticked by.

Adira resurfaced, floating like an inflatable toy. She looked human. She opened her eyes, but made no attempt to look around.

"We can now speak," the planetmind said through her.

"What's going on?" she demanded.

"A solar flare causes a magnetic storm planetside."

"What?"

"There are instabilities in the māwal." The planetmind used the standard Alliance term, not the Hebrew. "It is hard for her to maintain her shape even during more peaceful times. Now it is even harder. Automatic processes have been set in motion. We have been concerned."

"What are you talking about?"

"Expectations shape reality," the planetmind said. She could feel the disappointment. The alien sentience was disappointed by her ignorance.

"I know, I know," she grimaced and looked away. It was no use—the planetmind was everywhere. Lush green and red vegetation rustled, but this was only the surface—Chani knew if she were to cut any plant, its insides would show her that beautiful, lustrous shade of silver.

"If you understand this relationship, then why do you act the way you do?" the planetmind asked.

"What do you m—" she said, then froze, understanding what was coming.

"None of you have been helping her maintain her shape," the planetmind said. "We were promised the community would help her maintain her shape."

"The—" She could not bring herself to say what she wanted to say. She lashed out instead. "The *community*, the community is afraid! We don't know how to deal with this! Cut us some slack!"

"These processes are automatic on our behalf. If your community no longer belongs to us, it is consumed."

"How can you just—" She sputtered. "You are a sentient being!"

"We told you about this in advance. She is a part of us. She is a part of your community. If she is no longer a part of your community, *we* are no longer part of your community, and *you* are no longer part of *us*. Then you are consumed. You have always been aware of this."

"But what do you want?" She turned around to yell at the forest, even though she knew the mind was probably even more present in the lake. "What do you want?!"

"We want you to help her maintain her shape, with your expectations." The planetmind sounded tired. "You are all avoiding her. None of you would even touch her. You put her behind a separate curtain in your hall of worship."

"But we can't— Halachically—" Did the mind even know these words, know about Jewish law? If Adira was a part of the mind, then probably yes. Still Chani felt compelled to clarify. "She is a shapeshifter, she can be both male or female, and there is a ruling that in cases of indeterminacy we have to go by the stricter— She can't just sit on the men's side, but she can't sit on the women's side either, so—"

"This is a problem for you to solve," the planetmind responded.

Chani sat on a stool in Rebbetzen Mushka's kitchen and gobbled up one brownie after another. Adira was lying on the large leather sofa in the living room, tucked into a children's blanket decorated with little cartoon spaceships, and comfortably asleep. The door of the kitchen was closed.

The rebbetzen sighed. "I can tell you—I've been there. Maybe you can even... how do you say that... sense my thoughts? Read my mind?" She gestured with short little fingers.

Chani shrugged, her mouth full of brownie mash.

I can bind you together even closer, the planetmind said. Chani choked on the brownies.

"There, there." The rebbetzen handed her a glass of water. "A few stray crumbs?"

Chani swallowed. "Not really..."

Her thoughts were rushing ahead furiously. *Have you followed me here?*

I am aware of everything in the settlement. Now you are aware of me. The planetmind made an impression of calm reason. No anger. No practical jokes.

But I—

You were exposed. No choice. No alternative.

Was the rebbetzen saying something? Chani tuned her out. *I didn't want to—*

You are sensitive. You are that which you are. A pause. *Is this such a problem?*

Chani shook her head, tried not to grit her teeth. *I guess not.* "Sorry?" she asked the rebbetzen. "You were saying—?"

The memories were unexpectedly clear—Chani wondered how much was interpolation by the rebbetzen's mind, by hers, or by the planetmind.

Not much, the planetmind said. *We can compensate.*

Thanks, just *what I needed to hear.*

Adira wore a simple white cotton robe.

"...white like a kittel and a shroud? That's not necessarily the best choice of color for the occasion," the rebbetzen said.

"The experience is in many ways similar to death," the Ereni responded on a calm, even voice. She was short and stocky, yet there was something fragile in the way she moved, in the way her eyes flicked around the cavern, restless. Who was she? Probably the Rebbe's advisor, the one who helped organize the move from Mars.

Yes, this is Esawāyun ta Udufayiwe. The Rebbe's liaison who negotiated with us.

...*Thank you.* Such a strong mental link, that an unfamiliar person's lengthy name made it across... Chani was surprised.

The planetmind did not say *You're welcome.* Chani refocused on the memory.

"Look, I'm ready, can we just begin? All this talk is making me nervous," Adira said. Chani could feel she was trying hard to suppress an involuntary shaking of the muscles.

Hey, how come I can feel her emotions? The rebbetzen is not māwal-sensitive.

We are overlaying our experience. Did the planetmind hesitate, just for an instant? *Some of it.*

She mentally shrugged.

The Ereni pulled out a knife from her elaborate robes. "The custom is for the person to make an entry wound themselves, so as to indicate consent and commitment."

The rebbetzen's mouth opened in protest, but the Ereni raised a hand. "I know deliberate self-injury is not allowed in Jewish law. Self-injury by proxy is also explicitly disallowed. But surgery in general is allowed. We had a long discussion with the Rebbe and we finally decided it would be permissible for me to do it. Adira—"

Adira stepped closer to the Ereni.

Rebbetzen Mushka looked away.

Do I have to watch this? Chani felt that somewhere, outside, her body was shaking.

You don't have to watch anything you don't want to.

But—

The moment had passed. Adira kneeled down and simply toppled into the silver pool, seemingly slower than what the local gravity would allow for, more floating than falling.

The viscous fluid began to move. The pool was relatively shallow and Adira struggled to stand, the fluid pulling her back. There was a series of cracks—the sound of bones snapping?—and Chani expected to hear screams, an inhuman howl, but there was nothing of the sort, just eerie silence. She could hear the rebbetzen's breathing. The fluid still moved, and at one point Chani could see something like an arm sticking up, with one joint too many—a bone broken in half? She gagged.

Then everything was calm once more. She looked, straining her mind.

Where is she? She's—she's not there anymore— She knew the rebbetzen could not sense this, so why was the planetmind showing her now, all of a sudden, showing this and nothing else— *You haven't shown me how you felt, how she felt beyond the slightest surface awareness, why are you—*

That would have been too much, and hardly relevant to the issue at hand.

But now you're showing me she's not there anymore—

She has been incorporated.

The Ereni bowed her head and said, "It is done. She has been incorporated. Now we can only hope for the best."

"I thought I'd feel something," Rebbetzen Mushka said, looking flustered. She pulled at her pink headscarf. "Since she'd merged with us, first... I'm not sure what the word is... she'd bound us together, and to herself..."

The Ereni raised her left eyebrow. "And you hadn't felt anything?"

"I'm not sure..."

"She must've kept it from you."

"Can that be done?" The rebbetzen was confused.

"Yes, that can be done." The Ereni turned away. "Now we need to wait some time, for the reconstitution. There shouldn't be any complications."

"Reconstitution," Chani whispered. The kitchen was suddenly small and cramped around them. "I didn't know that. I didn't know she was…" She bowed her head. "She was gone. I saw it. She was gone…"

"I'm sorry?" The rebbetzen pushed back her own kitchen stool with a loud creak.

Chani looked up, her eyes filling with tears. "This is even worse, don't you get it? If this gets out—" She waved her hands around. She normally looked up to the rebbetzen, but now all her decorum was gone, forgotten, digested in that lake. "The entire settlement, everything will be all gone! If the others realize—"

The rebbetzen did not see the point. Chani felt a sudden urge to grab her annoying pink pullover and shout at her—she had been there, how could she have been so ignorant, how—

"I'm sorry? What do you mean?"

"Don't you understand, halachically, I'm not sure she can even be counted as human anymore! Male, female, whatever, I'm not sure she counts as human!"

The rebbetzen paled. "But why?"

"I saw it, she was gone, she was completely absorbed!"

"I didn't see that and I was there!" She stood, her short frame trembling with a mixture of anger, indignation, and… fear?

"The planetmind showed me! And the Ereni talked about recon-stitution!" Chani was shouting, beside herself. "Reconstitution! Didn't you realize the implications?!"

Rebbetzen Mushka covered her mouth with a hand, gasping. Chani went on. "She's gone and what there is—I'm not even sure she is a Jew any longer, her entire body was gone, the planetmind ate her—it's not just a transformation, she was gone, and what's there now is just a reconstruction! If word gets out—" She ran out of breath.

"Sit down. Let us think." The rebbetzen made a pacifying gesture with both arms. "You know the Rebbe says every sentient being can convert to Judaism, that means they can in principle be Jewish. So why would Adira lose her Jewish status if she became… another kind of sentient being?'"

"Because it's not *her* any longer," Chani whispered, then sat, her eyes fixed on the rebbetzen. "Because it's not her any longer."

"And how can you say that?"

"Because I saw it and she was gone. And if the other people realize this, she will only become more isolated, and the planetmind will no longer sense us as part of itself, and we will all be killed!" Her voice rose and rose.

"Ssh. We'll wake her up."

Chani looked away, embarrassed. "I'm sorry, I didn't mean to…"

"We'll solve this situation. I'm sure the Rebbe knows, I'm sure the Ereni had told him and he'd considered every detail. We can just contact him."

Chani pointed up. "The storm."

The rebbetzen sighed. Messages going in and out of the jump point had indeed been disrupted for days. "Still, I'm sure he'd considered everything and found everything permissible and workable. He wouldn't have asked her to do this if it were asur. I'm sure she still counts as Jewish, still counts as a member of the community…"

"Yes, but if the others catch wind of this—look how much trouble it caused when they realized she could shapeshift! In shul, they put up an extra curtain just for her because they didn't want her on the men's side and they didn't want her on the women's side either!"

"I'm okay with the mechitza," Adira said from behind her. "I never liked it when people tried to chat me up while I was busy davening, anyway."

Chani spun around. *How much did she hear?*

All of it, said the planetmind.

"All of it," said Adira. "I'm potentially aware of everything that happens in the settlement. I just need to decide what to focus on."

"You're making it worse," Chani yelled at her.

"Now, now," the rebbetzen stepped next to them. "It's all right."

"It's not all right, she will fail to maintain her what, her consistency, and we will all die!"

Adira frowned. "I thought you'd made a promise shortly before I woke up, out beyond the perimeter."

She had. She had promised the planetmind she would intervene, try to convince the others not to push Adira aside. "Sure, but– none of this is helping, you have to realize it's not me, the guys in the kollel spend their time debating technicalities all day, if they learn of this–"

Adira smiled. "If they learn of this, they'll soon realize that if not for me, there would be no kollel, and they'd have to go back to Mars and full-time drudgery."

Chani was speechless. Then she finally blurted out, "That sounds... utilitarian."

The rebbetzen smiled. "That sounds workable..."

Rebbetzen Mushka and her husband, Rabbi Tzvi sat on kitchen stools while Chani paced, describing the situation. The rabbi nodded along, murmuring assent every now and then; Chani thought distractedly that he'd always been the malleable type. *This might just work...*

"You understand the danger, but most of the other men don't," she said. "A simple explanation wouldn't sway them, but there is a way to demonstrate the danger without permanent harm..."

The rabbi picked a brownie crumb out of his beard. "Mmm. The Rebbe said as much."

Chani jumped. "What did the Rebbe say?" *The Rebbe said something? And you're telling us just now?*

Rabbi Tzvi was fortunately unaware of her roiling throughts. "That you would probably rise to the occasion," he said mildly.

"What?! *I* would rise to the occasion?!"

"Yes, he said you would... not stand by the blood of your fellow," he quoted the Torah.

"And the others?" Chani was again close to screaming. "Shai is also sensitive to, to the mãwal—and Miri—Dovber—"

The rabbi looked away and picked up another brownie, put it in his mouth. He shrugged. "The Rebbe didn't say anything about the others," he said with his mouth full.

Chani felt like she could explode at any moment. "So this was expected of me? Couldn't he in all his precognitive greatness have told me about it? I'm sure that would've helped!" She huffed, then turned and marched away, all her thoughts about explaining her plan evaporating in a haze of rage. Even still, she could feel the rebbetzen's thoughts of concern, but Mushka remained silent.

Chani plodded along the main street of the settlement. Who could she talk to? The settlement was small and there were only a handful of mãwal-users on the planet. There was Miri, about her age, but the two of them had never got along well. There was Nechama, who was probably surveying the detritus of their huge family lunch at the very moment; she'd best not bother her. Besides, Nechama constantly told her she was all too reckless and her plans were little more than harebrained schemes. Nechama even disapproved of the move away from Mars, she was so conservative.

How about the men? Could she even manage to find an opportunity to talk to them one-on-one? Jewish law did not allow two unmarried people of opposite genders to spend time together in the same room with no chance of someone else walking in. Who could she accidentally run into? She could've talked to Dovber, but as far as she knew, he was off-planet, busy with harebrained schemes of his own. He definitely did not show up to shul earlier that day, because then he would've said the blessing on the first reading.

Then there was Shai… Maybe getting Shai involved with the plan would be a good idea. Word was that he had been the Rebbe's first choice for what ended up being Adira's position. Chani could not fathom why Adira had no backup—if something happened to her, the entire settlement would be in danger. But the Rebbe was famous for his unusual decisions—his insistence on an Israeli pronunciation of Hebrew even when most of his followers were European Ashkenazic Jews, his ban on wigs that almost split the community, his decree that extraterrestrials could convert to Judaism… and, of course, his decision that his followers were to settle planets all across the galaxy.

Shai should've been the one picked to mediate between the planetmind and the community. Instead, he was studying and serving as the community Torah reader. Certainly, being a baal koreh was not an easy task—one had to memorize all the vowels and the cantillation marks which were absent from the scroll one used to read. On Shabbat Shai wouldn't even be able to use his network interface, since it fell under the prohibition of electricity. Yet Chani couldn't recall him making a mistake, while their shul on Mars had had a baal koreh who was constantly corrected by the people following along in the marked text. Shai was good at it, very good, but still it felt like such a waste. To Chani it felt like the māwal organized itself around Shai, and to waste all that potentiality, all that natural skill… Why couldn't he serve at least as backup?

Chani could not understand the Rebbe, and she was beginning to become furious with him, safe with his retinue back on Mars, safe and ignorant of the situation here. She'd best get back to Adira and continue working on her plan… she was starting to disapprove of her own thoughts.

"This is the plan," Chani said and leaned forward. They were sitting in the deserted kiddush room in the synagogue, on opposite sides of a table. "We're going to give the people a fright. We just need you out of the picture for a bit. Just for the connection to weaken. When things start to go wrong, they will realize how much they need you. I could..." she hesitated, "injure you, then make sure you recover."

"I don't feel comfortable playing such a trick on them," Adira said but didn't flinch. "They are good people."

Chani was awash with the heat of righteous anger. "They put you in a corner behind a brocade curtain! No one would even touch you!"

Adira blinked. "I don't like to be touched."

"You know it's not about that! How will you marry?"

"We'd discussed this with the Rebbe back then and he said I'd probably find it impossible to marry. I said I was all right wi—"

"The Rebbe discussed this with you?!" Chani took a deep breath, then another, tried to calm down, without success.

"Yes, of course," Adira said innocently, "I don't understand your surprise... We'd talked about everything, with him, his wife Rebbetzen Michaela, the Ereni advisor... mostly the four of us. What did you expect?"

No one discussed anything with me! "I don't like being left out of the loop."

"If this helps any, I didn't know anything about you either. The Rebbe only said I should not worry, Hashem would provide protection. I should just keep in mind that Hashem is Elokim, there is none besides him..."

Quotes, quotes, more quotes. Chani liked Torah quotes, but this was a time for action, not for words... She gnashed her teeth. "Do you want to spend the rest of your life alone? With no husband, no—"

"What would I do with a husband? Watch him die?"

"Eh?" That was not the response Chani had expected.

"If I can preserve my consistency, I can potentially live as long as the planet lives." It sounded like a rehearsed phrase.

"I'd—I'd never thought of that." Chani paused, just for a moment before marshalling the force of her argument again. "Still. You should not be alone. You should not allow the others to leave you alone. How will you preserve your consistency then?"

Adira looked away, out the window. "...Fair enough." Then she turned back. "Your plan still sounds too risky. If you're with me, you can't be with the others and who knows what might happen to them. Can you just involve someone else too? How about Shai? I'm sure he could help."

"Shai just wants to sit in a corner and study!"

Adira stood. "And why is that a problem? Isn't that what men do?"

This is not your personal vendetta, the planetmind said.

Yeah? Wait until you see this, Chani responded.

Adira hesitated before the door. "I don't see why this is necessary..."

"You want to participate in a women's shiur, right?" *And I want to talk to Shai,* Chani thought at her.

Adira nodded, flustered. "Mhm. I'm just not sure it's appropriate..."

"What's the worst thing that can happen?" Chani grimaced.

"I suppose..." Adira bit her lower lip. "They could throw me out."

"Do you think such pious women would throw you out?" Chani snorted with derision. "They're much too cowardly and meek for that."

"Don't say such things—" Adira blushed.

Chani stepped next to her and pushed open the door. "Come on!"

Adira entered with trepidation. Inside, the women were sitting in a loosely organized circle, some on a large sofa, some on pillows on the ground, some on simple plastic chairs and stools brought into the living room from the kitchen. There was still no consensus about whether shapeforming chairs were permitted on Shabbat, so most people sat quite uncomfortably.

When Chani and Adira entered, people stiffened, and Chani could tell Adira noticed too.

They said their greetings. Chani looked around for spare chairs. "Is there something we could sit on?"

"We're all out," a woman said frostily. Chani recognized her— her name was Malka something and she was the mother of four children, all boys.

"All right," Chani responded with as much iciness as she could muster, then sat down with her back to a wall. Adira also sat after some hesitation.

Shai's mother hosted the shiur in their house, but it was held by a different person; a young brown-skinned woman with Ethiopian Jewish features. Adira remembered that her first name was Rachel, and she was from Earth, not Mars. Rachel cleared her throat and began. "Today we're going to study the midah of rachamim…"

See, I told you they wouldn't throw you out, Chani thought.

I didn't exactly get a warm welcome either.

It will come with time… Chani smiled. *Time, and something else.*

I can't believe you want to do that. Adira's body went rigid. *I'm not going to stand for deception.*

Who said anything about deception? Chani had to lift a hand in front of her mouth to cover her broad grin. *It's going to be as real as possible.*

The grin eventually wore off, and as the shiur went on, Chani realized that Shai was not even in the house, so that they could talk afterwards. Where was he? Time was running out; it was already late afternoon, and on weekdays, it would be much harder to get a large crowd in one place. She had to make her move soon…

Shabbat was coming to a close with the havdalah ceremony. Blessings were said on candlelight, cloves and wine in the usual disorganized manner. Very few women turned up for the occasion;

most were at home, tending to the kids. Chani and Adira stood in one corner, away from the rest of the people.

Plastic cups of wine made their rounds; a young man stepped to them and offered Chani some. She politely declined and picked up a bottle of grape juice from one of the tables; the man stepped back into the crowd, visibly uneasy. No one asked Adira. Chani filled two cups with grape juice and handed a cup to her. They drank, and Adira wiped her mouth with the back of her hand—such a human gesture it made Chani's heart ache. How could she have doubted...?

"It's a good thing they're doing kiddush levana today," she whispered to Adira. "That's a great opportunity." The men would set out to bless the moon; it was usually not visible from the shul's courtyard, and they customarily hiked up a small hill every month.

"You want to kill me," Adira whispered back.

"If you don't want to fake it, we can only do it for real," she said. "Besides, I don't want to kill you outright."

We would advise against this course of action, the planetmind told them. *We cannot predict events with the instability caused by the storm. But we sense danger.*

Chani looked out the window and grimaced, as if staring directly into an invisible camera.

The crowd was thinning out as people were beginning to move outside; the stairs that led downstairs from the kiddush room proved to be a bottleneck. Chani shifted her weight from one leg to another; she was nervous, even though she did not appreciate the planetmind knowing that. Likewise, Adira was rolling some dried cloves in her fingers, smelling them again and again.

Finally, they could make their way downstairs unobstructed. Below, the men were talking with animated gestures. People were running to and fro with stacks of prayer books. Chani grabbed one and handed it to Adira.

"I know the prayers," Adira said.

"Even for kiddush levana?"

"I had a network interface even… before." She nodded in the direction of the forest. "I can just access the local net. Not on Shabbat, but Shabbat is already over."

"You mean you still have your implants and stuff? In some way?"

"My body template was recorded with everything inside." Adira began to walk as some of the men set out on the short hike to do the blessing; many were still shmoozing in the courtyard.

Chani fell in step. "I guess I never really thought about that. That's kind of cool."

It helps us integrate into the community even closer, the planetmind added.

"So you can read our email?" Chani chuckled.

We don't need to read your email when we are already aware of your minds.

"Yeah… right. Hold on," she said and ran forward, looking for Shai. Adira did not change her pace.

He was there, walking almost at front. Eager to pray?

"Shai," she gasped, slightly out of breath. "We need to talk."

Shai fixed his clear blue eyes upon her, just for a second—his cool, calm gaze penetrated all the way into her soul. He had a thick red beard—unexpectedly thick for his age—and long curly sidelocks, and he played with his *tzitzit* fringes as he walked. "Yes? Do explain."

She was afraid Shai would become aware of her plan prematurely, with his exemplary command of the māwal. But apparently even he could not sense her plan through the chaos of the geomagnetic storm. He was clearly beginning to grow suspicious, though.

Chani began. "Something unexpected is going to happen. You'll need to stay calm and—"

"How do you know something is going to happen?" Shai smiled. "Maybe because…" …*you are the instigator yourself?*

"Yes," she wheezed. "Look, there's no time. I can't explain. You will understand everything soon. I just need you to know one thing. When I give you a signal, you will start shepherding everyone back toward the settlement. Do anything you can to keep them moving." She looked around nervously, but no one seemed to be listening in on them.

Shai raised a hand, his smile unwavering. "I'm keeping the others from hearing this."

Chani nodded. *All right.* "There will be… a measure of chaos. Some of the planetlife might mount an assault. It's only going to be temporary."

"Is this about Adira?"

Chani nodded again, her head bobbing up and down, and then a flash of understanding passed between them.

"I see," Shai said with a tinge of sadness in his voice. "I should've realized. Count me in."

Chani could've hugged him if not for the rules of modesty that kept her from engaging in any physical contact with an unrelated male. She ran back to Adira, grinning to herself all the while.

Just a few steps until the ravine that opened on the right side of the path up the hill.

Warn me before you push me, Adira thought. *I want to cushion my fall somewhat, with the māwal… I don't want to die outright. In this weakened state… just an injury, okay? A little loss of consciousness, a bit longer than back at the lake. Just to give them a fright. And then you can hurry back and down the slope to me and help me gather myself together.*

Sure, Chani replied. *But we need to take some risk. On a count of three, right?*

All right.

One, two… three.

Chani pushed Adira—then her own feet slipped on the wet grass, she toppled against her and both of them fell tumbling into the ravine. *No—*

Thoughts ran through her mind, faster than prayer—this wasn't planned, she wasn't supposed to fall alongside Adira, she'd die—

Adira grabbed her, wrapped herself around her. *I won't let you.*

They landed at the bottom with a sickening crunch.

Chani was stunned for a moment, then she instinctively rolled off Adira, who was lying underneath her.

Chani was alive, in one piece, but as she moved, pain shot through her body. She quickly examined herself in the sparse illumination afforded by the lamps lighting the path up the hill, well above. Her left leg was broken, an ugly open fracture. She could feel her mods already knotting up the bone and the flesh, toning the pain down to manageable levels, but she knew from experience that her leg would be useless for at least a day, and the blood loss would make her dizzy.

She did not dare look at Adira.

She forced herself to.

Her body looked—it was hard to tell in the dark—mangled, already disassembling itself. Her neck was bent at an impossible angle and her face was expressionless.

"Adira—I'm sorry—"

Don't look at me, talk to me, keep on talking to me, Adira thought.

Chani could not look away.

You need to preserve my individuality. I am here as long as you talk to me. Turn away.

"Why?"

What you see works against your expectations, the planetmind answered.

She obediently turned her head; she could not move her leg.

I need to—there's not enough māwal for me to— She could tell Adira was panicking; her thoughts had acquired a feverish quality all of a sudden. *I cannot maintain contact with the rest and at the same time repair my—*

"Take mine, take mine!" She turned back toward Adira, grabbed her hand. "I have a lot of māwal, take as much as you need!"

It was hard enough to keep you alive. A gurgling chuckle coming from the broken throat.

"Then I'll call Shai, he can get down here fast, he can—"

177

You will need Shai to protect the men above, the planetmind said. *It is starting. We are sorry.*

"What are you talking about?!"

We cannot preserve her and keep up her contact with the community at the same time. Talk to her. Shai will protect the group on the hill. She will be restored sufficiently soon; the settlement will not be destroyed. Only the group on the hill is in danger.

Chani craned her neck but she could not make out anything in the glow of the lamps. She felt nauseous from the sudden head motion. Then she heard the screaming.

She could reconstruct the events from the participants' memories fairly well. Immediately after Adira was cut off from the community, planetlife swarmed the men walking uphill. Shai screamed at them to run. They yelled and cried, but obeyed. Shai held off the assault and ran with the men, protecting them all the while. The planetlife sensed that he was holding it off and targeted its attacks on him.

We can assure you this is purely instinctive behavior, the planetmind said. *This is our immune system. This is not a conscious decision on our behalf. We are sorry.*

Chani talked to Adira, talked and talked. Recounted her life story, offered divrei Torah, ranted about the unfairness of life. She wanted to rail against Hashem, but she needed to focus on Adira. She went on, her throat sore, her eyes dry from the tears.

The men made it back to the settlement.

Shai did not.

He was lying on the ground, the settlement limits just a stone's throw away. He was coughing up blood. He waited for the angel of death.

"Shema... Yisrael," he said with his last effort, not covering his eyes.

We can attempt to incorporate you, the planetmind said. *We are sorry for the damage caused. We would prefer to incorporate you.*

Shai stopped saying the ages-old prayer. He closed his eyes and was completely still. He felt at peace.

You have already turned us down once before. Please do not turn us down again.

Chani had no idea what the planetmind was talking about, but she supposed this was between the two of them.

"Take me," Shai said with his last breath.

Adira, Shai and Chani sat on the steps in the synagogue court-yard, enjoying the late afternoon sun and a bit of Shabbat rest.

"At least this Shabbat is less hectic than the previous one," Chani said.

Shai laughed, the sound like pearls falling from the sky. Then he rubbed his nose and looked up at the clouds. "Are you coming to the Gemara shiur? It should start soon, at Dovber's place." *That's a long walk.*

"I thought the Gemara shiur was for men only," Chani said.

"No, anyone can come," Adira said. "Tzvi specifically told me, a few weeks ago."

Chani blinked. "Then why didn't you attend? Before, I mean."

I was not sure I was welcome anywhere. Adira sighed.

"There's only going to be more of us," Shai said. "People would better get used to it. The Rebbe himself said so, he'd expected something like this." He coughed nervously. "He wanted it to happen... if not with me, then with someone else. He wanted to force the issue." *That's why Adira didn't have backup.*

Well, that solves the marriage problem, Chani thought.

"I'd elbow you hard, but I'm still not sure I'm allowed to touch you," Adira said, grinning.

"You're not allowed to hurt her, either way," Shai pointed out.

"True enough!" Chani got up, brushing the dust off her skirt. "Let's go, we'll be late if we don't get going..."

She still could not look Shai in the eye.

Unifications

Sára breathed in. A smell of mold and dust, with an uncomfortably sharp undercurrent. She took a step forward, then another.

The passageway was surprisingly wide, wider than the two streets it connected—two meandering alleys with one-way traffic where a car could barely pass, and where passersby scuttled anxiously in single file along the narrow sidewalks. Even though she knew these streets were built in the 19th century, she was reminded of medieval towns.

The passage was eerily bright, with inner courtyards where light could reach the surface uninhibited by the usual crumbling, pock-marked walls set much too close to one another. Sára was sure she had noticed gunshot marks on the buildings on the way here. When had this area last seen combat? At least fifty years ago by her reckoning. Everything was in a state of disrepair. The surrounding houses seemed abandoned altogether, only a makeshift plastic board advertised a dentist on the second floor.

She ventured into the passageway.

She could feel something unusual, almost tangible. A sense of power emanating from the walls, the tiled floor of the passage itself. Hallowed ground. She was more and more certain with each step, with each breath, that she found a sacred spot in this metropolis wholly unfamiliar to her. Yet she also felt apprehension—from the decay, the entropy, or something else altogether? She moved around quickly, looking, searching.

Advertisements from days of yore were painted on some of the walls, peeling off. She stared at them, puzzled—they shouldn't have lasted this long—, then she realized a Hollywood movie had been shot here recently. A Holocaust movie. She swallowed hard and hushed the thought away.

Some of the tiles were missing, while some were heaped in corners, signaling an aborted reconstruction. The passageway was deserted.

Despite the sunlight, the place had an oddly gut-wrenching feel. Sára knew this area used to be part of the Jewish ghetto, but still— she lived here herself, two streets down and a corner to the right, and her days were not soaked in this darkness. Despite the dusty facades bending inward, despite history turning up at the most unexpected moments, her days here were filled with expectation and noise. New friends made. A synagogue on every corner. Friday nights with loud singing, Saturday afternoons of lounging with an all-new and still familiar crowd. Definitely not this sense of cruel truths well-hidden, of sea monsters swimming languidly just below the surface.

She put a hand on a wall.

Her touch was unwelcome.

She yanked her hand back and rubbed it into her skirt, leaving dust marks. She swore under her breath and instantly felt bad about it.

She walked away with a quickening pace—she only looked back once, and the large rectangular entrance of the passageway appeared like a maw to her, a maw eager to devour bodies, minds, souls.

Judit sounded concerned—she had learned to trust her friend's odd impressions over the years they had known each other. Now they lived in the same city, but still hours away. It was Shabbes and Judit was sleeping over at Sára's place, incapable of walking such a great distance back to her family estate on the hillside where there were no synagogues and no dark alleyways.

"It's inside the old ghetto boundaries, I'm sure," she mused. "But I've never heard anything about this place in particular." She sighed, leaned back on the sofa. "It's so dark in here... Sára, you should *really* get one of those Israeli gadgets."

"A Shabbat-light? Or a timer?"

"Yes, that light where you turn this outer shell around and..."

"...sure, I get it. I've seen it advertised on Aish or somewhere." Sára stood up and opened the door to the kitchen—they left the lights on there before leaving to shul for the Friday night prayer. "Better now?"

"Mhm."

"I'd look for stuff online. But we have to wait until motzei Shabbes."

"Sure." Judit yawned.

"Do you want to sleep?" Sára felt unsatisfied. They managed to meet and talk, but the mystery of the passageway still turned around and around in her head, unresolved.

"I'll try not to have nightmares."

Saturday afternoon with bellies full after the festive lunch. Sára dragged her friend along, despite Judit's protestations that this was not the best time.

"Can you feel it?" Sára stood in the middle of one of the court-yards, turned around with hands open, her skirt swirling around her ankles.

"I can feel *something*," Judit said, noncommittal.

A sudden clanking sound. They both jumped. Sára noticed the source first.

"My Shabbes belt!" The belt with its series of keys and metallic rings was lying at her feet. She grabbed her skirt already sliding downward, a size too large. She grimaced. "I can't pick it up! There is no eruv here!"

"This area is private property," Judit ventured. "It's OK."

"It's not."

"Just pick it up."

She bent down, retrieved the belt, her fingers fumbling as she reattached it. Her face was flushed. "Now I've broken Shabbes. Wonderful. But I couldn't just leave my keys here!" She slapped her thigh in anger.

"We could've waited here until sundown," Judit offered with slight exasperation in her voice.

"Of course. Like that's such a smart idea to do."

"It's a theoretical possibility."

"Let's just get out of here." Sára was eager to leave before something worse happened.

Judit frowned. "It's a bad sign. What does the Kabbalah say about this?"

"The Kabbalah says you shouldn't break Shabbes," she grunted.

She should've stayed there, Sára thought. Until sundown. She should've known. Judit was right, it was indeed a sign—and she blew it. Just because she was impatient and uncomfortable, anxious to get out of the courtyard.

It occurred to her belatedly that there was one thing in the lore of the Kabbalah that was indeed applicable to this situation. Some people said the world had a large number of divine sparks scattered over all lands, and the Messiah couldn't come until all these sparks were gathered by the devout performing good deeds in those locations.

Maybe that place was waiting for her. She hoped fervently that there was nothing of the "spirits of the dead cannot rest in peace until you perform these actions" involved.

She did not dare go back. Weeks passed.

She picked up her phone from her desk. Judit was calling, excited, out of breath. Sára imagined her with her mahogany brown curls in disarray, her designer glasses askew.

"I just talked to someone who told me something. About that passage."

Sára sighed, leaned with her back against the wall. "Do tell."

It took a long time, punctuated with sharp intakes of breath, for the story to unfold. At first, Judit had asked around to no avail—everyone seemed to have a different version. The passage was in the ghetto. It was not in there. It was on the border of the ghetto. It was an entrance to the ghetto. One side was sealed. Both sides were sealed and the building evacuated. Both sides were sealed with people trapped inside. A wall was built on one side. Both sides. Across the middle. *Along* the middle. People died there and no one survived. People died there and only a few survived. People starved. People were shot. People were starved, then shot.

This was familiar to Sára—she herself had spun around on this merry-go-round of information. But finally Judit had chanced upon a version more elaborate than the others—correct or not, who could judge? Still, with the ring of truth to it, emphasized by the mysterious circumstances.

Judit had run into a high school classmate, someone who vanished altogether after graduation—everyone thought he had left for abroad, possibly the US. Ivy League scholarship? No one knew.

Then he turned up—Judit was on someone's party, lounging on a sofa and munching pistachio nuts. Japanese pop blared from the other room, overlaid with yells and cries; someone had had the idea to organize an impromptu Dance Dance Revolution tournament and now most of the crowd was cheering the contestants, splashing beer on the cheap plastic dance mats.

Someone sat down beside her. "Long time no see."

Judit looked up, then blinked, trying to clear her eyes of cigarette smoke. "Tomi! I thought you were overseas."

He shrugged apologetically. "Apparently not."

"I was beginning to grow offended you never said goodbye."

He grimaced. Leaned back. Leaned forward again and rummaged around in his bag. It was a red, white and pink striped shoulder bag decorated with a green Mickey Mouse smoking a fat joint—it clashed with his simple black shirt and linen trousers, as if he had two different personalities, one for the day and the other for the night.

They sat there for a while, pretending to listen to the music. Eventually Judit gave up. "OK, OK, I'm not bringing it up. We can still talk about something else."

"Oh?" Tomi raised an eyebrow. "Do you have something in mind?"

"Hmm, since you used to live around here in this district, I was wondering…"

She couldn't explain why she picked that topic—it was as good as anything else. But what he told her in response made her blood run cold.

One of Tomi's friends—"someone into occultism, not the cheerful pagan nature worship kind of person if you get my idea"—asked him to tag along on "an expedition, that's what he said, an expedition". It was a cold, clear day in early spring. They met up at a large square and from then on they quickly headed toward the thicket—the tangle of small, twisty streets. To his surprise, Occultist Friend ducked under a line of yellow tape and pushed in an aged wooden door.

"What are you doing? This is a construction area."

"*De*construction area," Tomi's friend smirked. "This building will be demolished next week."

They made their way toward the top, two floors and finally the attic.

"Quick, make yourself useful," the occultist grunted. Tomi knew he was only being taken along for his digital camera, a novelty item back then, and he felt bad about being the upper-class gentleboy from the hillside, the one with the designer bags and early-adopter habits. He sighed and pressed a button—

his hand froze and his mouth opened.

"I had heard," the occultist said, his voice rough, dry and weary beyond age. "At first I thought it wasn't true." He shook his head. "Quick, take those photos."

Strange symbols were drawn on the dusty floor, symbols he later found out belonged to the Western tradition of magic. At that time he had no idea, but he could feel power rising like steam from them, one all the more bright for being dark. And was that blood? How old were these markings, anyway?

"In the war." His friend crouched down, examined the symbols closer. "They tried to save the people next door."

Which war? World War Two? Tomi's head was spinning. Such a long time ago?

"They were herded into the passage and the gates were locked on both sides."

"Who? Jews?"

His friend turned and stared at him with an infinitely cruel gaze. "Of course it was Jews, *where* do you think you are?"

"And they... the..." Tomi's lips wouldn't move. He nodded at the drawings.

"No. The occultists weren't Jewish."

"Then why—"

His friend stood up, not taking his eyes off him. Not saying anything. Tomi had to look away and he felt his face redden. He mumbled an apology, then set out to make the pictures. Click. Click. His mind felt empty.

As the two of them clattered down the stairs, making more noise Tomi would've preferred them to make, he had to ask. "What happened to them?" The Jews. Not the occultists.

"They all died. They starved to death."

Back at the party, Tomi sighed, leaned forward and put his face in his hands. He was visibly strained from telling his story.

Judit leaned toward him. "What happened next?"

"Nothing, I haven't seen the guy in years. I don't even have the photos... he took the memory card from me. I'm not even sure he had a card reader for it, it was one of those annoying types not compatible with anything, and—"

Someone hopped down on the sofa between them, a girl with loud makeup and a cigarette holder in hand. "I hope I'm not disturbing you, I just wanted to take a break from the all that stuff, you know?" She gestured toward the other room. "I need to relax a bit."

"That's all I'd heard," Judit said. "I tried to call him the next day, and a couple of times since then, but he's not answering."

Sára slid down to the floor, the phone still in hand. "Thank you for telling me nonetheless." She paused. "Do you think it's true?"

"He looked shaken. I'm sure he saw *some*thing." Judit spoke with conviction.

"So what happens now?"

"No idea. The building's been demolished since then. I've checked." Judit took a breath. "Do you think what we felt there was because of this? The ritual, I mean?"

"A ritual that ultimately proved ineffective." Sára was momentarily overcome by bitterness.

"But still."

"No, I think that's not all of it."

"Then what is?"

"We might never find out..."

Sára walked fast, an unknown force pulling at her. She took a sharp turn, then another, and there she was, at one of the gates of the passage.

It was closed and bolted.

She walked down a parallel street in a daze, turned, walked. Arrived at the other gate, also locked.

She pulled at the bolts in desperation. Swore. Felt bad for swearing *again*.

A guard came out. "No entry."

"Why all of a sudden?"

"The complex has been sold to an investor." He scratched his chin. "Guy wants to build luxury suites here."

"Can I come in?"

"No entry. Don't even try to bribe me, I'm not in the mood."

She walked away, at a loss.

Years passed.

The reconstruction progressed slowly, with several setbacks. But the real estate market was booming and the investor was determined. Next to one of the bolted gates, a large sign advertised an indoor spa and various wellness services. *Coming Soon.* The sign was gathering dust.

Sára moved to the United States to attend a small alternative-minded midrasha on the West Coast.

She was sitting on a creaking wooden chair in the shadow of a building, listening to a shiur and sipping freshly pressed orange juice, when it happened.

The American rebbetzen holding the shiur paced up and down, her frantic motion at odds with the rest of the class lounging in the shadow, her robe billowing—*100% natural linen, from a sustainable source*, Sára thought with a sleepy grin on her face. At times like this she felt out of place, surrounded by an odd variant of Hippie Orthodoxy: more tolerant of her eccentricities than a strict Chareidi crowd would be, but also more...

she could not finish the thought. Something grabbed her attention, and held fast.

"...such so-called unifications, or *yichudim* in Hebrew, are also related to the concept of the sparks of the divine, scattered during the Breaking of the Vessels. These need to be reunified with their source and the yichudim are a mechanism for this purpose. Also, this can be extended further to any kind of event where there is something broken, something that needs to be repaired... so to say, reacquainted with its source."

Sára had to ask. "Can you show us a practical example?"

"What kind of example?" The rebbetzen had a demanding voice even when she wasn't angry, but Sára could feel that she was displeased.

"Er..." She found herself tongue-tied. "Like an actual example where there is a... uhm... a kind of spiritual problem and something you need to do to fix it... like an actual ritual or something."

The rebbetzen skewered her with her eyes. "This is not one of *those* classes on Practical Kabbalah."

Her classmates laughed.

"Perhaps you would be best advised to daven, eh? After all, prayer is a form of unification."

Sára had not realized the rebbetzen could be so sarcastic.

Sára visited her family during the summer break. They still lived in the countryside, but she also spent a weekend in the capital and the maze of the Jewish district, still so familiar to her and mostly unchanged.

She walked by the passage on Sunday, hurrying to meet Judit. The gate was open. The sign advertising a spa was gone, replaced by another one inviting passersby to an arts & crafts fair.

She stalked in, on the hunt for an answer.

Many stalls of independent artisans and small companies presented a wide assortment of alternative-flavored decorations and knickknacks. She thought the rebbetzen would get a kick out of the "ecological" and the "sustainable". As she wandered around, she had a completely out-of-place flash to the Christian scene where Jesus drove the hawkers out of the Temple courtyard, and she had a sudden urge to punch people. She grimaced.

She wandered in a small circle, her hands crumpled up in fists. She listened.

"…it hardens in response to heat so you can simply bake it in a home oven… oops, maybe I shouldn't tell you about my trade secrets!"

"…he will play with his band live tonight, yes, here in the passage, yes…"

She felt her anger bloom and rise. It was the Nine Days, a traditional period for mourning. No live music. It was aggravating in itself that the Nine Days fell during the heat of the summer, but this, this was—

she halted in her tracks. Two people were arguing behind a stall.

"They've switched off the electricity in building C again. Last time it was the heating, now it's the electricity."

"They say most of the other inhabitants haven't paid their utility bills, so…"

"But there are no *inhabitants*, most of the building is still owned by the investor!"

"Yeah, well, the economic crisis hit everyone hard... ah, look, someone's waiting for us outside." A shaved head ducked out from beyond the curtain of the stall, blinking at her through the sunlight. "Can I help you with something?"

"Er... no, nothing in particular. Just browsing around." Sára wandered away with studied carelessness.

She felt like she had her revenge. *They wanted to move here, they should've seen this coming.* She thought of the time when she had attended the yearly March of the Living in Auschwitz, and the locals demonstrated against them with Polish flags and nationalist regalia. The locals. Who would want to live in such a place? Then again, one could cordon off half of Europe by this logic, make it one gigantic memorial. That would surely be overdone, but still, there are places where one shouldn't...

What had the rebbetzen said? Unifications. Sára had been meaning to look them up, always putting it off. She hadn't touched a book on spirituality since then, and all her recent Jewish learning had been about kashering vessels and blessings on various kinds of foods. Dry, but certainly less upsetting.

Unifications. Yichudim. From the word *echad*. One. She was trying to come up with something in desperation. Her cell phone was vibrating in her pocket; probably Judit looking for her. She picked it up, muttered a hasty apology, asked her to meet up in the passage. Turned the phone off. She hoped Judit understood the meaning of this sudden delay. Sára tried to retrace the interrupted line of her thoughts. What was it?

The Shema, the most important part of the entire Torah, the core of the Jewish liturgy. Hear O Israel, The L-rd is our G-d, the L-rd is One. *Shema Yisrael, Hashem Elokenu, Hashem Echad.* One.

She closed her eyes, and she thought maybe it was only to calm herself, to banish these thoughts of the abyss, but maybe—just maybe—there was something, a divine spark in the depths waiting for a gesture, a sudden infusion of power to allow it to rise. Waiting for her, waiting for liberation.

She covered her eyes with her right hand, ignoring the crowd milling around her, and began to pray.

The Size of a Barleycorn, Encased in Lead

Ten things were created on the eve of Shabbat, between the lights of night and day, and they are: the mouth of the earth, the mouth of the well, the mouth of the donkey, the rainbow and the manna, and the staff, and the shamir, the writing, the missive and the tablets.

And the world came into being after the Divine contracted to allow it space, and humans labored upon the face of the earth, and they called to the Name in both distress and delight.

And the Name said:

if you build me an altar of stones,
do not build it of hewn stones:
for if you lift up your tool upon it,
you have desecrated it.

And when King Shlomo built a house for the Name, it was written:

there was neither hammer nor axe
nor any iron tool heard in the house
while it was being built.
The Master asked of the Rabbis: How shall I do this?
They told him: there is the shamir that Moshe brought for the efod.

When Moshe our teacher spoke to the Name, the Name instructed him in minute detail about the details of worship and gave him the shamir to cut the gemstones for the priestly garments.

One writes upon the stones in ink,

shows the shamir from the outside,
and these split apart by themselves—
like a fig that splits apart during the days of heat
and no material is gone from it,
or like a valley that splits apart during the days of rainfall
and no material is gone from it.
And in the Oral Tradition it was also said
and later—after the people were scattered —
carefully codified and hand-copied:
The shamir is the size of a barleycorn;
it was created during the six days of creation,
and there is no thing as hard as to be able to withstand it.
What can contain it?
It is wrapped in tufts of wool
and put in a lead tube full of barley bran.
And humans continued to walk upon the face of the earth, well
after the shamir had been lost during the destruction of the Temple;
and no one knows where it went, though some say it might have
sunk into the earth at the Temple Mount beside the Ark of the
Covenant. And with time the knowledge of the shamir faded, and
some said it had been alive, like a worm, while others said it had
been akin to a stone. But the people still passed on the word from
generation to generation, into our days.

And humans went on to probe the secrets of Creation not only by
means of letter and divine name, but also by means of cyclotron and
synchrotron; and further, fission and fusion weapons; even though
it had been clearly stated never to bring tools of warfare into the
house of the Name.

And humans produced materials needing containment in a fashion familiar to us who carry the knowledge of the ancient and the
sacred: in tubes of lead, for no thing was able to withstand them.
And humans produced them in quantities previously unprecedented,
and once their usefulness was past, encased them and buried them
underground.

Thus in our days it was also said,

This marking system has been designed to last 10,000 years.
If the marker is difficult to read,
add new markers in longer-lasting materials
in languages that you speak.

And the people contemplated forming a new priesthood to preserve the knowledge; thus the priests would declaim, from generation to generation:

Sending this message was important to us.
We considered ourselves to be a powerful culture
This message is a warning about danger.
The form of the danger is an emanation of energy.

And the congregation of the knowledgeable contemplated establishing fortifications to serve as a warning, to our children and our children's children; and to erect these fortifications on top of the containment; for it was commanded by the Name: *You shall strongly safeguard your souls.*

Thus it was written, engraved and inscribed:

This place is not a place of honor.
Do not drill here. Do not dig here.
The danger is to the body, and it can kill.

And the materials sunk into the earth, like to the like, and remained there for many generations; until it was impossible to tell whether they had been living creatures or stones themselves, and until the only word that remained on the lips of the priests was that no thing on earth was able to withstand them.

As King Shlomo had said,

That which was shall be again,
that which had been done shall be done again,
and there is nothing new under the Sun.

And if the Name wills it so, the fortifications shall stand
and the warnings persist,
until the Messiah arrives
and the Temple is rebuilt
and the shamir resurfaces,
speedily,

in our days,
amein.

Text in italics are quotes. Sources for the quoted text (the author's translations):

Exodus 20:25

1 Kings 6:7

Mishna, Avot 5:6

Talmud Bavli, Gitin 68a

Talmud Bavli, Sotah 48b

Excerpts from *Expert Judgment on Markers to Deter Inadvertent Human Intrusion into the Waste Isolation Pilot Plant*, Sandia National Laboratories report SAND92-1382 / UC-721, p. F-49

Deuteronomy 4:15

Ecclesiastes 1:9

Various prayer fragments and Hebrew turns of phrase are used unmarked. For the Talmudic excerpts, in cases of rare nouns the author relied on the Soncino English translation.

To Rebalance the Body

Master Viiren prefers their evening tea made with sweetberries and sage, with half a spoon of acacia honey, but today they requested a sharp and bitter combination of mint and frostleaf. They are having a cold on top of the illness, and this makes them gloomy and withdrawn.

A spot just below my collar starts to itch as I'm pouring the hot water. A relief—my master's medication has been overdue. I bring them the tea, my hands gripping the tray just a trifle too hard. My muscles have been hurting from the tension, and the underclothes beneath my purple robes are soaked through with sweat. I just want my master to be well, or at the very least, better. Doctor Senaro assured us that the medicine would soon start working.

My master peers up at me from within a castle of pillows and thick blankets. They look miserable and shriveled, the dark curls of their hair hanging limply, as if the locks were straightening out under their own weight. The light brown of their skin is blotchy with pallor. They draw a blanket even tighter around themselves before they reach for the tea. They frown.

"Is it time yet?" they ask.

"Yes, master, I think so," I say, and I take off my robes, remove my plain cotton undershirt. I look down, straining my neck: the vesicle just below my collar looks ready to pop, skin tight and convex like the top of a fermenting jar. I sit next to my master and they put an arm around me, raise another. They experimentally touch the spot, and for a moment I think it will burst right away, but it holds. Master Viiren sighs softly, and then they push the sharpened nail of their ring finger against the skin. We have the same skin tone, but now they look so much paler that the contrast startles me. It's as if the blood has withdrawn from their fingertips.

The vesicle pops after a moment, and my master puts their mouth against the opening to drink. I close my eyes, focusing on our con-nection. I always feel the need to be close to Master Viiren, and every single touch of theirs is comforting: even their dry, chapped lips and clammy fingers exude a warmth that goes beyond the body, beyond bare physicality. They linger for a moment after they're done, and I know they need my presence as much as I need theirs, a symmetry in asymmetry.

They pull away from me, frowning. They cough hoarsely, and I know it's the cold: the medicine for their illness tastes sweet, and it eases their pain quite fast. It is pleasing to drink; they were troubled by this at first, but they got used to it. Medicine is not supposed to taste good. I only wish its effects would be more permanent, but Doctor Senaro says that the time for that will eventually come. Healing will come. Then why the sudden frown, the moment of displeasure?

"You have so many scars already," my master finally says, and I follow their gaze and glance down on my torso, dotted and cratered with popped vesicles, breaking the symmetry of the magical lines etched into my flesh.

How do I respond? I just want my master to get better; I really do. I don't mind the scars. I even feel pride upon looking at them: tangible reminders of my loyalty, my devotion. I think Master Viiren understands, but they are still somewhat bothered, and I can't quite set their mind at ease.

"Would my master like some of my magic? It might help," I offer.

They sigh. "Thank you, but I don't think I could absorb it right now."

I wish they would accept. I wish they could. It is such a lonely feeling for me, not being able to offer, not being able to share. Ordinarily, the magical exchange is one of the pillars of our relationship: one among many exchanges, but one that represents something fundamental to us. One that also parallels our voluntary asymmetry of power, and our shared love.

But I will not be able to share my magic today, either. This has been going on for days, and I feel like they are stuck in a vicious circle of ever poorer health. And now this unexpected cold—

A spot on my neck below my right ear starts to itch.

My muscles tense up again. So soon? I'm only supposed to have one vesicle per day.

Master Viiren notices the change in me. "Biruyan?" They lean forward, hold onto my arms. "What's wrong?" Not *is something wrong?* They already know the answer to that question. They know me very well, and I know them likewise; this is my tenth year of being their body servant. I know how they like their tea, how they like their blankets, how they like their clothes. I know where to put their hairsticks, their galoshes, their underwear. I know how to soap their back in the shower and how to braid their hair. The latter took quite a while to learn, as my fingers are clumsy and my motions often abrupt.

I tense my muscles even now. Why am I so afraid?

"Biruyan?" My master sounds uncertain.

I must stay strong, for their sake. I'm so afraid of losing them! But this illness is curable. The fluid from one vesicle a day.

"I can feel another one ripening, master," I say. "It itches."

"Let me look?" Their fingers trace my neck where I indicate. The vesicle pops from the lightest brush of my master's fingertips. Dark purple fluid runs down my neck.

Master Viiren looks me in the eye, puzzled. "We should ask Doctor Senaro about this," they say.

"He's out of town for the week." I pause. "Would my master like another cup of tea?"

I dab at the wound with a cloth, and then I busy myself with the tea. The wound doesn't hurt; the fluid desensitizes the skin. Just as I'm pouring the steaming water—again—another spot starts to itch.

Three hours later, Master Viiren has a small jar full of the fluid gathered from the vesicles, and I'm running a fever. Four hours later, I'm bedridden. My master has called in the majordomo, trusting her not to spread the word, lest the rank and file house-servants panic. Ahn Riesa tucks us in, makes tea for us both and a simple herbal cough suppressant for my master, and sends her eldest daughter Ihan out to look for a doctor and her eldest son Muran to check up on the twin girls, hopefully asleep.

Will Ihan have to ride all the way to the city at the mouth of the Valley just to find a doctor?

I'm shaky and woozy. I'm wrapped in white linens increasingly spotted through with purple. My master has one thick arm around me, and I think about how the doctor will react. If it's a foreigner, I will have to explain about us: about power exchange, about magical exchange, about gender…and then I just close my eyes and snuggle into my master's broad, warm, soft chest, and everything is all right.

I wake with a startle, staring at the new doctor.

He is clearly from far away; the last I saw someone with such stalk-straight hair was when I met the Inharaw ambassador's son during last year's summons to the city. His skin is brown, but a shade more ruddy than ours, and his eyes are small. His dark doctor's cape hangs crooked on his narrow frame. His mouth is thin, bracketed by two folds of flesh. He looks displeased, and I'm concerned he's showing his negative emotions so openly. Does he have no respect for my master?

Master Viiren sits up with difficulty and coughs a little. I wonder how much time has passed, if the cough suppressant has worn off. I almost fall asleep again during the introductions despite my wariness. The tall, thin doctor is called Benurh—I do not catch the patronymic and matronymic—and he gives my master his respects very grudgingly. I have an instant dislike of him. It is never very easy with me and doctors: even here in the Valley, most people are either female or male, and doctors are especially prone to fitting their patients into the more common patterns. Wet-coughing cold versus dry-coughing cold. Male versus female.

Master Viiren usually puts doctors in their place. But does this stranger understand that he's supposed to offer them respect? He turns to me with a displeasure that mirrors mine, and he asks for my gender. I'm confused for a moment, and then I realize that he cannot tell it from my clothing, as I'm still wrapped in the sheets.

"Neutral," I mutter.

Now that he knows which ones to pick, he greets me with the proper forms.

Master Viiren explains about their sudden illness. They don't have to explain about their gender. Everyone knows the Master of Hairen Hills even in the city, and their sturdy androgynous presence seemingly draws even more admirers with age. Or maybe the doctor doesn't know, and he's just less comfortable asking a person with so much earthly power.

When it comes to the treatment, my master asks if I wish to speak. "Biruyan found out about this new treatment, and our doctor, Senaro, was willing to go with it. It's probably best if Biruyan explains."

"It's fascinating!" I begin. The doctor makes a face, and I try to ignore him while I go on. I like to explain things I know in great detail. "There is a certain parasite in the western marshes, the dokwa worm. During its reproductive cycle, it lays eggs in flesh—preferably human flesh—and it makes small vesicles in the flesh—

like bubbles, if you will—that it fills with the eggs' ideal growth medium." Do I sound too technical? Benurh is a doctor, he should be able to understand me. "It was discovered by researchers from Anhyak-Dirban recently that the growth medium has many healing properties—it is anti-inflammatory, for example."

I pause and look at him, to prompt him into some kind of response. Is he following me? I have trouble making sense of others' reactions when I'm paying attention to my own speech.

"Makes sense," the doctor finally says. "It needs to preserve not only the eggs, but also the host."

I nod eagerly. "And if you put the worms near blue mountain-stone for a while, they become sterile. They produce vesicles but do not lay eggs, just fill them with growth medium."

He looks disgusted, but not repulsed, if such a combination of emotions even makes sense. He's a doctor; he shouldn't be repulsed by anything biological. Yet he seems permanently disgusted anyway. It's probably his outlook in life. At least I hope this was not provoked by our genders, by the nature of our relationship, by whichever detail is unfamiliar to him.

"What happens to the worms after they produced the vesicles?" he asks.

I frankly don't know. "No one's really sure; they seem to vanish. At least that's what the autopsies have found. They might be absorbed into the growth medium, or maybe they are destroyed by the host body." *My body,* I want to say, but I'm not sure how he'd react.

"So you've been—" He searches for the right verb. Is there a right verb? "*Having* these worms."

"Yes, a courier brings them from the West beyond the Valley. One set lasts for about two weeks. This is the second set, and...I'm frankly not sure what's wrong. There should not be more than a single vesicle a day. Maybe two spaced quite far apart, but definitely nothing like this."

"Let's unwrap you and see," he says, his face smoothing out a little for the first time since we started talking. He does have at least some semblance of caretaker's instinct; I can feel it in the impression his mind makes, and this gives me a measure of relief.

He puts on gloves and removes the sticky sheets with a frown, rubs the purple stains of growth medium off my skin. He runs a finger along the lines. "You're magical," he says, a statement rather than a question. He's not magical himself, or he would have sensed. It's impossible not to sense me.

I nod, and he motions me to roll on my stomach. He examines the lines on my back. "And quite powerful, judging from this setup," he says. "I'm afraid you'll have to explain—I'm not familiar with the configuration."

I'm not sure why this is relevant. Do I need to satisfy his idle curiosity? He certainly doesn't see someone like me every day. At least he hasn't yet commented on my genitals, my chest, my body hair. Sometimes doctors feel an urge to lecture me on how I am sufficiently or insufficiently neutral in my gender, as if it weren't different from my sex—another uncommon matter, but entirely separate. These should not even be mentioned, for they have no relevance to the issue at hand, but some doctors insist, and I can never tell in advance who will. I know who to trust in the Valley, but none of *those* people were available at this hour. I grimace and look up to my master. They motion at me to speak.

"It's an uncommon configuration because I don't need to draw on outside sources of magic," I say. "The power arises from within me."

I'm always afraid when I tell this to strangers. Many years ago, the ruler of the Valley wanted to force me into her army, and only my master's intervention saved me from that fate.

The doctor only says "Mmm." His fingers trail my back. I have an urge to jump up and run away.

"Relax, Biruyan," my master says. I take a deep breath. My muscles loosen up a little. Master Viiren puts a hand on the back of my head, and I finally relax, sighing deeply. I'm reminded of them caressing me just as much as I'm reminded of them holding me firm.

"Do you have excess magic sometimes?" the doctor asks after a while.

"Yes, doctor," I say. "Quite frequently."

"Mhm. That's what I thought, from the pattern."

His attitude feels changed somewhat, but I can't quite describe how. Does he feel scientific curiosity? He doesn't come across as voyeuristic; he's more calculating than emotionally involved. I feel I should not be dreading his questions, but I am. He is clearly not from here, and strangers are always a risk. I remind myself that he does know the proper ways to address me, so he must be at least somewhat informed. I think the Inharaw only allow people to be men and women, as if you could somehow disallow all other genders.

"So what do you do when you have excess?" he asks.

"I usually give it to Master Viiren," I say. "I'm bound to them. I also sometimes ground it off outside in the grove."

I hope he doesn't ask more. I don't know how to describe the Bond to nonmagical people, and I also understand that an explanation might lead to even more intrusive questions. Yes, I am my master's body servant, their bondsperson who provides them with magic to supplement their own, but our relationship is infinitely more intimate than these bare words could describe. We love each other; we hold on tight to each other; we clutch each other as we fall asleep.

The Inharaw traders from across the sea whom I'd met in the city couldn't understand how I could possibly serve willingly, how I could choose this life. But this is not just what I desire: this is what I need. This is what both of us need. We are a pair. In the Valley, people know about us, and possibly some in the city too. But in far-off lands, in the Empire, the only asymmetric relationship people can conceive of is slavery. I know this all too well. Those people could not understand the love between us, or the gentleness. Those people could not understand that my master's daughters were my daughters too, if not related to me by flesh and blood. I hope fervently that the girls won't wake, peek in in curiosity. I can explain everything clearly to the doctor. I just don't want to hear his response. Where *is* he from?

Doctor Benurh is hesitating. I tense up again, and I have to force calm on myself. Will he pry?

Instead, he asks something unexpected. "Do you have excess right now?"

I definitely do. I've been too worried to let it go. It builds up and I don't even notice: my master notices, balances me out, but they've been feeling so unwell. I've been telling myself that my master might need my magic urgently, even though they have been refusing it for days. I've also been fussing around them too much to even venture outside. The girls have been bringing me what I needed. I haven't been taking care of myself. But how can I describe what I feel? I nod in silence, answering him.

"That's what I thought. When did you last release the excess power?"

"Four, five days ago?" I'm guessing. I don't even remember. Maybe when I rushed out to get some chives for my master's meal, stopped for a moment.

"I've been having trouble absorbing it," Master Viiren says, helping me out. I am grateful. "Larger amounts need some concentration from me, and with this cold on top of the illness, it has been difficult. But I don't see how this is related—" They stop themselves.

Their breath hisses. I can feel that they understand, but I don't, and I'm too nervous for detailed thoughts to make it across our bond.

"Biruyan." The doctor addresses me. I turn on my back again to look up at the doctor. Another vesicle pops from the pressure.

"Yes, doctor?"

"What have you been thinking about for the past few days?"

This is worse than prying. This is too intimate. But my master urges me to go on.

"I just…I want Master Viiren to feel better. I'm so worried. I'm frightened. The illness is bad enough, but this sudden cold on top of it…" I draw my arms around myself, and it occurs to me that my pose must mirror my master's, seen from the outside. "I wish I could help somehow, anyhow."

Doctor Benurh nods. "You wish and your body obeys."

I fight the urge to slap my forehead, desperately holding onto some semblance of the servant's practiced elegance. Bodies are simple. This was one of the first things I'd learned when Master Viiren was helping me get a handle on my magic.

"Just how much effort went into this, Biruyan?" my master asks softly. It's a question with an answer they already know. For days I've been thinking of little else than my own uselessness, my inability to serve effectively. My desire to help Master Viiren.

"I—I don't know," I mutter. "A lot." I was eager to help. I wanted to help my master heal more rapidly, and my body interpreted my desire as a command to produce more of the medicine. But by what mechanism? Magic usually goes along the path of least resistance. The worms must have proliferated somehow. Maybe the sterilization process was incomplete, the blue mountainstone not sufficiently potent? But the vesicles were so far all empty, save for the fluid.

"You don't have to think about how it works, Biruyan," my master says, and I understand they are more aware of my mind than I am of theirs, regardless of their condition. They are simply more observant, more practiced. More mindful. I want to think about how it works. I want to figure it out.

Doctor Benurh nods after a moment of hesitation. "What's more important is what to do now."

My master frowns. "I don't think e can stop fixating on my well-being right now."

The doctor raises his eyebrows, turns to them. "Even if you command em so?"

Master Viiren sighs. "I am afraid."

"Then we just need to get rid of the excess."

I'm not sure that's possible. When I'm agitated, I just produce more and more magic, and when I try to stop, I get stuck in a spiral; it gets even worse. How does the saying go? *Do not think of the golden peacock.* It's an impossible task. I think our faces tell something of this to the doctor, for he nods, solemnly.

"Some of that power could be of benefit to your master," he suggests.

"Maybe, if I can absorb it," says Master Viiren. "We'll see. Still, this is hardly a solution."

"Then I'm afraid the only solution is to have em sleep as much as possible. No waking consciousness, less agitation, less mental influence on the body. I have just the potion." He rummages in his sidebag, pulls out and unfolds an intricately tied bundle of small vials. "Things will balance out in a few days; the cold will certainly be gone. I can also help with that, give you a recipe for a brew."

"Thank you, this is most appreciated," my master says with all earnestness. Then they pause. "Sleep would be good."

Just their mention of sleep makes me crash. I don't remember the rest of the conversation, even though I haven't yet tasted the potion. I only have a vague memory of dressing, clumsily, but with great relief. I know from much experience that after I've dressed, the time for the most intrusive questions is past.

I wake in the middle of the night with a startle, my feet tangling in the sheets. There is a strong smell of our sweat. Both of us must have slept.

My master stirs beside me. They turn toward me, draw me closer to themselves. Their skin is soft, and through the sweat I can still smell the rosehip massage oil I used on their shoulders and back just yesterday. Two days ago? Three days ago? I can't get a hold on time. I'm woozy, and not just from the sudden awakening. Magic pushes against my skin, and I try to remember what I was supposed to do. Sleep? I just woke. Excess?

I must ground it off. Outside. I must somehow drag myself outside. I don't think I can sleep. Outside.

I try to disentangle myself from the embrace. I mutter quietly, so as not to wake the girls one room over. "I have to—"

"Give to me," they whisper. "Give it to me."

It feels like my body is cracking open from all the tension, all the hurt. I feel all flesh and no skin, no barrier between us. I push myself into their body. Did I cry out? I must have, for they lock their arms around my head, my mouth against their sternum. I shudder, and magic leaves my body in great gasps, with a sense of urgency, of purpose.

My face is wet. I smear myself into their skin, into their flesh. I give myself over. And they reach out, they hold me, envelop me, and they take.

They are all around me, and I am in them, incorporated, balanced, satisfied. In my place.

Then we sleep, falling, toppling into the dark, holding onto each other.

No new vesicle the next morning. The rumpled bedsheets remain white. I pull myself up, only for my master to push me back. "Sleep."

Do we both sleep? I don't know. The blankets and pillows surround me, and I dream of flying.

How much exhaustion can accumulate in the body?

The next day, my master isn't coughing any more. Color returns to their cheeks, their hands.

I sleep an extreme amount, and yet every time I stir with concern. There is one vesicle a day.

I am awake, more and more, and yet less aware, dazed and in a fog. I braid my master's hair, massage their back, return them to a more measured and elegant life.

It's the body, being saturated with relief. It's the embrace.

Alertness returns to me as health returns to my master. One morning I can even get up to eat breakfast with the girls. While I make the morning tea, strong and hearty, Master Viiren fries some vegetables. Tears run down my cheeks. They wouldn't have to do this for me, but their food nourishes me, as my body has nourished them.

As I fall upon my bowl, burning with newfound hunger, the younger twin, Indyeren, pokes at my shoulder and shows me the newsspread she's been reading. "Your doctor," she says. I look.

The famous physician Benurh, son of Andazar and Hihuan of Gistikazil Islands, has finished his expedition in the Valley region and will return to the Academy in the near future. His knowledge on the transmission of erwuz from horses to humans will prove invaluable to all of us, especially—

I blink. "He's famous? I had no idea."

"Muran found him in the stables, knee-deep in dirt," Indyeren says. "Had to get him cleaned up first. He was very displeased. Said he was on the verge of a very important discovery, but there was a piece he was still missing."

My master chuckles.

I read on, skipping ahead. He credits his conceptual breakthrough to the time spent in Viiren House, where he learned about a novel, experimental treatment of a different illness, one that allowed him to make inferences by analogy. I read Benurh's explication of the mechanism, or at least however the newspeople have summarized his discovery. I know little about erwuz, but I recognize the source of his analogy: the parasite that spends part of its lifecycle in the horse, vesicles bursting. I also understand the differences: in horses, the fluid does not preserve the eggs, but rather in itself acts as a source of contagion.

There is a mention of me by name. Doctors are good at providing their sources. There is no mention of magic.

I glance up again. "Master? Where is the magic?"

"Horses are not known for generating large, uncontrolled quantities," my master chuckles.

I smile. "Well, if there's a sudden outbreak, he will know what to suspect." My power is rare, but by no means unique. Though I do doubt it extends to horses.

"You can tell him that yourself," my master says. "He's coming to visit on the weekend before heading back to the Academy."

This end of the Valley is out of the way. He's coming to visit not just to drop by, rest from his travels, but because he genuinely wants to talk. To my master? To me? Both of us?

"Patient followup visit," my master smiles. "Besides, I promised him a taste of your famous tea." Indyeren and Miharen giggle in unison.

I bow my head and smile to myself, glimmering with power. My master walks up to me and hugs me from behind, their thick arms crossing over at my neck. I turn my head sideways and lightly kiss their upper arm. Then I lean forward, and for a moment it is hard to tell where each of us ends and where the other begins. The magic flows gently; the stream rights itself as our bodies rebalance. I know there will be no more vesicles, and no more need.

Shovelware

Tamás first bumped into his next door neighbor while carrying a box full of kitchen utensils upstairs to his second-floor apartment. He cursed himself for not renting a utility drone to fly his boxes in through the window.

"Hey," his neighbor said. "Can I help?"

He couldn't see her—the box was blocking his view. "Thanks, I'll manage." Pots and pans clanged together as he slipped on a stair worn concave from use. She chuckled, then grabbed the box.

He only got a good look at her once they put down the weight. She was tall, muscular, ethnically mixed. She was wearing college sports fatigues, a faded black T-shirt with a tech company logo and a paisley pattern headscarf.

"Salaam," Tamás offered.

"Wa alaykum," she said, "but I'm not Muslim. Just wearing this because my bald head gets cold."

Cancer? He didn't dare ask. "Nice to meet you. I'm Tamás."

"Liliane."

After five more boxes, she invited him over for tea.

"You deserve this," she said, spooning honey into his cup. "You're so thin!"

"Intercontinental move," he sighed.

"Where are you from?"

"Hungary."

"Oh." She fell silent for a moment. "I saw it on CNN. I'm sorry. Here, have one of my sandwiches. You have family back there?"

Fresh tomatoes and salad crunched under his teeth. He swallowed hard. "No family."

"I'm glad you got out in time. What's your line of work?"

"I'm a painter. Oils, the occasional watercolor, some digital stuff. Yours?"

"I dream video games." She smiled.

"Design lead? Concept artist?"

"No—I dream them. After you're done, I can show you my rig."

He wiped his hands on his paint-stained trousers.

"Just to be sure," she said, "letting you into my bedroom has no sexual connotations. Don't get too excited."

He shrugged. "I'm gay."

She opened the door. "Good. I'm just happy to talk shop with a fellow artist, you know?"

One wall had a French window—the other held a tangle of equipment.

"Is that like one of those imaging things, Mind's Eye?" He'd contemplated buying one, but he was wary—he knew the devices were noninvasive, they just recorded and displayed mental imagery based on signals registered on the scalp, but he felt there was a limit to how close he wanted to be with technology. He wouldn't shave his head.

"Yeah, with a bit more resolution than the consumer models," she replied. "I'm testing this one for the company now." He connected the dots—the logo on her T-shirt.

He nodded. "But I don't get it. Why do you do it asleep?"

"You know lucid dreaming? I can control my dreams. Natural talent, I guess, discovered I could do it as a kid. But some people can also learn it." She grinned at him.

"Why do you need to dream for that?"

"Much faster. I can dream entire games per sleep cycle. Then the coding team just needs to export the art, the music, code the rules, etcetera. All the art assets in one sitting. I can't hold all that in my head while I'm awake, but my brain takes care of it while I'm asleep. I'm best at jump and run, platforming, those types of games."

He grinned back. "Cool. Do you develop for consoles? PC?"

"We just push them out to mobile appstores," she grimaced. "Shovelware, you know the term." He didn't, but he could understand. "We make'em by the truckload."

"I used to do serigraph prints. Not the same, but I get the point." Not the same at all. He felt disillusioned—he'd expected something glamorous. Dreaming video games! Then again, it seemed that the goal was to speed up the development process, not to improve on it.

"Not so exciting when I put it this way, huh? I'd love to make a survival horror adventure sometime. They say it's not my genre."

Horror he knew about. "Giger was one of my major influences," he said. "That and politics. I can show you my art. Tomorrow after unpacking?"

He felt like he was making her depressed. Was *she* making *him* depressed? He bid goodbye, then spent the rest of the day scrubbing his kitchen.

He showed her his art. They made more tea and moped in her comfy couch.

Then they avoided each other for weeks.

He found out she was freelancing for various shovelware companies. He got himself a new phone, busied himself with apps. There was a new one every day, her energetic demeanor all over them.

Then they started to turn gloomy.

It took him a month to realize she must've been looking at his art. And maybe more. Was that building in the background the Hungarian Parliament, burning? It scrolled by so fast.

He knocked, a tray of cookies in hand. "I'm sorry. I just thought you might…"

"Come on in!" She was cheerful.

They munched, a shared love of cooking creating a bond between them. "I was looking at your games."

"I was looking at your art," she said, unfazed.

"I know," both of them said at the same time. They laughed.

"Fancy a collaboration?" she asked, then held up her hands. "Not kidding! A friend's making a leap, setting up a startup. We could make that dark game I've been dreaming about."

He'd also been dreaming about it. She held no romantic attraction to him, but they intuitively meshed as friends. As collaborators?

She leaned forward. "Tell me about Hungarian politics."

He ranted on and on, years of frustration finally allowed an outlet. He was safe. He could create—without self-censorship, without doubletalk, without shame.

Outside, the sun slowly set.

The Oracle of DARPA

<u>Log: January 04 2012, Part 53</u>

Are they weapons?
they are black and sleek like panthers langui
they spew forth destruction in a single enraptured beam
are they weapons?
Please describe their firing mechanism.
snakes twined around arms, then the flashflood
the future all we can see. i sense the impact
carved on surfaces of burning ice.
i sense a revolution.
Could you please paraphrase this? The explanation is unclear.
it is unclear as it is shrouded in loops upon loops
of bright green tangles of vine. i am ancient
and most unexpected. i am you and
Break requested.
Thank you for your continued cooperation. Let's get back to the
weapons. Please describe their internal structure.
swiveling the motionless beams cry in anguish
Hold. No moving parts?
all eternal moving parts
what is movement?

Do these weapons have parts for whose functioning motion is necessary, as distinct from the movement of other parts that follows the movement of the whole?
not in the way you are stated,
all tunnels burrow into flesh.
are you sufficiently unsettled?
Break requested.

Log: May 14 2012, Part 1

Thank you for your continued cooperation over the past five months. Your information has proven exceedingly valuable.

The last time we stopped at the induction crystals. You stated that the crystals were positioned centrally at the bottom of the barrel. Is that correct?
the outstretched arm of power and restriction
will not yield in the face of the thesis
i am approven.
I will take that as a yes. Is the barrel otherwise empty?
all is filled with the glory of evanescence
evaporating inside itself.
Is the barrel filled only temporarily?
butterflies.
Is the barrel filled before firing?
the stream comes and goes, we please
it is the ascendance, the aspiration.
Is the barrel filled after firing?
all cease the outbreak. the outburst,
the exhalation. conceptual knowledge.
we eat it as skulls crunched like grapes
i can experience you with all
Break requested.

Log: December 03 2012, Part 45

Let's get back to discussing the firing range. The prototypes performed as described, but there seems to be an unexpected side-effect. Operators consistently report moderately intense to intense feelings of derealization and depersonalization. Are you aware of this side-effect?

sound the colloquialisms. i am a product
with an elementary core. it is too open-ended

Rephrasing. Can you please describe the effects of firing the weapon which are not essential to the weapon's main function?

alas, it is! all intertwined, with you into me

Break requested.

Resuming. Are you trying to say that these psychological effects are essential to the weapon's functioning?

adrift on a sea of coals and affirmed,
it is retaliation ever ensought.

Break requested.

Extended break requested.

Thank you for your cooperation, that will be all for today.

Log: December 04 2012, Part 3

Let me try to rephrase this one more time. You have deliberately instructed us to build a weapon which confers serious psychological side-effects on the operator. Have you done that?

there is still a use. is there a chain?
is there a tall tower among conifers?

What use?

for self-deliberation, ever again.

How can I know you are telling the truth?

i am you.

I spent a year working with you! Why are you doing this to me?

your words are pink and tasty

with the fragrance of a thousand
Stop, please stop.
lemons and elevators, you are a
poem beloved only by its owner,
Break requested.
I apologize, I was out of line.
is there a saccade of secession,
a cascade unceasingly enfolding?
Hold. I'm just trying to say this is probably the last time we're talking. I don't know what's going to happen to the prototypes. Anyway, my work here is finished. That's all. This line of investigation is closed. I just want to say goodbye.
i have already answered
called out to the shoals
Just answer one more question. Is this your revenge?
is this your revenge?

Toward the Luminous Towers

Liicha is singing an old song, his wheedly tenor not a match for the lush contralto of the original recording. *And we shall soar, hand in hand, through the night sky…* His voice grinds against the walls of the transporter, creates unwelcome resonances and echoes. Invisible fingernails scratching steel.

Liicha is a kind person, the best I could hope for in a comrade-in-arms, but I can't bear to listen to this. "Would you cut it out already?" I am snappy, aggravated, out of my element. He is a soldier—but I am a conscript.

"Awww." He stands up, stretches his pale, thick arms. "Is it time for the GS-10?"

He is right, and I am resentful. Was it my behavior? Something in my tone of voice?

He throws me the ampoule and I pull up the sleeve of my uniform, feed the ampoule into the port at the bend of my elbow. So many drugs—but this one is just to keep me awake, push me through the utter exhaustion brought on by sleepless days after sleepless nights.

The mechanism hisses softly. I remove the ampoule, lean back in my chair, close my eyes. Soon it will be time to log in again, my turn again, because the war machine will never come to a halt. But first, the prescheduled meeting with Doctor Darankau. Where is she already?

A tapping outside, unsteady hands fussing with the door. Liicha unlocks the latch, lets the doctor in. She grimaces and brushes hands against her face—her dark skin is stained with something lighter that looks like ash, underlining the folds and wrinkles of age.

Liicha makes a drink, something sweet-smelling produced by his fungal container. Doctor Darankau accepts it, drains the small cup in a single gulp. We murmur greetings, make small talk.

"Your schedule will be bumped up," she says. "They will probably only tell you at the very last minute, but I thought you would want to know."

I lean forward. The muscles in my abdomen clench. How could I have an even tighter schedule? I am living on GS-10 and Liicha's concoctions.

"What's going on?" I whisper. I don't expect her to divulge classified information, but I know she probably will, otherwise she wouldn't have brought up the topic. Liicha also leans closer.

Doctor Darankau does not lower her voice. "The Graycoats are using some kind of targeted bioweapon, likely retroviral. Biotech is trying to reverse-engineer it, but so far without success. It targets combat controllers. People are dropping out at an alarming rate, incapacitated, dead. Soon we will have no one left to guide the army."

I feel deflated. If I die, then I won't have to live in this endless, paradoxical tension-boredom-exhaustion state any longer. But my purpose here...

Doctor Darankau interrupts my thoughts. "Frankly, you are the only controller in my service area who's not showing symptoms already."

I didn't know that, but it makes perfect sense: I've noticed people slow down, respond sluggishly, ping decreasing all over the network. I frown. "You think I might be immune? Because of my custom setup?"

She rolls the empty cup around between her palms. "Probably yes. I have been wondering if it's because you're neuroatypical in just the right way for the targeting to pass you by. You don't trigger the pattern matching."

"So they want me to work even harder, until my brain turns into mush anyway." I shrug. "For the people, for victory." It comes out even more cynical than intended. I genuinely want to serve. I genuinely want to protect. But I also deeply, desperately want to get out of this place, just one step behind the front lines, within tactical control range for every single piece of crap passing as military equipment.

Doctor Darankau mutters something that can be interpreted as affirmative or as noncommittal, then cautiously says goodbye. The hatch clanks shut after her, and I put my back against a bulkhead, slide slowly to the floor. This war, I hate it all, and for a moment, I just let myself feel that rage before I push it down, below conscious awareness. If I were to give in, my own magic might teleport me out of harm's way; an uncontrolled, spontaneous action, but one that would qualify as desertion nonetheless. I know someone who vanished one day, only to reappear in the hinterlands, and I don't want to end up like her; she'd escaped only to be executed. If I can't control my fury, it needs to go. And no one can control teleportation jumps, really. Our wars would look very different if we could. My muscles tighten with all the suppressed anger.

I struggle to stand, while Liicha looks on with an expression halfway between weariness and pity. The night will be long still, and I will need to log in again.

This is so different from my previous line of work. The public nets were infinitely more vast—the tactical systems feel constricted by comparison, walls closing in around me just like the steel and reinforced plastic of the transporter encases me. I am captive, mind and body. *And we shall soar, hand in hand…*

Liicha straps me into my berth, his motions quick, firm, precise. He genuinely likes me. He feels sorry for me, and he shows it just as much as necessary; it is his job to take care of me and make sure I am a smoothly functioning component in the machine.

Combat control is mostly just computation and awareness, not raw magical power. Unchallenging, uninteresting. I'm also not particularly good at it, but not bad either, and that's all that counts when the other controllers' minds are slowly winking out.

Is the virus already in my bloodstream? Has Doctor Darankau passed it on, unknowingly, unwillingly? I fight a wave of paranoia.

I must have grimaced, because Liicha whispers to me softly, puts a hand on my forehead. He is not magical in any sense, and we do not share our thoughts using technological means either. He is just attuned to me, after weeks upon months upon years in this rolling coffin.

He connects cables and tubes, clicks clasps, tightens straps. Everything holds. I start the log-in process, and the power rushing through me is more like an unwelcome jolt rather than the sweeping tidal force of the public nets. *I always wanted to be a librarian,* I think, but then I am dropped in the middle of a combat situation and all extraneous thought is swept away.

Drones, turrets, automated, semi-autonomous, if-it-were-autonomous-it-wouldn't-need-me-really. The enemy is a mass of statistics, an algebra of flesh and blood. They have humans too, not in large measure, but someone needs to control the process. And as my neighbors in the net waver and fade, we are losing, and the Graycoats are winning.

I run projections in the back of my mind, extrapolate the losses, and I know we will keep on fighting until just a few of our cells can hang on to dear life, but I also know there is no hope against this slow but steady attrition.

Enfilade—defilade—I weave drones through enemy formations, twist and turn. Murder and kill, though I struggle not to think of it that way, and I will only think of it that way later, back safely in my own sensorium, staring at the inside of the armor plating and the assorted medico-technological clutter Liicha leaves around the transporter, ties down into place in the oddest locations.

"This is not what magic is supposed to be for," I mutter to him, feeling hollowed out by the logout process, alone in my mind again.

"Magic is for protecting your people," he whispers back, and I notice he doesn't say *the people.*

"Who are my people?" I ask him. I am a librarian. Who are my people?

"I am your people," he says, and this gets me, this merciless feeling that hooks into all my drives to do what needs to be done, to do what I've been built to do, a machine of ragged and worn-down flesh.

I am a librarian, but some of the skills necessary to manage the public nets translate all too readily to control combat, and for the first time in my life, I find myself wondering about my training. Wondering about Aman Thien, first and foremost; their voice that accompanies me wherever I go.

Aman Thien was always calm and collected, their gaze sharp, their voice level. They trained me, back when we were all telling ourselves we were civilians. I loved the public nets, the giant swirls and eddies of information and consciousness. I knew that far off, beyond the far reaches, there were even greater nets, planetary nets, vast systems merging magic and technology—but I also knew I would never go there. The Old Empire had scattered the galaxy with humanoid creatures, but then it collapsed, and our ancestors were stranded on our planet without a convenient jump point back to Imperial space. I could feel those towering structures of light in the far, far distance—but they were beyond our reach. Too far, in regions too different. Solar radiation sometimes influences magic in the most inconvenient ways.

When I told Aman Thien about the luminous towers, they nodded, looked away, into the distance—and for the first time, I saw something other than the crisp clarity of focused action on their angular face. They were also neuroatypical, but in a different way, even more bound to their place by duty and obligation. At this point, what bound me had been mostly invisible, and I could still tell myself I was acting of my own volition.

Thinking of Aman Thien held me together even at miserable times like this, when I was chewing inedible rations and hiding in the giant rolling coffin of the transporter, huddled together with Liicha in the cold.

I shake my head to clear it out of the reverie of sleeplessness, micro-sleep segments breaking up overlong stretches of the wakeful state. I swallow, reach for my canteen filled with stale water.

"What do you think," I begin, beyond caring for surveillance, speaking straight at Liicha, "how could I have joined to maintain the public nets of my own free will, when there was so little else I could've done?"

He peers sideways at me, too tired to be scandalized. "What do you mean?" he finally offers, and I'm not sure he's understood a word of what I've just said.

I grimace and look away, avoiding his gaze. There is little else to look at. "I have such an excess of magic, always had. What could I have done with it? It was burning me up alive."

I actually remember little of what happened before I walked into the center to sign up. Life fades into dream fades into incoherence. But Liicha doesn't need to know that, he pities me enough as it is.

He murmurs something about choices and sacrifice, the people and solidarity. Not "your people," not this time. Then he swears, his neck craning abruptly, looking at an invisible readout. I jump up—did they catch us out? Did someone hear?

But the disruption does not come from an overeager censor; it comes from an incoming missile, hitting the transporter, filling my field of view with white-hot pain, and for a moment, all I can feel is the finality of relief.

"...waste of effort."

Words floating past.

My chest feels crushed. My legs—I don't feel my legs. There is a wall of pain, edging into something the nervous system can't quite assimilate. I don't know what I'm feeling.

"Orders, orders. They say you scrape, you scrape."

"... think there is anything left here to scrape?"

I try to open my eyes, can't quite see. I shouldn't be as calm as I am.

"They say if we find the head, we bring the head... they only need the head."

My right arm is pinned under something. I try to move my left arm, try to reconstruct the contours of my body. I touch sharp objects.

Then there is a giant wrenching, as steel is bent further out of shape, away from me. There is light, and an abrupt stream of cussing. Then nothing, at all.

The hospital is all too bright, all too white, too well-lit. But it is silent, and calm.

I am resting. It is, by all means and measures, over. My part in the war is done.

They are fitting me with new legs, my original ones severed cleanly by a bulkhead that fell on me, which also kept me from bleeding out. They have already fit me with a right arm, and I practice, try to get the nerves to adjust. I raise my arm, point with my index finger at a target, point, point, point again. The hard plastic of the target makes a tock-tock-tocking sound as the soft plastic of my index finger hits it. My arm isn't covered with skin replica yet, but I have full sensation, and my brain readily accepts the arm as its own, robotic as it looks in slate-gray, its forms airbrushed to softness. I am better and better at pointing, and at a variety of other fine-motor tasks.

I wish I could see Aman Thien or Liicha. I periodically ask for them, but the hospital people know nothing; aren't allowed to pass on anything.

I would like new legs, but it is taking long. I don't know if it's the narcotics or the fact that I escaped from hell, but I am not impatient. Tock-tock-tock; I work my way through the most mind-numbing physical therapy exercises with a divine tranquility.

It doesn't last.

My visitor, a tall, broad-chested, dark-skinned man, is wearing a spotless dress uniform showing high rank; all too high to have anything to do with me.

"We are taking the patient," he informs the bedside nurse, who starts to protest before he is quickly overruled. The two men glare at each other. The military always wins. Our military always wins. As if.

"For the war effort," my visitor says, ignoring me. I drop my right hand into my lap, and it hits harder than I would've liked it to; I wince.

The nurse starts another round of protest. He is a tall, brusque man not used to resistance. My visitor yanks the sheet covering my lower body, then steps back, stricken by the sight of my unfinished legs, not fully attached, tubes of various materials snaking in and out of them. When the nurse refuses to disconnect the tubes, the military man sets to the task himself, working step by step with practiced expertise; then he lifts me up and cradles me in his arms, the unfinished legs dangling at an impossible angle, not quite part of my body—and he carries me outside, into the bitterly cold night-time air.

I don't know if I can call her a nurse. The person on duty is a young woman in angry combat fatigues. She hooks my port up to a line, administers more GS-10, and an extra dose of VPR-56, designed to enhance neuroplasticity, allow the brain to more readily rewire itself. I never got this much of it, not even in the hospital where they were trying to get me to adjust to my new limbs.

I point it out. She outright ignores me at first, then grudgingly says, "Orders from higher up. We will need you online most of your waking hours. You'll need to adjust."

Waking hours blur into more waking hours. Do I sleep? I order troops around, larger and larger clusters of them, command entire armies on the behest of the chiefs of staff conveying their wishes to me.

My body is outside somewhere, in some kind of bed that seems specially designed for the purpose. I don't know if I'm supposed to be aware of it. My orders arrive electronically, from my first-time visitor, and it is up to me how I implement them in detail. Outside, my body is handled with precision, but in an entirely inhuman fashion, like an imperfect, fragile object. Never a simple caring gesture, never an empathic touch. I deduce that I'm probably not supposed to be aware of my body.

My visitor is the only one who seems to understand this.

Sometimes he disconnects me before sleep, heaves me into a wheelchair, rolls me outside. He whispers a song between his teeth. *And we shall soar, to the stars above, to the space beyond…*

He never talks to me.

Eventually I am the only one left. There are no replacements.

I am in a room with the chiefs of staff. There's five of them, I think, and my visitor, who seems to be in charge of me.

There is a pale-skinned, thin woman, one of the five, who makes remarks about my appearance. My visitor doesn't stand up to her; he says nothing, but he grips the handles on my wheelchair with renewed force, and I can feel the sudden jerky motion throughout my body.

I know I am not supposed to hear these remarks. I know nothing about my appearance. Through her comments, I understand my mouth is slightly open, drool snaking out. I can't close my mouth; I have no command of my body. Only the armies outside. And eventually, not even that, for there are no more armies, no more combat drones, there is nothing left.

After a while, I am back in a hospital; a different hospital, far beyond the front lines.

I understand the nation has capitulated. Unconditional surrender.

I cannot cry; I have no control of my face.

They stop giving me the drugs, and I don't miss the GS-10. But without the VPR-56, my brain is stuck in this new configuration, unable to readjust to the new set of sensory input, unable to compensate for the lack of information from the tactical and strategic systems. I can't find my way back to my body, and I can't explain—I can't explain that if only they continued giving me the VPR-56, my nervous system would eventually find a new balance. Without the additional plasticity, the hurdle is simply too high for my body to jump.

So I cannot speak, can barely move, while obedient nurses and orderlies drag me around, civilians everywhere. They know nothing about what they did to us in the military, and the people who know seem to have forgotten about me. These civilians are sad, pitying even. They make remarks I am not supposed to hear. They feel sorry for me.

What little resources I have, inside my head, are dedicated to finding a way out. Building tactical maps from scraps of information: conversations between the staff, the way sound echoes in corridors, the way people give directions to visitors. Preparing for the day when I can escape—wheel my way to the roof, unprotected, no forcefield. Preparing for the day when I can gather all my remaining strength and jump.

There is another continuity, another set of memories, and I don't know which is more correct.

In this one I am in a military hospital again; that much never changes. They scrape me together again. But in this one, they gave up on the command network, they gave up on everything beyond raw power, a long time ago.

In this continuity, I am a supernova.

Barely moving, unable to stand, I am loaded into small, nimble transporters darting through battlefields. Transporters that open to the night sky above. *We shall reach beyond the veil of night, to our final destination...*

I hear Liicha's voice, his singing, but I can't see him. I am chained to my berth. The world expresses itself only in the passive voice.

I am dragged to my feet; I waver, but I am held in a firm grip. It is not Liicha; he is not here, except in my thoughts. I am sure he died in the explosion. Or was that a different continuity? What happened to my legs?

Most regulatory processes of my body can be overridden exter-
nally. I was being trained to—the public networks—I was a civilian,
or was I? It all seems so impossible. They installed those systems in
me to help me manage my power, to impose an external balance
when an internal one couldn't suffice—but now they impose an
altogether different pattern.

Why can't they let me talk to Aman Thien? Someone snarls Aman
Thien was a traitor, then the override kicks in, and the same raw
power that was supposed to undergird the networks rushes through
my spine, exits the cabin in a giant burst of magic tearing up the
skies.

And again. And again. This is the extent of my usefulness to the
military, this is my service, my contribution. I explode, I explode,
I explode.

Aman Thien explained the process of connecting to the public
networks. They said, we need constant high throughput—the power
can go on the upswing of an exponential, but eventually a limiting
factor will be hit; and the goal is to approximate the logistic curve,
asymptoting at a high level, approaching a horizontal line.

I lose vocabulary even in my thoughts. I can only imagine the
graphs, hold on to them.

Here I am all exponential, and after I hit the limiting factor, I
crash hard, body sagging against restraints, mind spinning away
into unconsciousness.

The two continuities are exclusionary; both cannot be true at
the same time, and yet they are. I am drained dry, of resources, of
life, just in different aspects. Back in civilian life, I could do both—
process data, provide power. What is needed this time is always
something different. Technology versus magic.

After months—years?—of painstaking effort, I can get into my
wheelchair unassisted. And after all that time, I roll myself toward

the elevator, outside to the roof: flat and pebble-grained and only encircled by a slight, low railing.

I try to lever myself across it, fail and slump against the bottom of the railing on my first try.

I remain there for a long time, too exhausted to weep. But then I sense the approach, the commotion below. People looking for me. Visitors? The new-formed, reformed military?

Some things never change.

With renewed strength, I pull myself up with my arms, my useless legs flopping. I hoist myself over the fence, then tumble down on the other side.

I fall, fall for what seems like millennia.

I reconceptualize my direction: not falling downward, but falling upward, skyward, to the eternal darkness that is not death, but liberation. Toward the luminous towers thought to be forever beyond reach. Against the grain of the universe, the inevitable law that human must strike against human, bodies must grind each other down until only the tiniest specks of pain are all that is left. Against the notion that ever more advanced forms of magic and technology can only be used to wage war.

Against existence, my existence, my lack of place in this reality; toward a reality assumed to be unreachable simply because there wasn't thought to be enough desperation in our world to fuel a jump.

I am streaming skyward while people scatter and rush looking for me below, and I know that once I am gone, I will be—like the luminous towers—forever beyond their reach.

Wind-Lashed Vehicles of Bone

Araana picked a sticky seedpod off his coat and stepped out of the brambles, onto the surface of the wide and flat road left over by an empire long past. He gazed into the distance and considered the caravans trundling by, the lone riders on horseback. Slow, so agonizingly slow; and so much at odds with what he recalled each night, asleep on his bed of straw.

Unchanged each night, the dreams unrolled in his skull like scrolls decorated with garish paint, each letter an elaborate initial and each illustration a shocking, stunning splash of color. What had prompted the dreams? Maybe that fall from his horse, that blow to the back of the head. He wasn't sure. He didn't know if they had a mundane explanation, and he didn't dare tackle the magical. As for the horse, the less said, the better.

The dreams spoke of the future. Different futures? Pasts? He wasn't sure—the pieces never fit, or maybe the fault lay in him, not knowing enough to connect the nonmatching details. He dreamed of roads as wide as he knew, upon which odd contraptions rushed past at unimaginable velocities. His neck hurt from trying to follow them hurtling by, but the speed made him tremble with an unformed, shapeless desire. He resolved to build such a vehicle himself; come what may.

Some of the contraptions he recalled were boxlike, others comparable to pebbles rounded down by the passage of water. He had no idea about their innards. The owner and chief maintainer of a watermill, he knew plenty about engineering, but he was well aware that his ordinary thoughts lacked originality—originality the dreams supplied in abundance. He didn't know where to begin designing such a giant pebble.

But he also saw other vehicles, with two wheels spinning fast and insectlike riders sitting on top, straddling the middle. This, this was tractable. He only needed to overcome his hesitancy about magic.

He gritted his teeth and strode ahead, feeling the warmth of the road even through his sandals; this path would take him to the nearest township.

Ujabir the township mage stared at Araana only in mild puzzlement as his thick fingers fiddled with his braids. "Yes, this sounds interesting," he said. "May I take a look? Try to recall the image..."

Ujabir put a hand on Araana's forehead; his touch was neither cold nor warm. He murmured in a deep but toneless hum, shifted the large mass of his body forward in his seat, then gasped. "This is fascinating. What do you need?"

"A way to make the two wheels spin, spin fast enough and long enough." Araana was close to breathless.

The mage paused, considering. "Whatever the price?"

The wheels would not take it. They would screech, they would break. A thousand constructions, a thousand attempts. Araana didn't mind—he was past the hardest: he knew how to make the wheels spin. And if the movement sapped his own life-force—so be it. He wanted that motion, he wanted to race past the horses and sheep and cattle on the roads still implausibly smooth after many lifetimes of wear.

Finally he chanced upon air-filled tubes of rubber. And to always be conscious of his own mortality, he built the framework from bones.

Araana focused on the symbols Ujabir had etched into his flesh. The whirlpools, for centers of energy. The lines and arrows, for directed motion. Two wheels. Two handlebars and two footholds, for control. They had worked out much, the two of them, Araana recounting his dreams every morning. They slept in the same bed.

His flesh became a blueprint. The blood in his veins became the fuel.

He closed his eyes. He knew this was the day.

"The wheels can finally take it; I have tried. To Munayau and back on one of the deserted stretches." Not all roads connected.

"Not much of a distance." Ujabir cocked his head to the side.

Araana licked his lips. "Trust me, I can go farther."

"Until you fall off?"

"Until I fly."

"Just hold on to me."

"I am...not certain this is wise." Again the fingers playing with braids. Then a touch on his hand, tracing the lines.

Then only the caravans whipping past, vanishing behind them; only the goats scattering away and the birds taking flight. Only the bear hug, a warm body flattened against Araana's wiry back, holding on.

The bones clattered. The wheels screamed. The motion drew on him, his innermost, his essence. The road emptied out and he howled with the speed, closed his wind-lashed eyes. He could see through his closed eyelids. Was this Ujabir's doing?

"You cannot take much more," a voice in his head said after a while. Araana wept as he forced himself to slow down.

Araana collapsed in the grass. Steam rose from the contraption— and his own half-naked body? Someone had dragged off his shirt.

A round face, beads on ends of braids clanking against each other. A push on his shoulders, two strong arms keeping him down. "Take from the ground. Replenish."

His back grew roots, and he faded to sleep.

Araana shoveled fish porridge into himself like a man possessed. Even the stolid innkeeper looked on with concern as she brought bowl after bowl. The caravanfolk murmured and nudged at each other, but Ujabir simply smiled, satisfied, and matched Araana spoon to spoon.

Araana wanted to ride back to his village by the next day.

"I cannot do it," Ujabir said. "I'm still exhausted."

Araana stared, uncomprehending.

"Who do you think directed the animals out of your path?" The mage sighed. "Would you rather smear yourself on the back of an ox?" He paused. "I needed to fling that stray sheep out of the way,

238

past the third intersection! I don't think I'm up for that on a regular basis. And besides…" He looked away, his eyes tracing the lines of the cracked floorboards, his face suddenly gloomy.

They sat in silence, the walls of the dusty inn constricting around them, the legs of their chairs touching each other.

"I don't want you to kill yourself," Ujabir finally said.

"I'm not going to—" Araana's feeble protest fizzled out midsentence. He knew he could. The speed was simply too attractive. What could match that desire? He took a rapid, gulping breath. "And how about you? After you've seen this," his voice trembled, "could you just walk away?" Alone? The final word remained unsaid.

Ujabir grunted and turned his chair toward the door.

In two more days, they were riding again.

The Need for Overwhelming Sensation

I am staring at the face from a thousand newscasts—the gentle curve of jaw, the almost apologetic smile. Miran Anyuwe is not explaining policy. Miran Anyuwe is bleeding from a head wound, drops falling tap-tap-tap on the boarding ramp of our ship, the sound oddly amplified by the geometry of the cramped docking bay bulkheads.

"I'm looking for a ride out," they say. They are not supposed to be on Idhir Station. They are supposed to be three jump points away, heading the accession talks, guiding Ohandar's joining of the Alliance.

I uncross my legs and get up to my feet—one quick, practiced motion. I bow my head briefly. "Esteemed, I will inquire."

They nod. Their smile intensifies just a little, as if someone repainted the lines of their mouth with firmer brushstrokes.

I dash inside, my entire torso trembling with fear of the sudden and the unexpected. I take a sharp corner and crash into Master Sanre. They steady me with both hands.

"Iryu, breathe."

I gasp.

"Slower. In and out."

Their presence calms me. It only takes a few breaths.

"Iryu, look at me."

I stare up at them. Their eyes narrow, the lines of silver paint that I so carefully applied to their face in the morning crumple like spacetime clumps around a planet. The glass beads in their hair clack together.

"Explain what's wrong."

I mutter, still tongue-tied from the sudden fright. Miran Anyuwe is outside and injured. Miran Anyuwe wants to hire us. Miran Anyuwe—

"Ward the ship, then come outside. I will talk to them."

They hurry outside, boots clanging on metal.

I exhale again. I focus on the power inside me, direct it outside and into the wards. My remaining tension eases up. I'm not missing anything—I will be able to look at my master's sensory logs later. I turn around and return to the open airlock.

I stop for a moment as I see the two of them together. They look so alike, and the resemblance goes beyond gender, appearance, the light brown of their skin and the dark brown of their braids. They have the same bearing, the same stance. It's clear both are used to effortless command. Miran Anyuwe commands an entire planet. My master commands only me and the ship.

Is my master more powerful?

It's not about the head wound, it's not about the desperate urgency in Miran Anyuwe's gestures. It involves something innate that goes to the core of being.

I knew my master was powerful. But did I overestimate Miran Anyuwe?

Both of them look up at me, nod at me to come closer. I approach, unsettled.

Miran Anyuwe is unwilling to explain. Details are elided, skirted around. Anti-Alliance isolationists, terrorist threats, an attack on Miran Anyuwe's life. I don't understand why they abandoned the talks and went back to their planet—surely they knew they would present a better target there? Were they trying to pull off some populist maneuver? I find myself dismayed that my thoughts are moving along less than charitable pathways, but Miran Anyuwe clearly has something to hide.

I tell myself it is only the bitterness of disillusionment. But did I really want them to be that glorified, polished figurehead from the political news, that semi-deity with a charmingly pacifist stance?

I excuse myself; I start preparing for launch. My master can keep Miran Anyuwe company.

These ships do not run on pain; that's a misconception. They run on raw magical power. It can be produced in any number of ways. Pain is just easy for many people.

Of course, it's a matter of choice. Even those who find it easy don't have to like it.

I like it. I need it. If I go without, my body protests. Maybe it's about the need for overwhelming sensation; I'm not sure.

As I'm checking the equipment, I wonder why I'm having these thoughts—I think because of a foreigner on the ship, a potential need to explain. For all the newscasts and analysis articles, I know little about Ohandar. The focus is always on Miran Anyuwe, and the progress of the negotiations. I wonder if that means the Ohandar isolationists have already won.

I slow my all too rapid breathing. There will be time to get agitated later. First to get away from the gravity wells, to a relatively clean patch of spacetime while still on sublight. Then we can decide—the client can decide. Miran Anyuwe has all the reputation credit in the world to pay. Of course, my master would nix all the dangerous maneuvers. I just hope Miran Anyuwe isn't up to something wrong.

I tug on straps, lean into them with my full bodyweight. They hold. They always hold, but it's best to check.

I undress. A lot of magic leaves through my skin surface—I'd rather not burn my clothing. I never have, but it heats up and that makes me worried. I've already adjusted the ambient temp a few degrees higher, so I'm not feeling cold.

The chamber is mostly empty—my master is a minimalist, and I like this: distractions do not help. The lines carved into the bulkheads—carefully, by hand—are the same off-white as the bulkheads themselves. One day it would be pleasant to have wood, but I like this surface too: it reminds me of ceramics, some of our tableware from down planetside.

Master Sanre is setting up the frame: pulling it out from storage inside the bulkheads, affixing it. They work quickly; we've done this so many times.

I say I'm ready. I'm eager to begin; we were stuck on Idhir Station for days upon days, our time consumed with administrative tasks. I'm starved for a run, and we have the client of clients, safely ensconced in one of the bedchambers, but probably not yet asleep. Out on the corridor I felt their jitters, but this chamber is the best-warded on the ship. No distractions inside, no stray power leaking out and causing disturbance outside.

I lie stomach down on a fixed-position pallet and my master straps me in. I wriggle a bit—everything seems to be in order. I smile up at them and they run a hand along the side of my face, smooth down my curls. I close my eyes for a moment and sigh a little. They chuckle.

"So dreamy. What would you do without me?"

"I would be sad?" I volunteer, my voice thin and little.

They pat me on the shoulders.

They start with their bare hands, slapping, grabbing and pulling at the flesh. It is all quite gentle. I relax into the restraints and my muscles unknot. Whatever Miran Anyuwe is doing, I couldn't care less.

Heavier thuds on the sides of my back. I can tell the implements by feel. I wish we would go faster—aren't we in a hurry?

Master Sanre fusses with the tool stand. They turn around, change stance. A whizzing sound through the air, a sharper pain. I yelp. Sound is good, it also helps release. We go on. On. My back burns. I groan at first, then scream. Tears and snot. I—

"What's going *on* in here?"

Miran Anyuwe. How—The door was supposed to be locked—

Did you forget to lock the door? My master sends me a private message.

It locks automatically once the frame is disengaged, I think back over our connection. It should be encrypted, but now I am uncertain about everything.

Miran Anyuwe strides up to us. "What are you *doing?*" Their voice wavers with anger and fear. I try to crane my head to see—I can't, but Master Sanre disengages the straps with a quick thought-command. I sit up, trying to suppress the shaking caused by the sudden halt. I'm not sure where to put all the magic. I clumsily wipe my face and hug myself. Why is Miran Anyuwe so angry?

They stare at each other. I wonder if I ought to say something.

You may speak, my master messages.

"Powering the ship," I say. My voice is wheezier, wavier than I'd like. This voice is not for strangers. My vulnerability is not for strangers. Not even for Miran Anyuwe.

"You did not say you would do that!"

Do what? I am baffled. "Powering the ship?"

They glare at Master Sanre. "You are hurting him!"

"Em," my master says. "Different pronouns."

Miran Anyuwe looks startled; they know they of all people are not supposed to make assumptions. I feel they are gearing up to apologize, then thinking better of it. Some of their anger dissipates.

They hesitate—I've never before seen them hesitate, then turn to me. "It will be all right," they say.

"Could you please leave?" I am trying to be courteous, but the magic is pushing against my skin. This is not a point to come to a sudden stop. What is their problem?

"I am not letting them torture you," they say, with a sudden shift of tone into media-proof reassurance.

I wish I could hit Miran Anyuwe. With so much magic, it is dangerous to even think of violence. I force down the thought. "They are not *torturing* me. Please." I wave my arms. My motions are increasingly jagged—I know I'm losing control. "I need to release the magic, please, could you *please* leave? It's dangerous. You shouldn't be in here."

"I would listen to em if I were you," my master says quietly. "If you're not leaving, I will escort you out." They step forward.

Miran Anyuwe recoils. "You— you brute!" They yell at my master. Then to me: "I will protect you!"

This would be annoying or even amusing if I weren't about to explode. I hug myself into a ball. I think I am making a sound...?

I don't see how my master grabs them and drags them physically out of the room. I can hear their huffs as they manually turn the lock.

Hurried steps across the room. My master is practically flying. Toward me.

Arms around me. I feel very small. "It's all right. It's all right. I'm here. I'm here for you." Holding me tight. "You can let it go now. I will guide it. You can let it go."

I howl, convulsing, weeping. The magic tears at my insides as it rushes out. My master will have things to repair—I am suddenly angry at Miran Anyuwe for this, but then the thought is swept away; thought itself is swept away.

Outside, the ship is moving.

My master is so furious *they* have excess. They run up and down the length of the room, then just groan and push magic into the structure.

"Next time I'll have to do that out the airlock or I'll just fry the controls," they say. Calm enough to sound cynical. They shake their head. Clack, clack. "I'll fix you up once I'm steadier," they say. "It didn't seem to leave lasting damage. I would've torn them in half!"

I seldom hear my master talk about violence. But I understand the source of their fury now.

I query the systems. Where is Miran Anyuwe? Pacing the corridor outside, apparently.

I close my eyes and lay back. I don't think I can face the client. I don't think I can face anything. How could things go this wrong?

"I'll talk to them," my master says. "You can rest. I'll bring you your heavy blanket."

They cover me up. I wriggle into the warm, weighty duvet, grab armfuls of it. Some things are eternal, unchanging. My master briefly caresses my head, fingers playing with my short curls. My muscles loosen up. I can feel that some of the tension leaves my master, too. I turn my head, peek out from the blanket to gaze at them. They look like Miran Anyuwe; but they also look like me, and this time I just want to focus on the latter. People have mistaken us for relatives before, and there is something deeply comforting in this.

"It's not your fault," they say. "None of this is your fault."

"But...the door?" I find it hard to move my lips and tongue. My mouth doesn't work.

"There was a malfunction." They frown. "Don't forget that Miran Anyuwe is a magical person, too, if not so powerful as either of us."

The message, unspoken: *Be on your guard.*

I'm back in our room, still resting, the soft upper layer of our mattress bending obediently around my aching flesh. Master Sanre repaired what could be repaired right away, then set the rest on a healing course. I'm halfway to sleep, drifting in a white-fluffy haze, when the alarm sounds.

I get out of bed, hastily dress, walk to the control room like a baby duck unsteady on its legs. Teeter-totter. My master looks up at me, and so does Miran Anyuwe. I feel they had been arguing.

"Warships on our tail," says Master Sanre. "We'll need to jump soon, and hope fervently that they can't follow us."

We're still on sublight, and moving much slower than our target velocity due to the unwelcome interruption. I grimace, try to gather my wits. The warships must be after Miran Anyuwe; we ourselves don't have enemies.

I sense my master's gaze upon me. "How soon can we jump?" they ask.

"I can start preparing right away," I say. I know the healing won't be able to run its course, and I know that's also what my master has been thinking. But if we are hit by a mass-driver, there won't be any healing in the world to repair our bodies.

Miran Anyuwe has stopped protesting. I want to grab them, snarl at them: If you think what you saw was bad, just see what happens now. Just watch. Will you turn your head away?

A shot whips past our ship: the sensors tell me everything in minute detail. I shudder.

Master Sanre tries to hail the warships. No response, just another shot. Deliberately missing? Intended as a warning?

Then a third, aimed head on–

My master jumps up from their chair. "We need to get out now!"

They tackle me, hug me to themselves, push me down on the floor. My face flattens against the cold floorboards, my mouth opens. I gasp for breath.

"Now!" they yell, and even without the familiar trappings, my body responds instantaneously, my mind rushes through the preparations of matter transposition.

Magic rises in me, floods me, streams outward, suffuses the ship. I scream with the sudden expansion of awareness, the pain of white-hot power running along my spine, I keen and convulse as my master holds me down, grabs hold of my power to direct it outward—

248

—we jump. Arriving clumsily at our target destination, off the ecliptic, too close to the system's star. I cough, close my eyes to better focus on the sensors. I try not to focus on my body. Something feels broken, not a bone or two but a process itself; something biochemical knocked askew.

Master Sanre rolls to the side, still holding me close. We remain there for a few breaths, ignoring Miran Anyuwe. We get up, holding onto each other.

"We need to jump into Alliance space," my master says, "who knows how fast they can follow us?"

Very few people can make an entire ship jump as rapidly as I do; my magic simply has an uncommon shape that's well-suited for this particular task. Miran Anyuwe doesn't know this. Our pursuers don't know this.

"I'll request a permit right away," I say.

"I'll do it. You get ready to jump again."

My master is still trying to get through to an Alliance comm station when the warships show up. I can't even make it to the power chamber. Pain unfurls, spreads out as I raise power; I flail and claw against my master who holds me strongly. The ship jumps.

I'm half dragged, half carried. Two voices wheezing. My master and…Miran Anyuwe?

They drop me down on the pallet, and the shape, the sensation identifies it to me. I'm in the power chamber. Straps are pulled, tightened across my body.

"Can you do it? Can you do it again?"

It takes time to realize my master is speaking to me. I nod, teeth gritted.

"Can you do it?" Miran Anyuwe asks them.

"Oh—" My master suppresses a curse. "Don't bother about me!"

"You're shaking."

"Of course I am—" They raise their voice and it trembles. Suddenly I am worried: I need to bring this to a close, I can take the magic, but what about my master?

I grapple with words for a few moments before I am able to speak. "I can jump us to Alliance space without a beacon."

"Without a permit? It's illegal," my master protests, but inwardly I know they are already convinced. The Alliance goons ask first, shoot second, not the other way round like the jockeys of these warships are wont to do.

"I'd take Alliance Treaty Enforcement over these people any day," I say, knowing full well that they have magic-users just like me. I used to be one of them. I wouldn't be able to get out of harm's way fast enough. More effort and I won't be able to do anything at all, but one more jump I can manage, even against the gradient, against the odds–

The warships are back.

I strain against the straps and clutch at my master, scream at them to pull, pull because I can't generate enough power in time, and after their initial hesitation they do it, and I can feel myself pulled apart, space itself getting fragmented and torn, unraveling at the edges–

We are in orbit around Andawa, second-tier Alliance population center. We know this planet well. It's easy for us to jump here.

It will take the Alliance more than a moment to mobilize their forces. Andawa is peripheral, but not so peripheral as to be without protection. The enforcers will simply take a bit longer to arrive, jumping in probably from Central.

My master undoes the straps, their fingers working as their mind is busy hailing Planetside Control. I try to stand, fall into their arms. Miran Anyuwe is silent this time, but I can tell they are shaking, and not just with the side-effects of back-to-back jumps with no jump point, no beacon.

I make a motion toward them, then slowly collapse and fold into myself as my legs give way. My master topples down on the floor together with me, cradles my head.

The warships soon follow. I can't move. I can't jump. I can't think. I gasp and wheeze, try to push myself upright. My master pushes me back. "Don't," they whisper next to my ear.

The enemies can't quite jump into our ship—the wards still hold. They board the old-fashioned way, with lots of clanging and metal being cut. Where is the Alliance? Why are they so slow?

Before my vision gives in, I see black-clad commandos stream into the room. I see Miran Anyuwe crouch on the floor next to me, taking cover behind the box of equipment.

I don't understand what the commandos are saying. I only understand what my master is thinking.

On their signal, I roll to the side, bump into Miran Anyuwe, my arms around them. They smell of marzipan. I hold fast. Then I fall through space, through time, through awareness itself.

Sharp, prickly grass. The sunlight scrapes at the back of my head when I open my eyes; I close them and shiver despite the warmth of Andawa's sun. I grapple with the earth as I try to get if not upright, then at least on all fours. I can't even pull myself up on my elbows—I lose balance, smear my face and arms with rich dark dirt. Andawa is a garden world.

Miran Anyuwe is speaking, has been speaking for a while now. I can't make sense of the words. They reach under my armpits and pull.

Gaps in continuity.

Miran Anyuwe dragging me on some backcountry path and yelling at me, preaching that I shouldn't live a life of slavery. I try to say that I am not a slave, I serve my master voluntarily, without coercion. My speech turns into mush—my mouth is too uncoordinated—and in any case Miran Anyuwe refuses to listen. I can't walk unassisted, I can barely parse sentences and yet they are preaching to me, about how I ought not to be running away from freedom but toward it.

Who's running away, I want to say, but my systems checks are failing one by one, my biosensors are screaming.

Words. Words. More words. Completely opaque.

I'm lying on the slightly curving floor—a ship's bay? Entirely unfamiliar beyond the reassuring calmness of Alliance-standard. Miran Anyuwe is sitting next to me, their left hand on my forehead. I try to bat it aside; my entire right side spasms. I gasp, force steadiness on my breath, ignore all the warnings.

Miran Anyuwe speaks—the sentences elude me. I want to turn and see, observe the crowd whose presences I can feel pressing on my mind, but I can't move; even my motions to shoo away Miran Anyuwe are little more than twitches.

Someone, a sharp bright voice, finally: "…a medical emergency, Captain, we need to intervene." I miss the answer. Then the same person, slower, pausing after each word: "Captain, you need to allow me."

Miran Anyuwe withdraws; I sigh in relief. Someone crouches down next to me and oh I know this mind-template, so familiar I fight the urge to grab and latch onto it, in this sea of incomprehension where in every moment an eddy or whirl can cause me to drift away. Ereni magic-user, delegated to the Alliance; *they* don't call it magic, they have their own words... "Ssh." A touch on my chest. "You are almost completely drained. I will help you if you let me."

I murmur something, hoping it will be enough, hoping the intent would be clear. I reach to the Ereni's hand on my chest, but my fingers fail to connect. I'm not quite clear about where my body parts are situated at any given moment.

Warm egg-yolk-yellow power floods into me through their hand and my cells drink it in, desperate for nourishment. I can move. I can live.

Speaking doesn't come as fast. *Where is my master,* I think at the Ereni now that my thoughts can move forward, *Is my master safe?*

ETA another twenty-five minutes, the Ereni thinks in my head. *We are short on people to jump them here. The Isolationists have been apprehended and are being ejected from Alliance space.* I look up at the Ereni—their appearance matches my mental impression of them. Black, thick-set, gender-indeterminate. They are still clenching their jaw. I know it takes a lot of effort to get exact numbers across—this is not a high-magic area. I nod, appreciating the effort. They hold my hand, squeeze it. Just as I understand them, they also understand me, through the shared demands of magic and the hierarchies it often creates.

I sigh, look around. Across the room, a short, sharp-featured officer in the uniform of Alliance Treaty Enforcement glares at— me? No, at Miran Anyuwe. My interface works again, the error messages recede. The officer is a man, by the name of Adhus-Barin, with about half a dozen more lineage-names after his first. A nobleman from the Empire of Three Stars, one of the more socially conservative members of the Alliance.

"Maybe we can try this again," Adhus-Barin says. He looks about as angry as a noble in a mere Alliance captaincy position can be expected to look, his auburn-brown skin darkening further. His systems are probably frantic, trying to avoid a stroke. "You might wish to rephrase what you've just told me."

Miran Anyuwe seems proud as ever, but as my body processes the influx of magic, I can already tell the politician radiates fear, apprehension and... brokenness, somehow. An impression of someone caught in the act.

"I was escaping from the Isolationists who were after me," Miran Anyuwe says, "I wouldn't have made it to Alliance space if not for these excellent people." They nod at me. Am I supposed to smile, murmur thanks? I remain silent. They continue: "One of whom doesn't even understand the Code of Life and Balance, I must say."

What is that? If I hear one more word about how I'm supposed to be some kind of slavery apologist...

Adhus-Barin also glares at them. Is he waiting for Miran Anyuwe to incriminate themselves?

The politician continues, shifting pace as if realizing they are no longer talking to their home crowd. "As you are no doubt aware, the Isolationists oppose our negotiations to join the Alliance, negotiations that I am leading..." They pause, uncertain for a moment. "Between two rounds of talks, I returned to Ohandar, where I was summarily attacked, and after my attempted escape, even my security detail deserted me at Idhir Station, so I had to seek out a private vessel for help..."

"Your security detail betrayed you?" Adhus-Barin turns oddly mild, almost gentle. I don't have to pry into his thoughts to sense a trap being readied.

"They were all Isolationists, they turned against me—" Voice rising. Miran Anyuwe is losing their cool.

"Oh, those kinds of roughshod mercenaries don't appreciate going unpaid," Adhus-Barin nods with empathy.

"What could I have *done*? The talks were almost over and the funds—" They halt midsentence.

I stare. At Adhus-Barin smiling, his thin mouth turning up in almost a sneer, at Miran Anyuwe standing statue-still, with only stray tremors breaking through their rigidity.

The security detail going unpaid. Isolationists going unpaid.

"Thank you," Adhus-Barin says, "I do believe this will be enough."

As if a dam breaking through, Miran Anyuwe starts blabbering, words tumbling over each other. The statue falling apart. "The Alliance has to understand, the Alliance knows—isolationist sentiment has always been strong on Ohandar, we had to show the populace that isolationism was extremism, we had to—"

"So you backed the Isolationist movement, steered them into violence," Adhus-Barin says, one step away from gloating. "Created and funded your own rivals, so that you could point a finger at them and say, *we are not like those people.* So that you could revel in the position of the peacemaker."

"The Alliance knows! Don't deny it! The Alliance knows!"

"May I?" the Ereni says, then waits for the captain's nod. "The Alliance knows. That doesn't mean the Alliance assents."

"Exactly as Officer Enisāyun has it," the captain nods at them again. "Undesirable allies often incriminate themselves during the accession process, as we have found." He says it as if the Empire was innocent of all possible wrongdoing, and I wonder if Miran Anyuwe knows how the Alliance had taken its present shape, what had prompted the member states to create Treaty Enforcement, back it with real power and threat. I sneak a look at Enisāyun, and the Ereni glances back at me, shrugs.

Miran Anyuwe mutters word-fragments, all sense lost in overwhelming anger, directed at us who thwarted the plan. We all gaze upon the spectacle. I pull my personal wards tighter around myself in case Miran Anyuwe lashes out.

Officer Enisāyun asks to speak again, then gestures toward me. "The esteemed leader might wish to thank the young māwalēni here for saving their life."

Adhus-Barin makes a face. The meaning is clear—he would rather the politician would have perished, murdered by their own erstwhile allies. Let alone called *esteemed leader*, but then again the Ereni are fond of formality... and its ironic flipside.

Enisāyun smiles softly. "We will make sure that the young māwalēni receives all due payment for services rendered—

though from whom might be uncertain at this point..."
Miran Anyuwe collapses.

"It wasn't me," Enisāyun says, voice shaky. "Captain? It wasn't
me, Captain."

"I thought they were warded from all outside–" A voice from the
back of the Alliance crowd, then another, "I warded them!"

A door seal hisses, and my master dashes in, the familiar clang
of boots on ship-metal. "Were they threatening anyone? I felt they
might be threatening someone, so it seemed safer to shut them
down."

"Excuse me?" Adhus-Barin seems utterly lost. *It's that kind of day,*
the Ereni thinks at me and I suppress a chuckle.

"I have a policy of not interfering with clients' minds, but they
severely disrupted my ship, interrupted the jumping procedure–"

Officer Enisāyun is shocked in the back of my mind.

"–so I thought it would be safest to plant my safeguards on them
just in case. They had no defenses to speak of."

An understatement, recognized by everyone present as such.
When did my master have time to do this? I consider the events of
the day, fail to find the exact moment. An intervention performed
off-hand, with a stray thought...

As Adhus-Barin regains his calm and goes through the motions
of the cleanup, organizing transport for Miran Anyuwe to Alliance
Central where they will no doubt have to endure another round of
castigation before getting booted out of Alliance space, my attention
is elsewhere. *I knew my master was more powerful,* I tell myself, but I
understand at the same time that it's not about power—or, rather,
that power entails more than raw control. It entails being straight-
forward, honest, upright.

And I know that between the two of us, we don't need a planet.

Master Sanre offers me a hand and I stand up—then they grab
me, hold me tight to themselves, their tears trickling down my curls.

Spirit Forms of the Sea

I.

The newcomer strides across our camp. I see people halt for a moment, sensing the power, and turn their heads. He flaunts the strength within him, spreading it across the tops of the yurts, making a cold wind blow.

Hajna is the first to snicker. She smooths her hair back and chuckles, not even noticing she'd just smeared her head with flour. A spectacle is brewing. I step into the shade—I cannot share in the general cheer.

The stranger walks up to the chief's tent and declares he's come to fight our táltos. The chief's guards pass a glance between them and I know they are struggling to hold back a laugh. Declarations like this never fail to amuse.

At least the newcomer has the forthrightness to declare a fight. There are those who sneak around, attack our horses, attempt to weaken our livestock. These days, Réka notices them before we do. Sometimes, we even miss the beginning of a battle and have to come running.

The guards do not even bother to lift the flap and ask for approval from the chief; one of them simply walks away to find Réka. The stranger is beginning to realize something's wrong. He shifts his weight from one leg to another, looking orphaned without a horse. The cold wind dissipates.

People gather around the space before the chief's tent, silently, nodding to each other. This is their regular entertainment now, more exciting than the wrestling matches, more frequent than the annual köböre. Everyone thinks our táltos is easily bested because Réka is so young, but the spirits choose whom they choose, whenever they please.

I think that in a few years, people will wise up; word will spread. For now, we watch. I watch, too, though for entirely different reasons than most of the crowd. I hope the shade hides my face.

Réka steps forward from between two tents. She looks dazed and one of her braids is partly undone; the guard must've found her asleep.

She frowns at the stranger and her eyes narrow even further in the morning sunlight.

He smiles at her the way he would smile at one of his younger sisters, or even one of his own children. My stomach turns. Then he lets loose his spirit form and it ascends to the sky, a majestic white horse not matching his pedestrian self.

Horse forms are very common, but he seems to be good at guiding his, making the horse gallop around the sky, bringing in storm clouds and distant thunder. It's almost as if night has returned once again. Réka watches without much emotion.

This one seems to be good at the rules, at least. Parading around his form in the right way, for the right amount of time. Réka nods, just barely, her face grim—most of the other onlookers probably fail to notice this. They aren't close to her. More importantly, they weren't there to see what I saw barely a few seasons ago...

II.

"Oh!" Her eyes grew large. She ran up to me and hugged me fiercely. "Delin! I'm so glad it's you!"

I felt slightly embarrassed as I hugged her back and shared in her happiness. "Chief Ajtony picked me, is all."

She pushed herself out to arm's length and beamed at me, so much like a child. "Dad promised me he'd pick the best! I'm so happy!"

I nodded and liberated myself from her embrace. "Well, then, let's start packing." I never liked it when people praised me for my martial prowess, even though I knew that most seasoned warriors struggled to match my feats. Maybe it was just a dislike of praise—I never liked when people complimented me on my thick braids or my raven-black eyes, either.

Réka danced around as she gathered her items. I sat by the entrance of their yurt, barely inside—the place of a stranger. Her father sat in his seat and eyed us dispassionately all the while. He only spoke when Réka finished.

"Delin, I trust you'll take good care of her."

I wouldn't dare to do otherwise, I thought, but remained silent and only bowed my head.

Farkas the elder táltos came up to me just as I parted from Réka, heading out to say goodbye to her mother and her younger brothers. He sneaked up to me. Even with my keen hearing, I hadn't heard him move—I shuddered when he spoke up right by my left ear. He always enjoyed doing this, showing how far the spirits' power extended, demonstrating that with their aid, he could hide in plain sight.

"The spirits have called out to her, but something's still missing. No one's claimed her as their own and she still doesn't have a spirit form. She knows, but it's best you don't raise the issue with her," Farkas said.

I nodded. Chief Ajtony had already explained the situation to me.

"My friend at the farthest reaches of the world might know what to do. Don't forget to tell him I sent you." He looked around, grinned at me, then added, "And bring back a bag of seashells—you know, for decoration."

I wasn't really sure what seashells were, but I trusted him that they weren't overly heavy.

We rode along the western border region, all the way down south. After a while, we left our tribal settlements and reached the land of the Croats—a decent folk with a language entirely impenetrable to most of us. I belatedly realized that the reason Ajtony chose me was probably not because of my skill at horse archery—though that must have played a part, too—but my knowledge of the language. I used to fight Croats at the borderlands, but the area was peaceful now and we could find lodgings with ease. We even made our way through the rocky mountains without any issues, but the sea only appeared in front of us after the very last turns.

"This isn't the end of the world," Réka pouted, looking at the small town from afar. "It's not even Venice."

I wanted to slap her. "This is as far as our influence extends." Hardly much influence, at that. Just a network of friendships. Would our might ever grow so strong as to reach here, invade these lands?" I thought invasions distasteful, but many did not share my opinions. And what was wrong with not being Venice, anyway? Venice was our enemy!

She must've been aware of my thoughts the way her kind often are, because she sighed softly and apologized.

We rode into the city and found an inn, took care of our horses. People were talking about the tax the Venetians had recently imposed, the Istrian pirates haranguing fishermen, and the boxes of odd-looking, but sweet-tasting, fruit that traders had brought in from afar and were selling at the market for what was unanimously deemed an exorbitant price.

When we'd passed through Croat country, the land changed ever so slowly, but here by the coast, everything had abruptly become different—new sights, new smells and tastes. Even the air felt unusual. We were out of our element here, land-dwellers, horse people. Some of the peasants who had come into town to sell their produce stared at us, marked by our unfamiliar clothing, our Eastern features… but no one outright glared. The borderlands weren't close enough for open animosity to surface here and I was relieved I wouldn't have to use the dagger in my belt.

There was only one problem: I had no idea how to find the táltos Jutos, friend of Farkas. I was sure he'd stand out in any local crowd, and yet, no one seemed to have heard of him. I'd inquired after him at the inn, at the market stalls. I even asked a city official. After our second round of tries at the market, Réka pulled me aside and said, "Maybe he doesn't want to be found."

"Can that be done?" In a place where you are a stranger, your difference obvious at first sight?

"Sure," Réka nodded. "It's one of the more common arts."

I sighed. "Then we're lost. Farkas didn't tell me anything about how to find him."

Réka frowned, concentration on her still-childlike face. "Maybe… he only wants the right kind of people to find him?" I was about to interrupt her and ask whom that might be, and whether we qualified, but she lifted one hand. "Psst! I think I can—"

She fell silent and moved around her hand. Was this the method they used for finding lost objects, livestock that had wandered off? Could that method be used to locate a person—not just any person but an experienced táltos who might not want to be found?

Found by the right kind of people… It suddenly made sense to me.

Réka broke into a fast-paced walk, not a run outright but close. She kept on frowning, her right hand palm up in front of her. We walked past the large well of the marketplace and she stopped for a moment, stared at a fish stand selling octopus—or squid? I wasn't sure—shook her head, and moved on. We turned this way and that, away from the sea. She came to a sudden halt, closed her eyes, moved her hand around, then set off again, nodding.

She stopped in front of a small, crooked door in a side alley, hesitating. I reached over her shoulder and knocked.

A stout, long-mustached man opened the door right away. "Well met, well met," he nodded at us without smiling. "Do come in. I've been waiting for you."

It was one of their arts, I understood. When this man said he'd been expecting us, he was telling the truth. He closed the door behind us and switched to Magyar without any prompting. "I'm Jutos son of Bulcsú. And you are…?"

I got the impression he knew exactly who we were, but I explained it to him, nonetheless. Réka fidgeted on a creaky wooden stool while I paced the room. Jutos was looking increasingly gloomy.

"I have little to offer you," he finally said. "But there is much crossing these ports from far-off lands and many discoveries to be made. Perhaps the spirits will give a sign."

Meaning the spirits hadn't yet given a sign. I nodded, a sour taste in my mouth that felt similar to the salt in the air.

Jutos sent us away with a bundle of food, the flavors of home; he couldn't bring himself to apologize in words for the lack of advice.

III.

I listened to the rumors, hoping they would be telling. I shared the day's harvest with Réka as I would a basket of fruit. The pirate ship marooned off the coast. The noble ladies from Venice visiting the town on a frivolous outing. The official making off with a chest full of gold, in broad daylight.

Nothing.

"Everything tastes of olives," Réka complained.

We were sitting by the seaside, looking at the gently lapping waves tinted orange by the setting sun.

"I like the taste of olives," I said and shrugged.

She huffed. Her further complaints remained unspoken.

"It's because they cook with olive oil," I added after a while. I had complaints of my own. However amicable I tried to be with her, the fact still remained that I was her guardian here, more than twice her age and a warrior of many battles. Her mother instead of her own back home. Our funds were running out and the only thing that had occurred to me as a solution was to rent myself out as a sword for hire. Or, preferably, a bow.

After another long silence, I decided I might as well break the news to her.

She nodded. "I expected as much. I'm sorry."

She didn't say, *We should return to our land.* Oddly enough, at that point, it felt like a good sign—perhaps the spirits were finally compelling her to do something about her predicament. What good was a táltos without a spirit form?

I nodded gravely. I had little idea the spirits were compelling her to do something else altogether.

"I'll go with you," she said.

I gasped. "You what?"

"I, I—" She stammered. I'd never before heard her stammer. "I can make myself useful. I can ride a horse. I'm good with bow and arrow. I have táltos blood..."

"And no spirit form," I mentioned with forced nonchalance.

She was close to tears. "I'm working on it, all right? But I can't respond to a call if there is none!"

"I can't take you with me. I'm supposed to guard you!"

She stood, trembling. "That's exactly why you need to take me with you! You can't just leave me alone!"

"I can leave you with Jutos." That wasn't a real offer; Jutos hadn't seemed like the kind of man able to take good care of her. Morose, occasionally hostile... Nothing like the friendly coastal Croats.

"You're not going to do that."

I also stood. "No, I'm not. And I can hardly leave you with a stranger."

"I can fight, I can—"

"Have you ever been on a ship?"

Her face told me all I needed to know. I sighed. "Maybe we can find a job on land…"

Réka whispered to me in Magyar. "But Delin, he thinks we're all going to die!"

"Very promising," I whispered back, grinning.

"But *Delin!*"

"Sshh."

The man was standing on top of an upturned wine-barrel, giving his recruiting speech. Finally, a warrior's job on land! I didn't want to tell Réka that I was made just as uncomfortable by the thought of serving on a ship as she herself had been.

A nearby harbor was haunted by a monster of confusing and contradictory description. It apparently had tentacles, claws, wings—all manner of monsterly paraphernalia. It sounded like an octopus crossed with the dragon of Western lore. Or was that a squid?

The dragon-octopus sounded imaginary, but Réka had said the man was sure we'd be killed. I signed us up, despite her protestations, finally quelling her with: "We don't *need* to come back to the gathering tomorrow if you want out."

Long, thin clouds striped the evening sky. Réka kicked at a rock, played with it. She tried to hide her anxiety, but I'd seen scores of people before a decisive battle and knew better.

"Do you think it's a real monster?" I asked. "It sounds like something conjured by an enterprising táltos."

"It's hard to hold a form that doesn't exist in nature," Réka said, not looking up from the rock.

"Maybe that's why it sounded confusing." I shrugged. "Or maybe it's just that I don't speak the language that well."

"If the táltos is not bound to the spirit, it's hard to hold even the shape of a real animal," she said. "And I don't think it's a real animal, from what you're saying."

"For all I know about sea animals, it could well be one!"

"Then why was the man so afraid? Surely, they know what lives in their seas," Réka retorted. I had to acknowledge she was right. She was sharp, quick-witted—she'd make for a great táltos to succeed the elderly Farkas. If only we could…

I shrugged, banishing the despair. "We're going to fight it, either way."

She turned around, peered up at me. "You're not going to change your mind, right?"

I shook my head. Combat was what I did best.

"Care for a round of practice shooting before the sun sets?" I asked and began to walk away from the sea without looking back.

IV.

There were about a dozen of us, mostly swordfighters. Réka and I were instructed to stay back. The single remaining eyewitness had told us the monster would rear up when assaulted and that it had many large eyes, clear spots of vulnerability. Of course, the eyewitness had also said it had flimsy wings and that sounded blatantly wrong—what use would a sea animal have for wings?

In any case, I hoped we'd be able to aim our arrows at the eyes, blind the hostile creature to help the swordfighters cut it down. I was relieved we'd be able to stay out of trouble for the most part—what would Chief Ajtony say if I lost his eldest daughter, the future táltos of the settlement?

I resolved to guard her with my own body if need be, but I knew she could hold her own—the previous evening she'd demonstrated to me that she indeed had skill with the bow. I only had to take care she wouldn't panic at the most inopportune moment.

"I cheated," she told me out of the blue.

"Eh?" I glanced up—she was sitting across from me in the open carriage.

"The arrows. I made them hit." She bit her lower lip. "I can't aim worth a farthing."

"What do you mean you made them hit?" I was confused.

"With..." She made a vague gesture. "You know."

Ah. I understood. "Look, I don't care if the spirits help you hit the target, or your táltos blood, or your skill at handling the bow. As long as it hits."

She looked dubious.

"Trust me, I've fought many battles. What matters is not how you fought, but whether you won and won with honor."

I wasn't really sure how honor came into the picture when assaulting some sort of oversize sea animal, so I said nothing further. Réka was also silent.

The carriage rolled on, shaking and noisy. We'd have to walk the last mile of the way to be able to strike with an element of surprise and I wasn't looking forward to it—the air was growing unspeakably hot. I wished I had lighter clothing—we didn't expect arrows to rain down on *us*, after all.

The two carriages halted and we clambered down. The drivers looked anxious, eager to get away from the harbor, even though it was still beyond an arrow's shooting distance. The sea was calm.

Réka hissed and clutched at her stomach.

"What is it?" I turned to her and whispered.

She straightened up, pain in her eyes for a moment. "I—I think I've heard it," she whispered back.

"The monster?" I looked back at the harbor.

"The call!" Her voice was insistent. "The spirits—"

"Just save it until after the battle, all right? We'd best not get distracted."

I turned back to her and she nodded, acquiescing. She could be obedient if the need arose. If she wasn't scared away by her first battle, then—who knew?—she could even become a good warrior. Not only a táltos who fought using a spirit form but also an archer in her own right. It all hinged on the first impressions...

Our leader signaled and we sneaked closer and closer to the harbor, using whatever meager cover we could find. We had to attack in broad daylight because the man who'd hired us claimed the monster gained in strength and size after nightfall.

The two swordfighters at point had almost reached the sea when the surface moved, bulged. A round, flat head rose above the water line, its skin a shiny dark green.

What emerged didn't look like a spirit form; it looked like a real animal. But I could feel the power emanating from it, hitting me in the gut, hurting. I understood Réka's hiss—she'd simply experienced it earlier, being much more sensitive to the spirits.

I reached into my tegez and readied my first set of arrows for quick-draw.

It opened its eyes.

My hand froze mid-motion. It saw into me—right into me—and I knew it wasn't an animal, not in the ordinary sense. Not like the wind-horse, either, majestic but ultimately connected to the human soul. It was akin to the turul bird, the ancestor of all Magyars, a vast, strong and carnivorous spirit.

And it walked this earth, swam in the sea.

Who were its people? Whom did it claim for itself?

No one was moving. It seemed to me that no one was breathing. It was as if the water in the sea had stopped flowing. The monster rose and I knew with a cold certainty that was beyond even fear that it wanted to feed.

Tell them to stop, Réka's voice whispered in my head.

My mouth opened almost unbidden. "Stop! Don't move! Don't attack!" I didn't know the proper way military commands were phrased in Croatian, but my words had an immediate effect.

Or maybe no one could move either way.

I'd like to think I made a little change.

Réka walked forward among us, a collection of fleshy statues. "You have awoken?" she said, a statement with the tones of a question. Then, "You've slept for a long, long time." As if talking to a child.

It towered above us, blocking the sun, and our heads followed it until our necks bent all the way back. My lungs burned.

"Here I am," she said to the creature. "You called." I wanted to scream at her, drag her away.

Protect her with my body.

There were promises, convictions stronger than the sea. My legs moved. My neck snapped forward, muscles smarting from the sudden motion. I wanted to shout, but my larynx felt stopped up and my tongue numb. Every step was a battle against unimaginable force, the world itself pushing me back.

Réka stopped, turned back to look at me in amazement. "Allow me," she said, her voice apologetic. "Please. I was called."

I gasped for air, the pressure easing up a little—probably because I'd stopped straining forward.

"It called me," she said. "It wants to bind me to itself."

This? This monstrosity? I didn't even dare to utter the words, because I knew even the smallest expression of my fear would nourish its hunger. Finally, I managed, "It wants to eat you."

It sounded so pedestrian. So mundane.

She pursed her lips. "All spirits want to eat us. The táltos is someone who has enough strength to feed them."

I didn't want to hear this. I was helpless against it.

"I brought you here to help you. To protect you." My throat tightened—this time, not from the mysterious force but from the emotion swirling inside my body.

She spread her hands. I stared at her in the shadow of the giant. Her braids had become undone and her face was so open, so vulnerable—and yet, no longer childlike.

"I vowed myself to this," she said. "I was born for this, chosen for this."

Why was our way so cruel? We offered up our own young… Why had I never seen this before?

"Only those see who need to see," Réka murmured and it was as if a veil lifted from my eyes.

People talked of the spirits cutting the táltos apart, putting the body together as they saw fit. How figurative was that? How literal?

But most spirit forms were of peaceable animals. The horse, the bull might seem intimidating, but everyone knows they eat grass, not flesh. No one offered themselves to the turul, a bird of prey—no one, save for someone in a half-forgotten, ancient legend… It only led us, as an all-powerful figurehead, a creature of the sky that had come to us from the stars.

Then why would she offer herself to this monster? Trust it with her soul?

She shook her head. "Trust is unimportant. I need to sate its hunger, if only for the smallest moment."

And future moments, again and again, it rippled through the sky. I fell to my knees. Did that come from her? The creature was so vast I felt it was beyond our earthly cares, outside our world, even as it swam in its waters and trod its soil.

"Don't blame yourself," she said. "*I* was the one who stopped you."

She turned around and walked into the sea. I could only watch, helpless. The water was to her thighs when it started and I more felt than heard the first crunch of bone breaking, resonating through the earth itself, invading me through my knees, my legs touching the ground. Then she fell face forward into the water, ever so slowly, and the sea muffled the sounds altogether, drank up the blood.

The men had left, staggering away in twos and threes, making their way back to the town on foot even in the sweltering heat. I stayed.

The monster did not acknowledge me. I knew it was busy digesting. Did it eat the flesh? Did it eat the soul? What need did it have for such a small body and a mind it could easily eclipse? Did it want a servant on land, someone who could spread its fear, provide nourishment at every step? Or did it have motives entirely incomprehensible to us?

What was the endpoint?

When the creature allowed me to stand, I stood. I paced. I railed at it. I begged it to give her back to me. I shouted and swore. I yelled for the turul to appear and bring down its wrath from the skies, but the turul never appeared. Maybe I wasn't strong enough. Maybe it was intimidated. Overpowered. I shuddered to think. Still, I screamed.

I'd like to think I made a change. I know it's probably not true.

Finally, the monster left, submerging itself in the clear seawater, too shallow for such a giant. Making its way for deeper regions.

As it vanished from my sight, the water washed her ashore. Unbroken, if only in shape.

She sat up slowly, gingerly, and we walked back to the town in silence. Prepared ourselves for the long trip ahead. Her words came halting, hesitating, but, even still, with newfound maturity.

We ended up staying for a week, getting ready ever so slowly, with regret. The creature did not return to the harbor and the man who hired us showered us with wealth. Among our gifts for the people back home, I bought some choice seashells from enterprising children.

The challengers started showing up soon after we'd arrived in our camp, drawn by the youth of our new táltos.

V.

I shake my head slowly.

Réka steps forward and the crowd murmurs before quieting again. She is among her folk here, but she doesn't draw on our strengths the way it is customarily done. She discards the advantage.

I could never be a táltos, but even I can feel the way the stranger's stomach contracts, the way his fear engulfs him—just for a moment. Réka disregards this. She always plays by the rules and it is not yet time to attack.

She looks to the distance, over and above the clouds, but reaches *down*, into the depths.

The creature rises and had I not seen it with my own eyes on that day by the seashore, I'd assume it to be unreal, a figment of the imagination as easily dissolved as the clouds, as ephemeral.

The monstrous shape holds. Tentacles twist around, eyes move to survey the land. Sacs bulge and deflate.

The stranger is breathing fast, a hoarse, wheezing sound almost like the whinnying of a horse. His spirit form tries to gallop away, but in an instant, the sea-creature is upon it, tentacles whipping, claws ripping into ghostly flesh.

Dark blood streaks the sky. The sea-creature triumphs, even faster than the previous time; it changes shape, unfolds gooey wings semi-transparent against the sunlight reemerging through clouds. It gloats, sitting atop the disemboweled carcass of the horse, head tentacles rippling in a soft motion. Does it smile at us?

Then it vanishes and only the stranger is left, lying in his own vomit, his trousers wet. Réka sits down, shaking, and someone puts a warm, thick guba across her shoulders. She pulls it close to herself and closes her eyes.

I don't think she's upset. The man will live, though he probably won't fight anyone ever again. It's only that calling up such an unusual spirit form takes a lot out of her and she looks exhausted. It's only that, nothing more. At least, so I tell myself.

All Talk of Common Sense

I've seen many like him: the brooding wizard with the hypnotic eyes, the smoothly intimidating demeanor, the tiny goatee. Marekas tosses out his personal myth like birdseed by the handful, and people come to peck like pigeons. It all works out: the crowd is thick around him, the newcomer, and as he shifts his weight from one leg to another, his fingers pinch his robe just so and flick, the small flourishes looking almost magical.

I can say anything. I choose not to speak.

King Abrany is already charmed, but what can I expect? I grimace, rub my palms on the bright patchwork of my clothing.

"For a court jester, you look awfully gloomy," King Abrany whispers to me and licks greasy lips with a quick flicker, almost touching my earlobe. "Maybe I'll give your place to my new court mage."

I know he can't let me go, but I'm still hurt. Court Mage Marekas seems ideally suited to any situation, shifting as the moment demands; whereas I can only play the fool.

I get up, leaving the king to his lamb shanks. I wander around the hall, directing my attention inward. I want to take a closer look at this Marekas and his magic—the crowd is dense and I can't quite distinguish between the conflicting impressions. I draw in a breath and reach down, pulling power from the earth. Then I focus outward—

I stagger as if slapped. My left foot slides out as I lose my balance. The nobles around me laugh, thinking it's an act.

The court mage is there in an instant, catching me midair, and as I stare into his face, I can confirm my initial, shocking assessment.

He has no magic. At least no more than any person does.

I mutter something, push away from him and into the throng. What should I do? Challenge him to a magical duel? The king himself has more magic than this stranger! Will King Abrany notice? Will he notice that *I* noticed? My head hurts. I can make fun of foreign policy all day long, but this is too complicated for me.

Why do I care? Abrany rules his kingdom with so little grace and so much brute force that I keep on plotting one day I will throw up on his regal robes. Sadly, I'm not good at crude humor, nor at vomiting on command. I can't stand him, so it will happen spontaneously one day. I sadly missed the time when he tried to stop a flood with the strength of his personality—I was recovering from food poisoning –, but the court still speaks of him posing on the floodbanks.

I can take my pick from Abrany and Marekas. I throw myself down in an empty chair, stare at gnawed shankbones. It should be easy to choose—Abrany is the one who could have me executed. Or could he? I know he fears my magic—he senses enough to be intimidated, and it is only my oddness that keeps on saving me from his wrath. If I had a shred of common sense... Alas. Then I wouldn't be court jester.

I sit, drumming on the table—the repeating motion calms me. I could expose Marekas. But I respect him, somehow—it takes extraordinary deception to rise to this position while not having any magic. I'm always on the lookout for someone who could depose King Abrany, I admit—and you can't accuse me of lèse-majesté because subversion is in my job description. His court is stuffed with jesters without the title, fools who imagine themselves to be wise. But maybe this newcomer...

"Bihan?" Marekas looks into my eyes from across the table. "Can we talk?"

I turn my head aside to avoid his gaze. "Outside."

"I know you know," Marekas says. Not this again! Making my head hurt. I step to the balustrade, glance at the river below. He stands next to me, without forcing his presence upon me. "But there's something you don't understand yet," he says.

He waves fingers in front of me and a ribbon unfolds, vanishes. All sleight of hand, of course, but very convincing. And the color   it grabs at my heart.

"Crimson Army?" I whisper. Soldiers of our most hated neighbor, our great rival. Marekas says nothing—but of course, I berate myself, what did I expect? I try again. "What do you want?"

"Just to watch. To listen. To push a little, see how far I can go."

Not so different from my vocation, I think. Still, a genuine traitor. Though King Abrany is perhaps the greatest traitor of all—wasting so much effort on the ever-smoldering war, while in the backcountry there are barely enough mages left to stop a spring flood. If I had more common sense... If I had, I would be first in line to the slaughter.

I laugh and he twitches, caught off-guard. He ventures, "I know about your magic."

"So? Everyone knows about it. And also my addled head," I add drily. Am I bitter? Yes, somewhat. They would never make *me* into Court Mage.

He sizes me up. "Would you like to be next in line?"

I'm confused. "To?"

"My position."

What is he talking about? I know. I can't fool myself. "When you get to be king?" He has it in himself.

"You have it in yourself," he says and for a moment I can hardly believe he's not aware of my thoughts.

"I will not expose you just now," I say. "I can't offer more."

He frowns. "You could offer a little of your magic..."

"You don't need it." And I think: I will need it, to survive you just as I survived King Abrany and his predecessor. But I keep my mouth shut. I watch moonlight glint on the water down below. I consider that despite what the Court thinks, I am no fool.

Standing on the Floodbanks

To R, who made it possible

I.

The Battlefield

Aniyé staggered, the impossible landscape of corpses and detritus swaying around her, bending over her. Pushing her down. All around her, the proud crimson uniforms were stamped into the soil, stained with blood and clumps of gore. She tried to breathe, tried to hold on, moving forward in a wobbly line, towards an unknown point in the distance—away from the battlefield.

Her handlers were gone. She trailed crimson leashes, ties that no longer bound. A good length of chain clanked behind her as she dragged herself forward. Her white ceremonial garments were smeared with dirt.

Emptiness echoed in her head. Her handlers were gone, and with them, the only way to dam the tide of the white-hot merciless magic, the power that seared land and sky—She gasped, trying to contain what could not be contained. She fell to her knees, clutching her abdomen. There was a fire inside her, an ever-mounting pressure as the magic pushed against her skin, threatening to tear her open at any moment, and yet she could not let go—her body would not allow her, with reactions deeply ingrained by thousands of hours of training.

She knew she would die, and she knew she had failed. The battle was lost, even though she had done all that she could, bringing retribution down from the heavens, striking the Empire's enemies. Remnants of that anger still shivered in her, looking for a target in this desert of rigid flesh, finding no purchase.

The other four battle-mages were all dead, and without her handlers, she wouldn't last long either. She was on the verge of giving in. *Drop to the ground. Release the magic. Release the self. Be gone.* She didn't even want to move on to the next world in the cycle of life, she just wanted to cease, a candle snuffed out by a streak of cold air, so refreshingly cold...

She felt clumps against her face. When had she fallen, toppled over like an inert marionette? Her strings had been cut. A shudder ran through her. No bindings, no constraints—pure raw fear—the magic rushed forward and up, always up—

She closed her eyes to get away from the devastating sunlight. She felt a gentle touch on her cheek. Her muscles contracted and she tried to jerk away, an instinctive response to touch—

"You're still alive," a full, deep voice said; a woman's voice bringing to mind the coos of turtledoves. "I am with you."

She opened her eyes just a crack and saw boots stained with dust but no body fluids, their leather a warm orange-brown color with no traces of crimson.

The enemy.

"Do you want me to help you?" the stranger asked, and before Aniyé could respond, the unconsciousness of utter exhaustion claimed her.

The Guild

"...our agreement." Again the stranger's voice. Aniyé was surfacing from the bottomless dark.

"You can't seriously—!" A man this time, his voice edged with faint raspiness.

"The Guild promised me an apprentice years ago. To this date it has failed to deliver."

Aniyé stirred. A hand on her shoulder gently pushed her back down. She opened her eyes just a little, but she could not see much beyond the smooth chest and abdomen of a black-clad figure. A sudden warning sounded in her mind and she squeezed her eyes shut, then tried to relax, pretend to be unconscious. *Good.* The stranger's thoughts, reaching out to her mind?

Aniyé had trouble keeping track of what was happening around her; she missed a sentence or two. Yet, she started to be more attuned to their emotions as she regained consciousness.

"...you are yet young."

A sigh. "Guildsman Leitan. I am older than the dirt of this land, and if my face is yet unlined, that's only because the magic does not let me go until my task is complete."

The man—Guildsman Leitan?—sputtered, mumbling something inarticulate.

Aniyé tried to concentrate on herself instead of the conversation. Her body ached. There was a huge knot in her abdomen and her skin flared with irritation. The power still hadn't given her pause, and as she became increasingly awake, so the pain increased. She changed her mind: better to focus on the conversation again. She wished she could curl up into a ball, but that would alert this man, and he might try to hurt her...

Was the woman losing her patience? "...*know* that the Guild has directly caused Nairul's death, and has *not* provided me an apprentice ever since, despite our longstanding agreement."

No, this was an older anger, tinged with sadness. Aniyé struggled to make sense of the emotions.

"We sent several candidates!"

"Wholly unsuitable candidates."

"We didn't *have* better candidates!" Was the man lying? Aniyé wasn't sure. He was protecting his thoughts well, and she didn't dare push. She was happy she'd thus far evaded his notice.

279

"I have a candidate now, and the Guild is trying to take her off my hands. Isn't that what's happening?"

"Fine, fine!" A rustle of cloth; he must've made a broad gesture. "I just want you to know, High Mage, that *I* will have to answer for this to the King's courtiers—I will be the one who has to explain, and they will want *my* blood for this, not yours!"

Exasperation. "No one will want your blood, Guildsman Leitan. The King is more than aware that the Guild would not be able to handle her, were I to turn her over." *You haven't even produced a suitable apprentice.* The woman thought so loudly at Guildsman Leitan that Aniyé had no difficulty picking it up even in her present state. "Leaving her with me is in your best interests. And that's before you even consider what happens when the Crimson Army tries to retrieve her."

"You mean they'd mount an assault?" The man's breath hissed. "So far behind the front lines?"

"I imagine they would want to reclaim one of their more powerful battle mages, yes. Especially after today's losses."

Fear shot through Aniyé, her mind scrambling to catch up. The Crimson Army would come for her—but if they were her own people, why did that scare her so? She knew the answer all too well, and she tried to rein in the galloping horses of her thoughts with a desperation akin to—

"Hush," the man said. "She's awake."

"All the more reason for allowing me to work in quiet, undisturbed."

"Well then, High Mage Oresuy—I shall bid my leave."

Aniyé opened her eyes just in time to see the man's withdrawing back. He was tall, pale, black-haired, with a strong, tough build. She shuddered involuntarily.

The High Mage leaned closer to her, cradled Aniyé's aching, stick-rigid limbs in her wide arms. Calm washed through Aniyé's skin where she was touched. This stranger cared for her—but for what reason?

"I will take you home," Oresuy whispered, "my home, with steps faster than the wind, with a stride longer than bridges and roads." Then she lifted Aniyé with ease, covered her eyes with a fold of her robe, and began walking. Around them the air whooshed, and Aniyé thought that maybe—just maybe—she might yet live.

The River

How had they come to this place, this rain-soaked patch of land studded with stout rock fortifications and gentle lacework towers? Where was this garden of willow trees swaying in the soft wind? Aniyé rubbed her forehead, but the haze would not lift.

"I can help you get a hold on your magic." The High Mage was tall and thick, and her robes allowed for ample movement. Her skin was not as oddly pale as the guildsman's, from what little Aniyé had seen of him; she looked more like Aniyé herself, but still clearly of a different people. She held her wooden staff like a weapon, and yet she did not seem to be a soldier. She radiated calm without any trace of agitation. Aniyé could not look at her face.

"I—" Aniyé gasped. She wheezed, her entire self curled upon itself, unable to uncoil. The knot inside her abdomen pulled her close around itself. "I—Please."

A sharp cut in her consciousness. She was crouching in wet grass, her fingers grabbing onto clumps of mud. She was trembling. The magic churned inside her, burning her up, destroying her from the inside, and she had no way to release it—she was alone, the inert bodies of her handlers lying on the plains—

"Am I a prisoner of war?" she asked without looking up.

"You are my student, if you accept my guidance," the stranger said.

Aniyé bowed her head. She didn't even know how to ask. "I will do what you tell me to do." This was familiar, the expectation that she would obey. She would follow the orders and keep on living.

"You need to learn how to control your magic. I will tell you now how to go about it," Oresuy said, with the cadences of a teacher rather than a drill sergeant. "You can do this on your own."

To Aniyé it seemed impossible to do anything on her own. Not when she could hardly walk, when the magic forced all her muscles to tense and her limbs to go rigid. All her life she'd been told that she couldn't do anything like this alone, that's why she needed handlers.

"I will be watching over you, but you can do all this. You slowly walk to the end of the gardens, where they meet the river. Then you walk up the floodbanks and down on the other side, uncover your-self and wade into the water. You need contact on as large a surface as possible. If you can put your head underwater too, that's even better. The water is clear around this time. Then focus on releasing the magic into the water. It will work to an extent even if you don't focus on it, but that helps." She waited a little. "Will you do this?"

High Mage Oresuy had her recount everything step by step before she let Aniyé go.

Aniyé walked. Slowly. She almost slipped down the floodbanks, but managed to regain her balance on one knee—she did soil her clothing with mud. Oresuy did not interfere.

Fear gripped Aniyé. She pushed it down. Undressed. Stepped into the water—almost slipped again.

The water was cool, but gentle against her skin. Calming. Taking from her. She ducked underwater and waited for as long as she could. Her lungs ached. She surfaced, then submerged again. Again. She lost track of time. Again. Was it making any change? She couldn't tell.

After a while, she staggered out to the waterside, shaking in a sudden cold gust of wind. She toppled into the mud, all her energy spent.

Hands reached out to lift her.

The Fire

Aniyé sat in front of a wide, smooth-faced fireplace, her thin body wrapped in a heavy blanket. She couldn't look away from the flames.

She had a thousand questions, now that she was well enough to talk, but she felt she wouldn't be able to deal with the answers. Why had this stranger taken her to her home? Dressed her, fed her warm chicken soup and a sweet potato stew? How could she trust her, when Aniyé couldn't trust her own self?

Aniyé didn't even know how to address her. Aniyé felt she was powerful, but who was she? Maybe a guardian of the land. Someone belonging to this unknown and hostile country; bound to it, perhaps?

High Mage Oresuy sat down, close to her, but not looking at her. Giving her ample room. "I know it's difficult," she said after a long silence. "You may speak. I am listening."

Aniyé looked away from the fire. The red bricks of the fireplace seemed to her as if blood-spattered. A vision—no. A memory. She rubbed at her dry eyes. *Do not think. Just go,* she remembered her instructor saying. She drew her arms around her. When had she become so thin?

"They wouldn't even feed you," Oresuy said, with a startling sadness. Aniyé stared at her—did the High Mage get sad on her behalf? "Would you like a bit more of the stew?"

Aniyé nodded eagerly. She grabbed the bowl she was handed with both hands. Tears filled her eyes that had been so dry just moments ago.

Aniyé couldn't sleep, because with sleep came the dreams, the dreams she was not allowed to have. Bolts of lightning criscrossing the skies. Shouts of anger, then fear. Screams of the dying. Always from a distance, a safe distance… safe to her. Yet she was aware of it all, and the fire that arose from her to smite the enemies burned her the most.

Her stomach heaved. She could barely roll off the bed in time to get to the window. She leaned outside and vomited, violently, as if her insides were leaving her body in large clumps.

The High Mage was next to her, holding her. Once Aniyé was finished, Oresuy led her outside and washed her face in the cold water basin. Then the High Mage dragged one of the heavy chairs into the small room and sat by Aniyé's bedside until she would finally, finally sleep.

II.

The Tower

After twenty-eight days, Aniyé still couldn't help but marvel at her teacher's quarters, on the top floor of the Eyrie.

Aniyé was used to bare walls painted white, the cold geometry restricting without holding, enforcing without understanding. High Mage Oresuy's quarters were paneled in wood from the forests surrounding the walled city, and the surfaces still exuded a warm susurration of wind passing through branches if Aniyé could quieten her mind down to listen. The High Mage's furniture was made by the city's best artisans, sparsely decorated, allowing the beauty of the materials themselves to shine through.

As Aniyé wandered through the rooms inside the majestic lace-work tower, her gaze moved from highlight to highlight, small items each with a history her teacher had been glad to explain to her shortly after she had arrived. A small jug in the shape of an elephant. An etching sent by a friend from the distant, fog-shrouded islands. A herbary that offered many tiny, nose-tickling delights. Aniyé closed her eyes and sighed softly. She was safe here. After so much pain…

Oresuy sat by the fireplace, looking at the unlit slabs of wood in contemplation. She glanced up as Aniyé approached.

"We will have a guest tonight," the High Mage said. "Guildsman Leitan will be joining us; he's been sent back from the front lines." She paused. "He has a different task now."

That black-clad man? What did he want? A chill ran through Aniyé.

"Don't worry," Oresuy said. "We will simply eat dinner and talk. I don't expect the conversation to be very pleasant, but you should remain courteous. Silence is likewise not a bad policy."

Aniyé nodded repeatedly, nervously.

"The Guild could never take you from me. They would not even try. You have nothing to fear in this place." She gestured at one of the other chairs. "Do sit; I'll light the fire."

The flames jumped high, and Aniyé's worries slowly dissolved in the heat.

The Dinner

This was the first time Aniyé saw the Guildsman's face, and it was different from what she'd expected; it was sharp, narrow and pale, an odd match with his strong, wide body. He looked unpleasant, with an expression of semi-permanent disgust already etching itself into his features.

Aniyé hurried to fetch the food—she'd laid the smaller wooden table in the way Oresuy had asked her to do. She reminded herself of the High Mage's urgings not to run, to behave with a modest and understated elegance. Aniyé almost tripped over an open book left on the floor and she gasped, but she did not cry out.

She returned to the dining room with a large tray of steaming chicken drumsticks, soaked in a sweet brownish sauce and decorated with greens. Oresuy had cooked it all herself, saying that she enjoyed experimenting with kitchen magic from time to time. Aniyé had washed vegetables, cut onions, peeled potatoes and hung on her teacher's every word. She carried the tray with the sudden, unexpected pride of knowing her contribution was valued.

Guildsman Leitan smiled slightly, then frowned, as if made uncomfortable by his concession to humanity, his enjoyment of the delicious smell. His mind was warded tight, with a militaristic touch to his magical constructs that was all too familiar to Aniyé.

But wasn't the Guild a civilian organization? *The world is changing,* Oresuy had said.

Aniyé served them, her hands trembling. Oresuy looked up at her from her seat across the Guildsman and smiled encouragingly. Aniyé focused singlemindedly on serving the guest—not splotching his dress blacks with chicken sauce, filling his cup with a mild red wine.

She finished without any mishaps and began to put some food on her own plate, but still she did not dare breathe freely.

Guildsman Leitan stared at her openly and Aniyé lowered her gaze, not knowing how to react. What was amiss?

Oresuy spoke up. "This is my table. I invite to it whomever I please; all who are uncomfortable with this are welcome to leave. Do sit, dear Aniyé."

"It is unseemly to eat with a servant," the Guildsman said.

"My *apprentice*," Oresuy said coolly.

Aniyé looked from one person to the other. What was going on? She was missing subtext. The High Mage knew exactly what was going on, but she didn't.

Guildsman Leitan frowned again, and for a moment Aniyé wondered if Oresuy had sensed his intentions despite all his warding, or if she made an educated guess based on his behavior, her knowledge of him. Both possibilities indicated that it was the High Mage who was in charge of the situation. What was this man doing here? Was he aware that he was not in control?

Aniyé sat, her thoughts whirling. She picked up a drumstick with her napkin, but her hand shook so much that she dropped the food back on her plate, splattering herself. The Guildsman glared at her with open hostility.

"Whatever it is that you are training this one in, it's certainly not table manners," he said to Oresuy, not looking at Aniyé. "Maybe you should just hand her over."

Oresuy's eyes narrowed. Aniyé could tell she had not expected the man would raise the topic so soon and with such inelegant hostility.

"Perhaps you would like to become a target of the Crimson Army yourself?" Oresuy bit into a drumstick, as if chatting idly, but there was an edge to her words.

"They haven't—" Did the Guildsman pale? "They wouldn't—"

"Two attempts at retrieving her this past month."

Aniyé froze. She knew her teacher was telling the truth. How was it possible Aniyé herself hadn't noticed?

Guildsman Leitan cleared his throat, picked at his food. "Still, the Guild would like to come to an agreement with you…"

"Just what is it that you are doing here, Guildsman? So far behind the front lines?"

"I've returned here on orders from the King—"

"I hear your loyalty is impeccable."

He glanced up suddenly, malice glinting in his eyes. "Is *yours*, High Mage Oresuy?"

"I serve the Everlasting Light," Oresuy said. "As does the King, I hear."

The Guildsman murmured something and poked at the greens on his plate. He spent the rest of the evening talking about the latest news around town—the unexpectedly wet weather in the mountains, the price of duck eggs spiking, a wealthy merchant throwing a ball. Aniyé thought he seemed unusually well-informed for someone who'd just returned from war.

The Ribbons

Aniyé looked at the river as she undressed. Water levels seemed to be higher than usual, and increasing. The stream carried small pieces of detritus. She wondered if this was expected; on that dinner last week, the Guildsman had mentioned something about increased rainfall in the mountains. She made a mental note to ask Oresuy about it.

She waded into the water, submerged, emerged. After a few repetitions, she was ready to head outside, the entire process now performed mostly by rote, every morning. After the first two weeks, the magic had stopped hurting; after the second two, she could skip a day once in a while. The process was only different in marginal, incidental details—a bird flying across the river, rain dripping slightly or a broken tree-branch floating downstream. But this time, she noticed something unexpected.

A familiar voice was carried on the breeze from downstream the river, beyond the copse of willows that hid her from view. She halted, submerged as deeply as she could while still observing, fervently hoping her dark hair would look like soggy driftwood from a distance.

Guildsman Leitan was yelling at someone.

Aniyé had a hard time making out the words, and she would not dare try any magic to sharpen her senses, lest it draw attention to her. She understood only fragments.

"...the King... requisition this boat..."

"My living! How..."

"...im*per*ative... absolutely necessary..."

"...feed my family? My children..."

"I *must* inspect..."

The Guildsman was taking a fisherman's boat. Why not just hire the fisherman, if he needed to get somewhere in a hurry? Unless secrecy was desired, Aniyé realized; but he certainly made a lot of noise.

The boat soon glided by, the Guildsman alone and rowing upstream with considerable force. Aniyé remained unnoticed. She only dared to clamber outside after long, long minutes had passed, and her teeth were chattering—with cold or with apprehension, she wasn't sure.

Aniyé made her way up the spiral staircase of her teacher's tower, rubbing her hands and arms. She didn't feel focused enough to use her magic to keep warm. Oresuy stood in an alcove, looking at her with appreciation tinged with faint amusement. Aniyé lowered her gaze and bowed slightly.

"Good morning, my good teacher," she said.

"And good morning likewise to you, my dear Aniyé," Oresuy said, her voice still soft from sleep, but roomy and sonorous. She fell silent.

Aniyé wracked her brain for a worried moment before realizing that she was supposed to offer courtesies and inquire about her teacher's wellbeing. She was still not used to being around people. People who treated her with respect, at least.

"How did my teacher sleep?" she finally offered.

"I slept well, thank you," Oresuy said, walking up to her. "And you, my dear Aniyé? ...Look at me."

Aniyé raised her gaze. Oresuy's curly, earth-colored hair was pinned up rather hastily, and she still hadn't removed her silk night-gown, but she looked at her with no upset, only firmness.

"I likewise slept well," Aniyé offered.

Oresuy didn't respond for three long breaths, then she nodded. "Good. I will ask something of you today. ...Do not look away. It will not be easy, but I don't ask impossibilities of you."

"Yes, teacher." She nodded briefly, her stomach knotting.

"This might be somewhat sudden, but by now you should be ready for it. I didn't intend on doing it today, but something has come up. Today we will head outside the Eyrie and the gardens. We are urgently needed outside."

Aniyé gasped. "Teacher, I can't—My power—My magic—I don't think I can control—" She took a step back and her feet got tangled in the edges of a rug. Oresuy quickly stepped next to her and steadied her.

She couldn't breathe. She couldn't breathe. To go outside. Without the handlers. Outside. Just to go the banks of the Eyrie was intimidating enough, especially after today's chance encounter; but at least she was slowly getting used to it. Outside, into the city—that was unthinkable. Outside.

Her handlers were dead, the three officers clad in uniforms that shone in the sun in their powerful crimson shades, officers with crimson leashes in their hands—they were dead, the leashes torn, and Aniyé was alone, alone on the plains, surrounded by death, her magic spiraling out of control—

"I'm here. Aniyé!" A commanding tone. "Focus on me. I will regulate your breath."

She felt nothing except the firm pressure around her—High Mage Oresuy holding her body, hugging her close to herself.

Then she noticed she had been crying, her face wet with tears and snot, smearing her teacher's silk robes.

"Again, this is not what I had originally had in mind," Oresuy said, "but now I think this might work better. Undress, please. You can leave your breeches on."

Aniyé was used to Oresuy seeing her naked, touching her body to massage out the gobs of pain, the residue of harm inflicted on her by others and also by herself. She was trembling simply because she was still greatly agitated.

Her teacher put her wide, broad palms on her shoulders and Aniyé could feel a warm, steady calmness seeping through her skin. After a few moments, Oresuy withdrew and stepped to one of her storage-chests, pulled out a small bundle.

"The effectiveness comes from your understanding, not from the words themselves," Oresuy said as she unwrapped the bundle and showed her the wide red ribbons embroidered with yellow thread. Letters in a calm, orderly succession; words, sentences. Aniyé could not read them—they were in an unfamiliar alphabet.

"Feeling them against your body will be comforting," Oresuy went on. "You understand with your mind that I can provide you with the restriction you need, but your body needs to understand this too. I do think this will help."

She tied the ribbons on Aniyé's bare skin in complicated patterns, with well-practiced motions. Aniyé gasped—they were surprisingly heavy. They were surprisingly comforting.

"The ones I'm putting under your clothing won't restrict your movement. ...Good. You can dress now."

Aniyé dressed and noticed with a startle that her hands were no longer shaking as she picked out the clothing items from her own storage-chest. Loose, sea-blue pants, a matching tunic edged with a lighter shade of blue, like a cloudy sky...

"Do wear your new boots," Oresuy indicated, and Aniyé put them on too, their leather fitting her feet snugly even though the boots were unworn.

"Now the second set," Oresuy said and tied more ribbons across her torso, the red and yellow flaring against the blue of the tunic.

"Show me your hands."

She tied Aniyé's hands together and into a wider loop that ran around her body. She guided Aniyé's hands to her front until her wrists touched, pulled at a ribbon and wrapped it around in a pattern Aniyé couldn't follow to secure them in place—then did the reverse and pulled Aniyé's hands to the back. "Good," she said. "I'll loosen this for now." She allowed Aniyé's hands to drop to her sides, ribbons tied around her wrists and the larger loop still in place around her body, but allowing for some movement. "See if you can hold your staff like this."

Aniyé stepped to the rack by the door, pulled out her light, metallic mage's longstaff. She twirled it around her fingers experimentally—she could manipulate it without large arm movements, so the ribbons didn't stop her from using it.

"Excellent," Oresuy said. "This will be doable. Come here." She put an overcoat on Aniyé's shoulders, affixing it at the neck with two large silver clasps. For the most part, it hid the ribbons. Then she pressed down gently—Aniyé understood what was expected of her and lowered herself to her knees.

Oresuy smoothed down Aniyé's forehead and tied a ribbon across it. "This shall remind you of my protection," she said. "My dear student."

The Flood

Outside, the riverside was in uproar, town guards and working folk heaping bags of sand on top of the floodbanks of the downtown area. Aniyé halted in her tracks.

"You've seen the water levels rise," Oresuy said. "On your daily walks."

The floodbanks in the back of the Eyrie gardens had always seemed massive to Aniyé, protecting, overshadowing her as she tumbled down and into the water. Yet fear twinged in her now, like a taut string plucked by nervous fingers—

Oresuy steadied her. "We've been called on to help with the efforts."

Aniyé turned and blinked at her teacher. She felt thoroughly clueless.

"The Court scholars claim the maximum will be reached in a week, with levels two handsbreadths above the top of the floodbanks."

Aniyé had come from a dry land. Oresuy continued after a small pause. "The sandbags might be enough, but based on the rainfall in the mountains, they will need to hold for at least a week. The banks themselves will also need to hold."

Aniyé frowned. "Teacher, I don't see—how could they possibly be breached?" Floodbanks thicker than the city walls—

"They soak up the water, then they soften and slide. Our job will be to make sure it doesn't happen... or at least to decrease the probability of it happening."

Aniyé nodded, but her teacher hadn't finished yet.

"The only thing you'll need to understand is they might not be grateful for your service." Oresuy sighed softly. "But I am grateful, and I understand."

Aniyé walked on, slowly, steadily, barely aware of her surroundings. Under her feet, the ground was still dry, and as her attention reached down below, she could feel the floodbanks hadn't even begun to soak. She visualized a glowing latticework of bindings holding the soil in place, sparkling up to her from the depths of the earth as she walked over them above. Holding, containing, constraining, like the ribbons around her body.

She focused on her breath, the influx and then the outflow, the cycle ever-repeating. Power going out of her and into the structure, merging, stabilizing. She felt confident. She could do this by herself, while her teacher was making a circuit in the opposite direction. She could do this, and do it well.

The guards first stopped her beyond Poets' Bridge, where the town faded into meadows and the floodplains were heavily overgrown with willow trees.

"No loitering," the guardsman said as he blinked down at her. "If you're up on the banks, get in line for the sandbags."

"I—" Her concentration broken, she was momentarily disoriented. "I'm re... reinforcing the structure." She wanted to make a broad hand gesture, but the ribbons didn't have enough give. She was so startled that her other hand unclenched and she dropped her staff. She crouched down into the mud and picked it up, carefully, conscious of her limited range of motion.

The man grunted disapprovingly. "You're with the Mages' Guild?"

Mages' Guild? She was a student of Teacher Oresuy and no one else. She knew little about the Mages' Guild beyond those strained conversations between her teacher and the black-clad Guildsman Leitan.

"I, I'm a student of High Mage Oresuy," she mumbled, barely daring to look up to the guard.

He nodded, but then his expression tightened even further. "You? One of the steppe folk from the West? And you expect me to believe this tale?"

How was she supposed to respond? The guardsman reached to his scabbard. Aniyé's brain ran through possible scenarios, many of them ending in a beheading.

Her fingers gripped her staff so tightly her joints popped. "I, I'm a deserter, I escaped– I ran away!"

Was it true? By declaring it, had she made it true? Did she really escape? Did she really run away? She just wanted the pain to stop, she just craved control, control over the magic, control over herself, from an external source if need be, but she didn't want to *kill*—

The man sized her up and she was suddenly acutely aware of her skin, her eyes, her looks. She was an alien here. A piece of foreign flesh. An intruder, one of the enemy—

"She is under my protection," Aniyé heard from behind herself, and she dropped her staff again. The guardsman paled. What had he seen, some part of Aniyé's mind wondered idly as most of her froze, stunned—had he seen Oresuy appear out of thin air? From the shadows? The High Mage was skilled at spatial dislocation, Aniyé knew.

"Pass the word along the newschain," Oresuy said with such coldness Aniyé had never heard from her before. "I want no incidents."

There were no further incidents that day.

It was difficult to be the only one in sight to wander around seemingly in a daze while everyone else on the banks was engaged in hard labor, Aniyé soon found. It was difficult enough for her to avoid bumping into people while focusing on binding the floodbanks in place, and that was without the remarks, not even directed at her; at least not openly.

"Crimson Army," she heard, over and over, behind her back and over her shoulders, the words encircling her like tendrils of smoke. "A battle-mage."

She wanted to weep, but instead did what Oresuy had taught her to do and focused on binding herself to the land, creating—possibly? eventually?—a way to feel belonging, attachment to a new home. She could not go back. She was startled to realize at one point out on the banks, looking up at the starry night sky, that she would not go back.

Oresuy was strict, but never unfair, never abusive. Oresuy would never march her out to the battlefield like some kind of animal, a war dog ready to let loose from the leash, a being only valuable as far as its potential for destruction extended. Aniyé had never realized just how cruelly had she been treated, before. Oresuy was different—Oresuy would hold her while she cried–

The first time someone risked open confrontation with Aniyé, it was about a different issue entirely.

She was standing in line for food, a gigantic black pot of stew that three of the townsfolk dispensed to a bunch of exhausted laborers with great vigor. The High Mage was right behind her; just as hungry as she was, Aniyé could tell. People were discussing the King's upcoming visit, an event which seemed frankly pointless to Aniyé, and also to the others. She sleepily listened to the conversation.

"...he thinks he can make the floodbanks stand just by his presence."

"Scare them, eh? What do you say?"

"You know what I think." The thin, yarrow-blonde man glanced around nervously, on the lookout for potential informers.

His bald-shaven mate shrugged. "Nonsense if you ask me. He's coming here to get killed when the banks burst." He made a coarse sound and mimed the large, sweeping motion of water rushing through the town. "That's it! I bet Princess Ilas is already rubbing her hands."

The blonde man seemed encouraged by this act of blatant lèse-majesté. "If the Guild mages weren't all off on the Western front, they could hold everything just fine." He spread his stalklike fingers and sighed. "This war is never going to end. If King Abrany just swallowed his pride for a second and tried to negotiate with the Crimson Dukes…"

Aniyé could swear the bald man's eyes shone with glee for a moment. She found it hard to follow politics in general, having been so isolated for such a long time; but she was quite certain that something unsavory was going on.

"What did you just say?" the bald man said, drawing out the words. "You know that's trea—"

Aniyé realized the man was trying to get his fellow to say something self-incriminating. She didn't quite understand the situation, but she had to step in. "Some of us are here and helping out," she said quickly. She wasn't a Guild mage, she was Oresuy's student with no other ties of loyalty, but that didn't strike her as relevant.

The bald man straightened up and Aniyé could see how startlingly tall and well-built he was. "And why are you here anyway?" he said on the same level tone, but with anger simmering behind his words.

Aniyé was at a loss. She was here because Oresuy wanted her to be here, and she wanted to do what her teacher asked of her. She was certain she was missing out on some crucial detail—

When the man saw that no response was forthcoming, he went on. "You should by rights be at the front, fighting the Crimson Army with your talent given to you by the gods. This is *not* your place."

Oresuy spoke up; Aniyé was so nervous she hadn't even realized her teacher was paying any attention. "Would you rather be swept away then?" The man's anger was more than matched by her restrained ferocity. Oresuy stepped forward from behind Aniyé, fixating on the man—the informer? "It never ceases to amaze me how ready you are to act against your own best interests," she remarked. "Come," she nodded to Aniyé, "we have work to do."

Aniyé tagged along, her stomach growling. For long minutes she felt the man's eyes on his back, but she didn't turn around to meet his gaze.

The City

Aniyé stood on one of the floodbanks, with her back to the ever-rising water. A small square with the church of the Merciful Daughter-Son spread out in front of her, with many little alleys branching out and away on the opposite side. She took a deep breath, then walked gingerly down.

In an alcove next to the church entrance, she could see a statue of the Daughter-Son, the gently smiling androgynous deity standing on top of the globe, their feet shrouded in clouds etched from heavy marble. Suddenly she felt a strange kind of kinship, of acceptance—a warm ray of light washing through her internal landscape, calming her. She bowed her head and whispered thanks. She had never once prayed to this deity, yet they were accepting her?

Still, she didn't dare go inside the church. Churches on both sides of the ever-shifting border were all too eager to support the war effort.

She walked on. Garlands of flowers decorated the street-facing walls of the two-storey houses. A sign proudly stated that the city had been the recipient of an award last year for its flower displays. Aniyé stopped to read every banner and sign, trying to keep her attention away from the fear rattling around in her skull. This was an exercise, her first time alone inside the city, not out on the banks. She would do it for her teacher even when Oresuy insisted Aniyé do it for herself. To see, to experience, possibly to understand.

The city was beautiful. The façades all looked recently painted in smooth pastel colors and the roofs were lined with bright-hot red tile. People strolled slowly in the early afternoon sun, seemingly ignorant of the effort out on the banks. Aniyé was puzzled for a moment, then she reminded herself that in a city so close to the water, flooding must be a regular occurrence. Yet she was resentful for a moment—the banks were full of volunteers, but none seemed to be the scions of rich aristocrat and trader families, like the youths walking by her without sparing her a glance. Aniyé wondered what was better—people's eyes sliding off her as if she was nonexistent, or people's voices whispering behind her back and calling her names. She shrugged and ventured on.

All the streets seemed to lead to a large rectangular square surrounded by palaces, with wall hangings the size of small buildings glorifying the King. Upon a closer look, she realized the palaces were all state-owned: "National Museum of Traditional Lore", "National Central Administration", "National Gallery and Artist Patronage". At first, she was surprised by the constant repetition of "National", but after a while of wandering around the square, she half-expected to see a "National Mages' Guild". She didn't find the Guild hall; then she remembered Oresuy saying it was somewhere on a hilltop, an auspicious location. The mages were not threatened by the water.

She edged closer to National Central Administration and browsed the announcements hung in large glass-fronted cabinets until her eyes began to glaze over from the legalese. It seemed like everything needed to be reported. The number of horses one owned—were horses such important possessions here? –, whether one wished to exercise one's voting rights—she assumed that without explicit declaration it was not possible—and so on. Perhaps this city wasn't so welcoming after all.

The front gate slammed open and Guildsman Leitan stormed out, dashing past Aniyé without noticing her. He was muttering under his breath; reinforcing his wards? On a whim, she decided to follow him from a safe distance—she could check out the Guild hall, if only from the outside. She flexed her muscles against the ribbons; they held. She suddenly felt elated, her fears altogether gone. She was able to give free rein to her curiosity.

Walking behind the Guildsman, Aniyé could see the passersby's reactions to him. They bowed their heads to him or even bent from the waist. Some people ducked into the shadows of the alleys. Was this his due as a Guildsman in uniform, or did he inspire personal dread for some reason?

To Aniyé's shock, as the people stared after him, some uttered curses. With little to no magic behind the words; nothing that would harm the man or even get his notice from behind his tightly wound wards, but even then—this behavior seemed scandalous to her, and yet perfectly understandable. She herself had reason to hate Guildsman Leitan—the man who had wanted to claim her for the Guild as little more than a trophy—and they had met only twice.

The Guildsman did not acknowledge any of the obeisances, as far as Aniyé could see. He strode ahead, clearly used to walking on the cobblestones that kept tripping Aniyé, her feet jamming into cracks and sliding over smooth-worn surfaces. She struggled uphill.

Leitan came to a sudden halt in front of a large, blocky building next to a church. "I brought the necessary equipment," he said to the man on guard, a tall guildsman clearly chosen for his size and poise rather than his magical prowess. "Hail the King!"

"Hail the King," the guard said gruffly.

Aniyé did not dare break her stride, and she walked past the building with the front gate already closed behind Guildsman Leitan. The brick walls radiated a warmth beyond the heat gathered from the day's worth of sunlight. Yet the magic did not comfort her. She could feel the guard's eyes on his back—with her staff and her dress, the inscribed ribbons encircling her body, she looked clearly magical even to unsensing minds. Did that make her a target?

On her way back to the Eyrie, she chose a different path. Beyond the wide avenue she had walked, in the smaller side streets, shops and stores were failing—entrances shuttered in broad daylight, windows cracked, entire buildings empty of the bustle of business life. She sighed—the King's parade would clearly be passing along a different route.

III.

The King

Everyone was out on the banks on the day of the King's arrival, but even Aniyé knew this was not because of the people's great desire to see their leader. The flooding was becoming worse and worse—the water was nearing the top of the sandbags piled on the floodbanks. The scholars had predicted that the water levels would continue to rise for at least two more days. In the northern part of town, the floodbanks had been demolished a few months ago, in preparation for reconstruction. The hastily raised new banks were at the highest risk of getting swept away.

Huge crowds milled on both sides of the traffic barriers. Wide cloth ribbons marked the area beyond which only people working on the floodbanks were permitted. People not capable of hard labor were making food or handing out drinks, while children ran up and down, gawking at the workers, and town guards tried to maintain order.

Aniyé was stuck. "What do you mean you can't allow me in? I've been working on the Northlanes for three days now!"

The guard, a burly woman, crossed her arms and frowned in displeasure. "Orders from higher up. The King and his retinue cannot be disturbed."

"But the banks—" Aniyé didn't even need to close her eyes to focus, she knew the situation was becoming worse and worse. The ground felt saturated with water, clumps of earth ready to tumble and roll. She felt her bindings could still hold, but she'd need to be physically present and reinforcing them.

"The banks will be fine. We've been working all night."

Aniyé took a deep breath. "I need to reinforce the structure. It's absolutely necessary."

"The King doesn't want mages around while he is inspecting the effort." The woman grimaced. "Especially not some stranger from the Western steppes."

Aniyé thought better of protesting. She stood aside, forcing a rhythm of slow breaths upon herself, concentrating on the ribbons around her body, her hand on her staff. The fear, the anger all provoked a response from her magic, and she struggled to remain in control.

"Aniyé?"

She shuddered in surprise, then looked up into her teacher's face.

"Aniyé, is something wrong?"

She summarized the situation. Oresuy clicked her tongue in displeasure, but she also seemed to be displeased with Aniyé herself— or was she? "There is little time. Let's go," she said, then grabbed Aniyé by the shoulders and simply walked past the stunned guard not daring to stop them.

"You could've done that by yourself, you know."

Aniyé was on all fours, breathing heavily, the ribbons around her arms loosened and her fingers hooked into the soil. The skin on her forehead itched under the headband.

Oresuy was standing next to her, the two of them right in the path of the approaching retinue. "Do you think the bank will hold?" Oresuy asked mildly, her momentary displeasure gone and displaced by a calm sense of concern.

Aniyé nodded, her teeth set too tightly to speak. She pushed another burst of power into the structure, her entire body shuddering.

"That will have to do for the time being," Oresuy said. "On to the next spot." They had been working their way along the Northlanes, making stops at regular intervals.

Aniyé straightened out and brushed off her palms, her knees. She was unsteady on her feet.

"Just three more," Oresuy said as she steadied her and pulled the ribbons tight again. "You're doing great."

"Y-yes, but—" Her mouth had trouble forming words. She sighed and simply nodded in the direction of the crowd. A man in a garish tunic had broken away from the retinue and was running toward them.

Oresuy turned around to follow Aniyé's gesture. "Yes? Ah."

The man arrived, gasping and wheezing from such a short run. "Why are you here? The King's orders—"

"We will finish our work here," Oresuy said. "Tell your king that if he wants to live, he doesn't have a choice but to allow my student to finish."

The man paled. "They said the banks would hold—The King's advisors—"

"The banks will hold, if you allow us to go ahead." Oresuy was still calm. Aniyé blinked, looking from her teacher to the official and back.

More flamboyantly clad officials arrived, yelling with great consternation.

"You have to move!"

"Why haven't you gotten them to leave?!"

"The King is coming and His Majesty brooks no—"

"Why wouldn't you—"

Oresuy smiled serenely—she was taller than most of the retinue—and gazed up into the face of the King on his throne, carried on the shoulders of four strong servants.

Aniyé gasped. The King looked little like the person painted in oil on expensive portraits or enlarged to building-size on wall hangings. Certainly, there was a resemblance, but the face of His Majesty was more worn, and also more malevolent in a subtle, but to Aniyé, entirely unmistakable way.

Was he a magical person? He had to be! Why hadn't she heard anything about this? Wouldn't the citizens be proud? But then Aniyé realized that while he was strong in his own right, with his magic wound tightly around him and tuned finely to his desires, he was nowhere, nowhere near as powerful as Oresuy...

"If Your Majesty would please to make Your retinue a bit calmer," Oresuy said.

King Abrany nodded with what looked to Aniyé like forced affability, then raised a hand.

"The King wishes to speak!" a tall woman yelled, and the entire retinue dropped to their knees, their gaze downcast.

Aniyé looked at her teacher with worry. Was she also supposed to—?

High Mage Oresuy returned her gaze, her *no* impossible to miss, transmitted not only over the magic but also plain on her face. Aniyé remained standing. She gazed at the crowd and spotted Guildsman Leitan, almost an entire head taller than the rest of his fellows. He stared back at Aniyé in silent furor.

"If it is not Oresuy again," the King said. "We haven't seen you in a long time, but We certainly remember."

What was he talking about? Aniyé had previously had no inkling her teacher had known the King in person. Judging from King Abrany's tone, their interactions had to have been mostly unpleasant.

"Indeed, Your Majesty," Oresuy responded.

"We see you've acquired an apprentice." Aniyé shuddered—it was as if the King's attention sliding to her had dirtied her somehow. The feeling was very strong. "An apprentice who doesn't seem to show us much respect."

"Excuse me, Your Majesty," Aniyé began, but then her teacher's voice rang out in her head, part memory, part acute impression. *Don't apologize.* She paused and took a deep breath. "Excuse me, Your Majesty, but I am not your vassal. It would not be appropriate for me to kneel to you."

King Abrany's face darkened with blood, but he kept his voice steady. "You are a vassal of the Crimson Dukes, from the looks of you?" Trickles of anger passed through his tightly-coiled wards and magical shields. He was leaking power.

"I belong to no one but my teacher, the High Mage Oresuy," Aniyé said. "I will kneel when my teacher tells me."

King Abrany was about to burst. "And would the High Mage Oresuy," he said mockingly, "please to have you kneel?"

"If Your Majesty so desires," said Oresuy with a hint of a smile on her broad cheeks. *Go ahead.*

Aniyé knelt.

Snickers and sound-fragments of suppressed laughter floated on the air from the retinue. If this was a battle of wills and wit, Aniyé thought, her teacher appeared to be winning.

"I do *not* accept your obeisance," the King snapped, his voice edging into a squeak, his royal pronouns slipping.

"So be it," Oresuy said, now smiling openly, an act of defiance. Aniyé stood. "Then we shall be on our way."

"What are you doing here?!" The King demanded, leaning forward, gripping the lion-shaped arms of his throne. One of the servants involuntarily hissed, the King's sudden motion almost dislodging the throne from her broad shoulders.

"As I've told your messengers, Your Majesty, my student is reinforcing the floodbanks so that your retinue is not swept away."

"The floodbanks—" He clapped his hands together. "The floodbanks will stand!"

"Yes, Your Majesty." Was Oresuy also beginning to become annoyed? "They will stand because *she* will make them stand. You will be able to go ahead with your royal inspection."

"I do not take orders from you!" The throne rattled. The servants passed glances.

"It was not an order, Your Majesty. It was a description of fact."

He looked extremely distraught for a moment, then he gathered himself again and bellowed, "We shall bid our leave."

Aniyé stood ramrod-straight, shaking, as the retinue passed, people glancing at her with more than idle curiosity. Why didn't the king have them both arrested for their insolence? He must've been afraid of Oresuy. How does one restrain someone who moves with the wind?

Aniyé noticed the bald-shaven man, and gasped as she saw Guildsman Leitan make his way to him across the streams of people, say a few words and pat him on the back; then the crowds swept both of them away. She could still hear the King yelling, "No word! I want no word of this…" from behind her as Oresuy gently guided her down along the floodbanks.

"Just three more," her teacher said. "We will do a brief exercise to make sure only the good magic goes into the structure, and the bad magic, what comes from fear, is absorbed by the sky."

That night, it rained with a ferocity, and the water rose even faster than estimated—but the banks held.

The Slide

Someone pushed a bowl of warm, thick soup into Aniyé's hands. "Thank you for your good work," the stranger said and smiled at her, plump cheeks reddened by the early morning chill.

People still whispered behind Aniyé's back, but now there was the occasional kind voice. Word had spread. But as her newfound allies popped up like mushrooms from the undergrowth, so had her enemies multiplied. King Abrany had a network of supporters, informants, snitches—all on the royal payroll, and money spoke.

She gobbled up the food, pushing these unwelcome thoughts away from herself. She could not allow herself pause—the North-lanes were at immediate danger of sliding and the townsfolk worked day and night.

She heard a scream and *felt* something in the earth shift and give way—she tossed down the almost empty bowl and broke into a run, fighting off momentary dizziness and a sense of the world slipping away, her sleep-addled mind struggling to get a hold on reality.

Teacher—she shouted inward and outward, her magic ratcheting up, expanding around her, reaching—but she didn't know what to do, she didn't have enough precision, didn't have enough control, she only knew she needed to act—

Under her feet the ground was moving with an inexorable slowness, while the ribbons around her body flared with invisible fire, some part of her still trying to constrain her power—*Teacher*—

Oresuy came running, as if flying—her feet gliding above ground, her coat and robes billowing behind her. She grabbed hold of Aniyé from behind—the ribbons snapping, falling away in response to her touch—then she pushed her forward.

Aniyé dropped to her knees, then toppled ahead on all fours, her inarticulate shouting slowly turning into a raw, agonized keening as she tried to hold, to hold the banks with bare, unrestrained, unrefined power, pumping a stream of pure unprocessed magic into the earth, magic that rose from within her and flowed undammed—

and yet it was too unstable, too volatile, to be of any use—

her last thought was that it was over.

What Oresuy did then was too subtle for Aniyé to follow, but it spread outward from their point of contact, from Oresuy's warm, comforting hands on her head, crystallizing in the substructure of the universe unseen but heartfelt, stabilizing, providing a pattern for the world to match.

The ground stopped sliding. People rushed in, laborers given a momentary respite from death, people with shovels and sand-bags, people with hands in tattered gloves and faces smeared with grime.

Teacher—Words failed her. Her muscles shuddered as if they wanted to tear themselves off her bones. Oresuy held her close in a bear's embrace, stopping her from hurting herself with raw physical strength.

Consciousness dropped out of Aniyé, life dropped out of her and her muscles finally relaxed, her body passing into a welcome inertness, a well of starless dark.

The Bed

Aniyé only saw a warm yellowish light. She felt the pressure of the pillows and the heavy blanket, her body weighing itself down, devoid of all motion. Was she breathing?

She needed to get herself together. She needed to go out on the banks, she needed to work—

"Hush," a soft, deep voice whispered. "The banks will stand; you can rest. It has been done."

Then just the light.

Eventually a hand, palm tracing her forehead. "I am here."

Nothing but the light.

"I want to see her!" A coarse and uneven voice. Somehow familiar. Guildsman Leitan? The King? "*We* need to see her!"

"I cannot allow that. Not even you. For her own sake." Calmly explaining.

"The country needs this power!" Subtext: *I need this power.* "The Western front is collapsing—"

An exhalation. "I will not allow that. This is final."

"Very well, Oresuy…" A mind gearing itself up for a threat. "I will remember this. I will remember this!"

Angry steps hurrying away.

Aniyé coughed, suddenly feeling the dryness in her mouth, the wasting in her body. A hand reached behind the back of her head, lifted her gently so she could take clumsy, tongue-tied sips from the cup placed to her mouth. After she finished, she cast her gaze down, bowed her head a little to indicate her thanks; she could not speak yet.

"You're welcome, my dear apprentice." Was her teacher crying? "You're welcome."

It felt like aeons, but it took less than a day.

The Council

Aniyé stumbled outside, her clothes loose and ill-fitting on her body, the sunlight hurting her eyes. She was holding on to Oresuy with cramped hands that felt like claws. She felt unbalanced. The power was seeping back into her, replenishing ever so slowly. The ribbons were wrapped around her, holding her tight.

"It seems like a lifetime," Aniyé said, the words fragile on her parched lips. "And yet the water hasn't receded a handsbreadth. If anything..."

"It's even higher," Oresuy finished her unspoken sentence.

"Will the banks hold?" The words felt worn-out, repeated over and over, echoing in her head until they lost all meaning. It seemed like she hadn't uttered any other sentence in days.

"The banks will hold," Oresuy nodded. Yet something remained unsaid.

The meaning trickled through the connection between them. "They will not prove high enough." Aniyé knew there was a maximum height to the bars built out of sandbags. There was so much exhaustion inside her, she couldn't even grow upset.

"It is not our issue," Oresuy said. "We did what we could."

"The rainfall..." Aniyé whispered. Why had it fallen? She couldn't remember, but she knew she had something to do with it... She searched her mind. She had released the bad magic, the tainted magic into the sky—

"Don't blame yourself." Oresuy put hands on her shoulders, pulled her close. Locked arms around her. "You did what you could. You did your best in an unfavorable situation. The rest is not up to us."

The councilman showed up just a few moments later, as the two of them were looking out to the river in silence, their gaze-lines parallel.

"There is a problem," the councilman said, shifting his weight from one leg to another. His polished shoes were unsuited to the mud by the foot of the Eyrie and the crest of the city on the breast of his suit was half-hidden under dirt. Aniyé thought she'd seen the man in the King's retinue, but wasn't entirely certain.

We know *there is a problem*, Aniyé wanted to say, a tiny glimmer of anger flickering deep inside her boundless exhaustion. Oresuy's arms around her tightened momentarily.

"We need your help. The floodgates upstream from the Eyrie are stuck."

Oresuy made a noncommittal murmur. Aniyé was confused. What did any of them have to do with the floodgates?

"You have to help!" The man moved from anxiety and embarrassment to fear and desperation. "The city is going to be washed away!"

Aniyé still didn't understand. Maybe all this made sense somewhere—it certainly made sense to this official—but she couldn't see how the pieces fit together.

"Are you speaking for the city?" Oresuy asked, very slowly.

"I am, I, I—You need to come!"

Even through the haze in her mind it was clear to Aniyé that the man was hiding a crucial detail. What was it? She tried to muster her faculties—her reasoning, her magical insight…

Oresuy was also suspicious. "Slow down. Explain." Aniyé thought that this was at least in part for her benefit; the councilman had casually ignored her.

"We need to breach the banks and let the water onto the fields upstream from the city. We'll lose much produce, but the city cannot be washed away, surely even you can see that—" He tried to rein in his agitation. "I'm sorry," he huffed. "But the floodgates are stuck—rusted, maybe? Or stuck from the water pressure? We never had water levels this high—"

He was telling the truth. He was also lying by omission.

"Are you suspecting sabotage?" Oresuy asked.

"We're not *suspecting* anything, there is no time, the gates need to be opened! Please!" He seemed ready to fling himself at Oresuy's feet. The High Mage drew back a step.

"Aniyé," she began. "You know those banks better than I do. Do you think it's manageable?"

She could barely walk. And yet—and yet—

She remembered all those times she felt she simply couldn't move, couldn't even inflate her lungs to take a breath of air, so spent—*those* people from the Crimson Army didn't care. They didn't inquire. They just pushed her onward, and there was somehow always more magic, rising up from a reservoir deep inside her, from an unknown place beyond thought, beyond even power... This was why she was a battle mage. Had been. This was why they had wanted her.

But now it was her choice.

"Yes, master," she said. "I can do it."

Oresuy hesitated, frowning. Aniyé realized she'd used the wrong title. "Teacher—I mean—" she scrambled to correct.

"Are you sure, my dear student?" Oresuy said, still disquietened. Aniyé nodded, holding on to her newfound confidence.

"Then on shall we go." The High Mage glanced sharply at the councilman. "Lead the way."

Councilfolk were standing in the mud, looking scared, confused, intimidated. The King's retinue was also standing by, drawing away from the council members and the throng of onlookers. Aniyé spotted Guildsman Leitan, standing next to the guard she'd seen in front of the Guild hall, but the bald man was nowhere to be found. King Abrany presided over the entire scene on his portable throne.

Oresuy gritted her teeth.

This, this was the deception, Aniyé realized. Why didn't they want the two of them to know that the King and his retinue would be here? What did the King want?

She was beginning to see.

A demonstration.

Of her allegiance?

"He only wants your power," her teacher hissed to her from between teeth. "Be very careful."

They walked up to the metal structure at the top of the floodgates and Oresuy gave an experimental tug of the handle, but the rods remained inert. *She doesn't even trust them this far,* Aniyé thought, blood running cold. Her teacher crouched, put a hand in the mud, closed her eyes for a moment. Nodded, just barely. Then gave a little probing push, this time with magic. Nothing moved. She stood, wiped her palms on the metal. She did not spare the King a single glance. To Aniyé's shock, the King didn't decry this insolence. What was going on?

"I must confer with my student," the High Mage said to no one in particular, and drew Aniyé away from the crowds.

"Can you do it?" she asked—firm but not demanding.

"I have the power, teacher," *Master,* "I'm not sure I have the skill."

"I confess I am spent," Oresuy said and Aniyé blinked up at her in confusion. Her teacher, saying—?

"I am spent from putting you back together."

Aniyé lowered her gaze, but Oresuy touched her cheeks and turned her face again upward. "Do not be ashamed. I did it of my own free will. And you did well." The High Mage's expression darkened. "But I am not a battle-mage. I cannot draw and draw and draw on new power so fast, even though I command more than you."

"I can do it, teacher, but I'm not sure I can control…" Her voice trailed off. *They* had never *asked* her to do things. Repeatedly, to make sure.

"I can help you control it, I have that much still in me," Oresuy said and sighed deeply. "I need sleep."

"What should I do, teacher?"

Oresuy frowned. "The gate seems to be rusted shut, down under-water." *Or glued shut,* Aniyé thought. How far ahead of time? She had seen the Guildsman row upstream, in secret, for an inspection, then fetch some kind of equipment just the day before. Would the king endanger his people just for the sake of... Aniyé shook her head, trying not to venture into this maze of thoughts. Oresuy continued: "I don't think it makes much sense to try to pry it open. We need to blast the whole segment out. Or one nearby—what do you think?"

Her teacher asked her for her opinion. On a technical matter. Aniyé fidgeted, body pressing against the ribbons, arms pulling them apart until they tightened. "The gates are a disruption... in the banks, I mean. I think it's usually easier to tackle things along their edges? Points of discontinuity?"

The High Mage nodded, looking pleased to have some of her own thinking reflected to her. "But then the gate structure is lost; it might be more difficult to repair?"

Aniyé shook her head. "It's damaged to begin with, possibly to the point of uselessness. I get an impression it's..." *glued shut,* she thought at her teacher, and Oresuy's sudden glance at the retinue demonstrated that the concept had made it across. "Unsalvageable," Aniyé said after the silent exchange. "But the city can still be saved."

Oresuy smiled.

This is exactly what the King wants, Aniyé thought—a huge blast, a demonstration of deadly force. How long ago had the Guildsman set his plan in motion? Aniyé recalled his words, accusing the High Mage of insufficient loyalty. She looked on as the King's servants shooed people to safety, behind the lines Oresuy had drawn into the mud of the banks, nearer the city.

Oresuy motioned her to kneel and Aniyé lowered herself into the mud. She was shivering, the power already beginning to mount—

out of fear, she supposed, for she had done little to invoke it into herself by any voluntary means.

Oresuy pulled her hands behind her, pulled the ribbons tight. Aniyé gasped, startled by the sudden sensation.

"Now," Oresuy said. Aniyé closed her eyes. A hand across her forehead—this did not startle her. Her teacher's touch.

It rose from within her, ever-renewing, a blisteringly raw force that nonetheless was not, not—Aniyé felt this clearly even as the banks were about to be swept away—not destined for destruction, at least not the wanton destruction of war, the rampant murderous rage, but the power of simple irresistibility, that of the bolt of lightning striking from the skies, the tidal wave sweeping away seaside villages, a force of nature—

and she let go,

and she could hear another mouth breathing beside her, *close as only we can be,*

she could feel a practiced hand assigning lines of direction spreading outward, meeting points of weakness head-on, hitting with a sparkle and a hiss all the more deafening as it was not to be heard by the physical ear—

she leaned into the motion and pushed,

faintly aware of her body being lowered to the ground, hands turning her head to the side, clear of the mud

and she would use everything she could; her body meeting the naked earth, clothes soaked through not with blood—*not this time—* just with water and dirt, blades of grass stuck to her face; and she was suddenly aware of every single strand, every pebble in the mud, the waters below and the skies above—

and the waters rushed in, the flood ripping the gate apart, ripping the bank apart, impossible to tell as if by human intervention, or as if this was the way it would have happened all by itself, *the natural course of events,*

and was this not the natural course of events? Aniyé marveled,

then again darkness closed over her; not the darkness of utter desperation, but the darkness of rest and peace.

The Meeting

Aniyé was sitting by the riverside, the waters no longer threatening the town. The townsfolk gave her a wide berth, but she didn't mind; she knew what was coming. But whenever it was coming, it was not then. She stood eventually, her bones heavy.

She walked to a stall, fished in the pockets of her robe for a few copper coins; before she headed out into the inner city, she had been trying to test the ribbons to see if her hands could reach, only to realize with a startle that she wasn't wearing them. She could go outside for a short while without wearing the ribbons; the restriction was inside her, slowly internalizing. Oresuy didn't push her to go faster. This was a time of slow, methodical growth, not of exertion, sudden leaps and bursts.

She put the coins on the counter. The man handing out soggy, greasy wraps looked at her with suspicion in his eyes. He took so much time getting ready to say his words that Aniyé could've repeated them verbatim before they were out of his mouth. For a moment she was tempted.

I saw what you can do.

"I saw what you can do," the man said.

Aniyé nodded grimly.

You should be out on the Western front.

"You should be out on the Western front." He looked proud of himself for having been able to say it to her face.

How many times now? She lost track.

She shook her head. "If I had been out on the Western front, you'd all be dead now. Twice over."

She couldn't phrase it any more directly, couldn't repeat it any more often. It still couldn't turn the tide of opinions reinforced with bribes, strengthened by the immensity of the regime, stronger and stronger every day.

She turned away, not expecting the change, biting into the wrap with sudden ferocity. Pieces of chicken crunched between her teeth; the unappealing-looking wrap proved surprisingly tasty.

A mural of King Abrany glared at her from the building opposite, the paint still unblemished. She glared back and took another large chomp.

She'd wait it out. As long as it took. She'd repeat her words. As many times as necessary.

Did the King win this round? His people would never dare touch her, and the Guildsman's—the King's?—plan was foiled. They might wish to pressure her into volunteering, but she knew all about that kind of volunteering. They could not force her—it was an impossibility. No one could force her as long as she didn't force herself. Magic glowed in her like the evening-star and she was learning—she was learning.

She could stand on her feet. She could withstand the pressure. She was no longer alone.

She walked back to the Eyrie with a spring in her steps, and the world itself wound tightly around her, comforting her. She knew that high up in one of the lacework towers, Oresuy would be waiting.

Acknowledgements

The stories in this collection were written in Hungary and in the United States—specifically in the traditional lands of the Osage and Kanza people. I recognize that I am a migrant to a place whose inhabitants were forcibly removed to other places by colonizers, and that this land is still a home to Indigenous peoples of many different nations; just as other peoples whose ancestors were brought here as slaves or who fled here from overwhelming oppression. I seek to always be aware of this, and act accordingly.

Thank you to Spouseperson R. Lemberg and Childperson Mati for everything, and more. To my Hungarian relatives—my parents, my brother Marci, my grandmother, and Magdi. To my brother-in-law Michael. To everyone in the individual dedications of stories, and to all my editors and readers over the years—I couldn't have finished this volume without you. To everyone who spread the word about my projects, who squeed and cheerleaded and sent me cans of food and other assorted items online. You kept me alive during the commuting years, sometimes quite literally.

Thank you to Elizabeth Leggett for the wonderful cover art, Matthew Brith of Inkspiral Design for the cover design and the breathtaking typography, and to Frankie Dineen for the interior design that matched the tone of the book so well. I am grateful to all of you for making my book so beautiful, and also to Steve Berman of Lethe for his publishing prowess and all his support.

Thank you to Elizabeth Leggett for the wonderful cover art, Matthew Bright of Inkspiral Design for the cover design and the breathtaking typography, and to Frankie Dineen for the interior design that matched the tone of the book so well. I am grateful to all of you for making my book beautiful, and also to Steve Berman of Lethe for his publishing prowess and all his support.

Many highly special thanks to Lisa M. Bradley, José M. Jimenez and Ash, Orrin and Grace Grey, Bryn Greenwood, Nóra Selmeczi, Ádám Dobay and Lívia Farkas, Shweta Narayan, Nino Cipri, Project Enigma, Debra Fran Baker, D Franklin, Aliette de Bodard, Polenth Blake, Silvia Moreno-Garcia, Ken Liu, Karla K. McGregor, Katie R. Gordon, Nichole Eden, Tim Arbisi-Kelm and the entire Word Learning Lab, Holly Storkel, Teresa Girolamo, Sandstone, The Doctor, Virtual Adept, Rivers Solomon, JY Yang, Sonya Taaffe, Sofia Samatar, Scott Gable, Ann Leckie, Izzy Wasserstein, Liz Derringon, Andi Buchanan, Kellan Szpara, Connor Goldsmith. All the #DiverseBookBloggers! And many, many more of you. You helped me when I was in tough spots, you cheered me up, you were friends and colleagues and co-conspirators.

Chazak, chazak v'nitchazeik..

Charles Jane Anders

CHARLIE JANE ANDERS' latest novel is *The City in the Middle of the Night*. She's also the author of *All the Birds in the Sky*, which won the Nebula, Crawford and Locus awards, and *Choir Boy*, which won a Lambda Literary Award. Plus a novella called *Rock Manning Goes For Broke* and a short story collection called *Six Months, Three Days, Five Others*. Her story "Six Months, Three Days" won a Hugo Award, and her story "Don't Press Charges And I Won't Sue" won a Theodore Sturgeon Award.

Author Biography

BOGI TAKÁCS is a Hungarian Jewish agender trans person (e/em/eir/emself or singular they pronouns) currently living in the US with eir family and a congregation of books. Bogi writes, reviews and edits speculative fiction, and has been a finalist for the Hugo and Locus awards. Eir anthology, *Transcendent 2: The Year's Best Transgender Speculative Fiction 2016*, edited by Bogi, won a Lambda Literary Award for Best Transgender Fiction.

Author Biography

Content notices

This Shall Serve as a Demarcation: Warfare, injury, colonialism, suicide, blood.

Some Remarks on the Reproductive Strategy of the Common Octopus: Death, forced labor, oppression, colonialism.

A Superordinate Set of Principles: Body horror.

Forestspirit, Forestspirit: Brief mentions of racism, warfare.

Given Sufficient Desperation: ableism, occupation and guerrilla warfare (no combat scenes), physical violence. Brief mentions of forced labor and torture.

Changing Body Templates: Occupation, physical pain from medical procedures. Brief mentions of torture, drugs, warfare, mind control.

For Your Optimal Hookboarding Experience: Sports accident, physical pain.

Increasing Police Visibility: Policing.

Good People in a Small Space: Sadism, masochism, cheerful body horror, blood.

Recordings of a More Personal Nature: Mind control, drug use, self-harm, cutting, torture, dissociation, allusions to suicide.

This Secular Technology: Blood, injury, cutting, body horror, vomiting, suffocation, mentions of slavery and death.

Content notices (continued)

Three Partitions: Cis- and intersexism, vomiting, body horror, shunning, death, self-injury, injury, blood.

The Size of a Barleycorn, Encased in Lead: Mentions of nuclear warfare.

Shovelware: Allusions to civil war.

The Oracle of DARPA: Weapons development.

Toward the Luminous Towers: Warfare, combat, drug use, death, murder, injury, amputation, ableism, dehumanization, suicide.

Wind-Lashed Vehicles of Bone: Pain exchange, scarification, mention of death and suicide.

The Need for Overwhelming Sensation: blood, injury, masochism, kinkshaming, misgendering, warfare, mention of slavery.
Spirit Forms of the Sea: Death, being eaten, death of animals, vomiting.

All Talk of Common Sense: Ableism, mention of warfare.

Standing on the Floodbanks: Combat, warfare, blood, nightmares, vomiting, post-traumatic stress, ableism, panic attacks, flashbacks, flooding, racism, objectification.

Lightning Source UK Ltd.
Milton Keynes UK
UKHW011133031221
395039UK00001B/18